A "Gaston" The Poodle MYSTERY

I0549171

A
Glint
in
Her Ice

Janice Detrie

A Glint in Her Ice
Copyright © 2020 by Janice Detrie

ISBN: 978-0-9987342-1-7
All rights reserved
Printed in the United States of America

No part of this book may be used or reproduced in any manner whatsoever without the written permission of the author except in the case of brief quotations embodied in critical articles and reviews.

This is a work of fiction. Names, characters, places, and incidents are either a product of the author's imagination or are used fictitiously. Any resemblance to actual events, or persons or locales, living or dead, is purely coincidental.

Published by
Janice Detrie

Cover Design by Eric Labacz
www.labaczdesign.com

*Dedicated to my daughter, Megan,
for her love and encouragement*

Chapter 1

VLAD CHOMSKY'S FIRST MISTAKE was leaving the brochure featuring riverboat cruises where Norm Clodfelder, his handyman, found it after he fixed the leak in the kitchen sink. Norm hauled himself up from under the cabinet where he'd placed a Dutch oven borrowed from Vlad to catch the leaks when he removed the pipes. He stood up, stretched, and cracked his knuckles. After three trips to the hardware store for missing pieces of pipe, plumber's putty, and the appropriate wrench to finish the job, the zigzag connection was fixed. He wiped his greasy hands on the back side of his even greasier jeans and pushed back his sweaty Green Bay Packers baseball cap with his forearm. His grey ponytail hung limply down his back.

"I think we got 'er fixed," he said. "The third time's the charm."

"I'm ready this time," said Vlad, who waited on high alert with a host of bathroom towels just in case this third time really wasn't "the charm." The first two tries had sent waterfalls through the supposedly fixed pipe, and he'd spent an hour mopping up the deluge while Norm ran to the store for the proper materials.

With the cabinet door open for observation, he turned on the faucet. This time, however, the water flowed through the pipe with nary a drip.

"Success at last!" Vlad exclaimed. "Thanks for taking care of it. Tell Sandra all is well."

He moved toward the outside door in the small efficiency, hoping to usher Norm out as quickly as possible. Vlad watched as he picked up the scattered tools, slamming the well-worn hammers and wrenches into his metal box. Rusty pipes and plastic rings were flung into the mix along with the newly acquired putty.

"No problemo, Doc," he said with a jaunty wave of his hand.

Vlad had long resigned himself to Norm's calling him Doc instead of the requested Dr. Chomsky, or even Vlad.

As Norm passed by the end table, he noticed the colorful brochure with a long, flat ship nestled beneath a majestic cliff, a hilltop castle gleaming in the background.

"What's this, Doc? Ya planning on a trip?" He set the battered toolbox on the end table and picked up the brochure. Thumbing through the glossy photos of romantic destinations, he let out a low whistle.

"Wow! Will ya look at this classy ship? This sez: 'Rooms with verandas, an outdoor café, luxury private baths, and shuffleboard on the open deck. Even an elegant suite. Unprecedented levels of comfort.' I could dig a vacation on one of these babies."

"One of my colleagues at work passed it on to me. He and his wife took a cruise two years ago, and he gets these brochures almost monthly. I thought Beatrice would like to view some of the educational opportunities."

"So you're thinking of taking her on a trip?"

"Yes, maybe move our relationship to the next level. She's a wonderful woman, and I'm definitely falling for her," he said but he thought, *When you're twice a loser at love, you're a little fearful to try for a third rejection.*

"Why don't you just tell her?"

Vlad put his head down and started pacing, hands folded behind his back, then said, "It's not as simple as all that. I'm building up to it—waiting for the right moment."

"Like when you're on the ship?"

"Yes, like when we're on a romantic cruise," he said, but he couldn't say this aloud: *I even bought her a ring, a small diamond, just in case.*

"Yeah, a classy lady like her would like this: 'state-of-the-art ship with the elegant dining room serving regional wine with gourmet meals.' Ya think they serve any Wild Irish Rose?"

"Wild Irish Rose is made in America, and you're looking at European cruises. They probably feature Chardonnay, Riesling, or Cabernet Sauvignon. Wines like that."

"It's hard to find the good stuff ever since they quit making

Pagan Pink Ripple. Sometimes I guess ya just gotta go with the flow."

"Speaking of going, I have a lot of papers to correct this afternoon before I pick up the kids for dinner at the Pizza Lodge. It's Nicholas's eleventh birthday."

"Tell the kid 'Happy Birthday' from his Uncle Norm. I think Auntie Sandra has a little present for him so be sure to stop downstairs before you leave."

Norm was an uncle by friendship, not by blood, but as an only child himself, Vlad figured you take relatives where you can get them. Since moving to this one-room efficiency, he had become close to his elderly landlady and her diamond-in-the-rough handyman.

Just then, there was a knock on the door. Vlad hurried to answer it before Norm intervened. He had a habit of making himself at home in whatever domicile he found himself, which included emptying the refrigerator, using the last clean towel, and answering doors and phones.

Beatrice Krup, the librarian at Crawford University where both Vlad and she were employed, and a classy lady in Norm's esteemed opinion, stood in the hallway. Her pixie hair hung in short, shaggy layers, making her look young and delicate; her oversized glasses added to the fragile appearance. However, her appearance was deceiving; she ran the Reserve Room with a steely authority and efficiency that broached no arguments. Today she was wearing a fluffy peach and tan knit hat with matching scarf, looking like a hint of spring on this grey February day.

Then Vlad made his second blunder.

"Come in, Beatrice," Vlad said. "Let me take your coat. Norm was just leaving." He arched his eyebrow and gave Norm a pointed look.

'Didja see this brochure?" Norm waved the river cruise booklet in her direction. "Your dude here is going to take you on a trip to Europe. Look at these luxury rooms."

"A trip to Europe? This is the first mention of a European vacation," she said, her grey eyes knotted in confusion. "I would think that's rather pricey." The unspoken thought was how Vlad could afford such a trip on his meager professor's wages and child support payments.

"There was a reward on Waco's head," said Vlad. "He bombed an administration building at Drake University, and the regents authorized a reward for any information that led to his capture. Apparently, they've awarded it to me."

Vlad remembered the terrible night when Waco, the fire bomber, broke into his apartment and held a knife to his throat, threatening him to change his testimony. He thought he'd be killed by the elusive terrorist, but Gaston, Sandra's nasty-tempered poodle, fiercely attacked the intruder. The dog distracted him so much that Vlad was able to disable him with a lamp blow to the head. Norm called the police in the meantime, and they hauled Waco away—currently to jail where he awaited trial for several acts of terrorism on college campuses.

"Why Vlad, that's wonderful." Beatrice's eyes shone with pleasure. "I'm so happy for you."

"How much ya gonna get, Doc?" Norm eagerly asked.

"I'd prefer not to say until I know for sure the cash is in hand," Vlad answered, shifting his eyes to the ceiling to avoid Norm's scrutiny.

"Bet it's a bundle."

"It's enough to take a trip in May after the spring semester ends." He stepped toward Beatrice and took her hands. His dark brown eyes stared deeply into hers, and he struck what he hoped was a romantic tone. He had spent the whole sleepless night rehearsing in his mind exactly what to say to her. "I'd like to take you as my guest. A room with a balcony, the Romantic Rhine River Getaway. Sailing aboard an intimate cruise ship. We can watch the sunset over the water, just the two of us."

"Oh, Vlad, that sounds wonderful. I've always wanted to visit Europe and see a real castle. But I don't think I can leave my parents for that long. You know how difficult Dad can be," she said regretfully, withdrawing her hand to bite her knuckle. "I check on them daily to make sure he's behaving. Mom's getting too old to put up with his shenanigans."

"Not to worry, fair maiden. I've got it covered. Your friend Nora will take over the parent surveillance duty." Vlad smiled reassuringly.

"But who will get the reserve room ready for the summer session? It's total chaos with professors changing their curriculum at the last minute." She shook her head in dismay

"Your assistant, Kate, promised to stay on top of things."

"Ya see, the doc thinks of everything. Ya really should go with him and not worry—have a good time." Norm winked at her and nodded his head vigorously.

"Norm's right. I thought of everything. I may not have a windfall like this ever again."

Both Norm and Vlad looked at her expectantly. After a long moment of silence, Beatrice broke into a smile. "I suppose I could take a vacation in May. But you're much too generous. I insist on paying my own way."

"No, I want to do this for you. It's a great opportunity to see castles along the Rhine, to travel together." He reached for her again, cradling her hand in his. "Just the two of us. No parents, no kids, no work schedules. A voyage of discovery, so to speak."

Norm broke in. "Special sale, two for the price of one. Airfare included. What a deal. Ya wanna see?" He stepped between them and shoved the brochure at her. Vlad reluctantly relinquished her hand and moved back, scowling at Norm's shabby ponytail. He stifled the urge to push him out of the way and toss him out the door, throwing his dirty toolbox after him. Instead, he took three deep, calming breaths, placing his hands on his diaphragm and feeling the movement as he serenely inhaled and exhaled. Better his hands there than around Norm's scrawny neck.

"Looka the names of these ships," Norm said. *"The Illumination, The Expression, The Vista.* Here's one for you, Doc. *The Passion."* He pivoted to face Vlad and gave him a broad wink. "Don't it sound like a helluva trip?"

Beatrice flipped through the shiny pages. "It certainly seems like my dream vacation. Pristine medieval cathedrals, quaint villages. And we sail by the rocks that originated the legend of the Lorelei." Her eyes had a faraway look, like she could see beyond the shabby room into a brighter vista, sunlight dancing on blue water.

"Whaddya say? Fancy meals. Free wine. Yer own private bath. And the doc's willing to spring for it, ain't ya, Doc?"

Always the grubby Cupid at heart, Norm enticed her with the brochure's fine offerings.

"I will seriously consider it. What are the dates available in May?"

Vlad moved next to her and thumbed through the pages to the back of the book.

"See, these dates coincide with our interim break. Maybe we could take a few extra days in Amsterdam. Visit the Rijksmuseum or the Van Gogh Museum. See the Anne Frank House."

"We could see the Dutch Masters' works in person—Rembrandt, Vermeer," she said. "My favorite artists."

Vlad could tell from the enthusiasm in her voice she was considering the possibilities of his proposal.

"The majestic cathedrals. The magnificent artworks. We'll see it all together. It will be unforgettable." He reached for her forearm and gave it a gentle squeeze.

"Amsterdam? Ain't that where they sell pot in coffee houses?' Norm said. "I read some place that you can buy marijuana right in the restaurant like booze." His face lit up. "And ain't hooking legal there, too? Prostitutes with storefronts like any other business. Not that you'd need to take advantage of those services. Ha-ha."

He jabbed Vlad in the side with his elbow and gave him another wink, ignoring Vlad's frown and indignant sniff. He stood in thoughtful silence for a moment before he spoke again.

"Ya know, I might want to go there myself. And you know who else is in need of a vacation?"

Vlad gave a little frown, sending Beatrice telepathic signals not to encourage him, but she asked anyway. "Who might that be?"

"Sandra, that's who. She's been feeling a little peaked since her accident with the fire. She could use a break."

"Do you think it's wise for a woman of her age to be traveling to Europe?" Vlad tried to inject a little sanity into the conversation.

"Nah, she loves to travel. Went all over hell in her burlesque days. And on nothing so fancy as a ship named *The Illumination.* She'd love it. Besides, I'll be there to help out. Only problem is coming up with the dough."

My good luck! Mrs. Tooksbury lacks the money for a trip. For once the gods are smiling down on me, Vlad thought. Then he turned back to Beatrice, grabbed one of her hands, and said, "Will you come with me on the Romantic Rhine River Getaway?"

"Yes, I will." She smiled happily at him. "But only if you agree to my paying for my fair share," she said. "I'd love to travel with you."

"What a splendid opportunity for us to get to know one another better." Only Norm's presence prevented Vlad from gathering her in his arms and kissing her.

Norm held out his hand and waggled his fingers, "Ya mind if I borrow the travel book for a day? I'd like to show it to Sandra."

She dropped the brochure into his waiting palm. "Of course, you may borrow it."

"Just let me jot down the number for reservations. I want to call today. May's only three months away," said Vlad as he grabbed a pen from the kitchen table, jotted down the number emblazoned on the cover, and handed the brochure back to Norm. He dumped it on top of the toolbox and strode toward the door. He paused with his hand on the knob and spoke.

"I was just thinking, Doc? Ya had a little help capturing that terrorist."

"Thank God for Gaston. Luckily, he was still with me that night." Not in his wildest dreams would he ever have predicted he'd utter those words.

"Yeah, thank God for Gaston," Norm heartily agreed. "Glad ya get my point. Don't ya think the little fella deserves some of that reward money, too?"

Chapter 2

A FEW MOMENTS LATER Vlad and Beatrice stood before Sandra Tooksbury's front door.

"I can hardly believe we're going on the Romantic Rhine River Getaway," he said. "Too bad all the cruises starting in Amsterdam were filled."

"I don't care if we start in Basel and end in Amsterdam," said Beatrice. "I've never been to Europe so any country we visit is exciting to me. And I insist on writing a check tomorrow for my room. If I'd known what you were up to, I'd have brought my checkbook." She demonstrated her gratitude with an especially lingering kiss, not caring if any of the neighbors opened their doors.

Reluctantly, Vlad pulled away and rapped on the door once, which precipitated a loud yipping. Before he could knock a second time, a broadly smiling Sandra opened the door with Gaston, the source of the yips, at her heels. Like an old, defective vinyl record, the little poodle just kept yipping and yipping.

"Norm says you're planning a trip down the Rhine. It sounds wonderful." She stepped back to usher them in. "Won't you sit down and tell me all about it?"

At the sight of Vlad, Gaston's yips turned into a low growl. After weeks of living with him while Sandra was in the hospital and the nursing home, Gaston had fallen into an uneasy truce with him, allowing Vlad to feed him, take him for walks, and share his bed. They tolerated each other for the sake of Sandra and the kids, but the only warmth between them occurred when Vlad brought him a Cheese Danish. Now that Sandra was back in action, the hostilities were revived.

Sandra settled herself down on her pink flowered couch, while Vlad took the powder blue chair and Beatrice the matching love seat.

Decked out in a lavender tunic top trimmed with lacy ruffles, and matching lavender canvas shoes, Sandra resembled a stuffed Easter bunny that just escaped from a dollar store clearance rack. Of course, Gaston had his own oversized pink pillow on the couch where he was enthroned like doggy royalty, wearing a matching lavender bow instead of a crown.

"We just made the reservation," Beatrice said excitedly. "It's for the third week in May."

"How lovely! Spring along the river. I've always wanted to see Germany," Sandra sighed. "Will you be taking the kids, too?"

"Oh, heavens, no! It's not a romantic getaway with three kids along," Vlad said. "Besides, this is a riverboat cruise—mostly for older adults."

"Some cruises allow kids. I see the ads for Disney on TV all the time—waterslides, swimming pools, and Mickey Mouse."

"I'm afraid the only sports on this boat are shuffleboard and practicing your golf swing on the top deck."

"Oh, I love shuffleboard. Did I tell you once Howard took me on a ship when we were first married? He promised me a trip to Paris for our honeymoon. It was so romantic. Of course, to economize, our cabin didn't have a window, but at least it had a bed, if you know what I mean." She tittered. "We didn't see daylight for a week."

"We have two rooms reserved. Beatrice wanted her own. But they both have a window," Vlad said as he shot a speculative glance at Beatrice, but she had a faraway look on her face.

"To each his own, I always say. Howie couldn't keep his hands off me. Of course, I was much younger and prettier—practically a child bride." She fluffed her blue tinted hair with a coquettish gesture and smiled. Despite the garish purple eye shadow buried in folds of wrinkled skin, her rouged cheek bones and plum lips held a hint of her former beauty.

"You still are pretty," Beatrice said as she reached over to pat her hand. "How was Paris?"

"Paris was wonderful—everything I ever imagined. It was fall, late September—but the flowers were still blooming. We walked all over the city. The sculptures in the park were magnificent, especially the bare-bosomed Greek goddesses! Howard said they were flat-chested compared to me. Little sidewalk cafes where we drank wine until the wee hours. I'd go back in a second." Her voice had a wistful tone, and a brief sadness filled her eyes.

"Did you ever return?" Vlad asked.

"No, sadly, we didn't. He had just been promoted to vice president of the bank, and his job was so demanding. We were busy those first years trying to make babies, but sadly, that didn't happen either."

"I'm so sorry," said Beatrice. "I'm sure you would've made a great mother."

"Oh well," Sandra sighed. "Some things were not meant to be. Like Doris Day sang, *Que Sera Sera*. I do have Howie's travel vest somewhere. It has inner pockets to guard against pickpockets. I'll dig it out for you."

"Thanks. That'd be much appreciated."

Then the elderly lady reached over and caressed the sleeping poodle. "I had my puppy for consolation. That would have been puppy Pierre, Gaston's great-great-great grandfather. But it was hard getting over the real tragedy."

She sighed again, and this time tears started to well in her eyes. Then she vigorously shook her head and said to herself, "Stop that, you foolish old woman."

"Tragedy?" Vlad said. "What sort of tragedy?"

"You've seen the publicity photo of me when I was on the stage? The one with my two dogs—Fifi and Pierre?"

"Yes, I remember when we first met. You showed me your old photos." He recalled the picture of a younger, prettier Sandra in a sequin-covered costume. The two poodles, balanced on their hind legs, had matching bows and doggy smiles.

"Fifi was really the star of the show. She was the smartest dog on the circuit. Gaston inherited his talent from her. I could do a mean hoochie coochie dance, but she stole the show with her flaming hoop trick." Her voice cracked at the last part, and her lip trembled. "Foolish me to try to recreate it with Gaston."

Just the mention of the flaming hoop trick was a painful reminder of the terrible accident that resulted in third degree burns to Sandra's hands and arms and caused a mild heart attack. Vlad reached over and gently tweaked her shoulder.

"That's all in the past. You're a tough lady. You survived the accident and are thriving better than ever."

She met his eyes and smiled bravely. "You're right, dearie. But it brings back memories of the first tragedy when I lost Fifi."

"I'm so sorry. How did you lose your dog?" Beatrice asked.

Sandra rose and tottered over to the credenza, which held a box of tissues. She pulled one out and dabbed at her eyes. She stood with her back to them for so long Vlad began to worry that she had forgotten they were there. Even Gaston began to whine and rose up on his paws in a piteous manner.

She finally turned and spoke, "We left Fifi and Pierre with Mildred, Howard's older sister, when we went to Paris. She didn't have much experience with dogs, but I figured it's only three weeks. Little did I know…" Her voice trailed off to a whisper. "I never saw her alive again."

"Oh, dear. What happened?" Concern reflected in Beatrice's voice.

"It was that time of the month for Fifi. She went a little crazy when she went into heat. I had learned to lock her in her kennel until she got over it, but Mildred hadn't a clue. When the dog started bouncing her bum on the carpet, she thought she had worms or something. She started whining and scratching at the door, and Pierre ran around barking so Mildred figured they would get tired out after a long walk."

Sandra shook her head sadly. "She just didn't realize what a looker Fifi was. When she went out in public, all the male dogs came over to sniff her. But Fifi was fussy; she growled at the other poodles and spaniels. She was attracted to the strong, muscular types. When she saw the male Rottweiler walking across the street with his dark, good looks, she couldn't help herself. I never thought to warn Mildred about what Fifi would do when she wanted a little action. She yipped at the Rottweiler, and he barked back. Then she pulled the leash clear out of Mildred's hand—nearly knocked her over."

"Just like Gaston. The dog biscuit doesn't fall far from the box," Vlad mumbled.

"She dashed into the street. Of course, she didn't care about traffic. She just wanted to mate up with that hunky stud. The poor dear got hit by a Nash Rambler. She dragged herself to the curb. Pierre was howling, and Mildred tried to wave down some help, but it was no use. She was gone just like that." Sandra did an imitation of a snap with her arthritic fingers.

"I'm so sorry. How horrible!" Beatrice covered her mouth with her hand. Vlad patted Sandra's arm.

"Mildred knew how upset I would be if I didn't get to say good-bye to Fifi so she carried her home, Pierre barking all the way. She couldn't just throw her in a dumpster, and she couldn't fit her in the ice box, so she did the next best thing."

"What was that?" Vlad asked.

"She wrapped her in butcher paper and took her to the butcher shop. She told the butcher someone had given her a little lamb for a special dinner, and could she rent a locker to keep it in until her birthday celebration? The butcher said sure, so she put Fifi in his freezer until we came home."

Sandra stared off into the distance, reliving the memory. "I'll never forget unwrapping her ice-cold body, her stiff little legs sticking straight out, her eyes staring, her tongue protruding like a dead salmon. We had a funeral and buried her under the lilac bush in the backyard. At least Mildred gave us those last precious memories of her memorial."

Beatrice rose and gently put her arms around Sandra, "You poor dear. I can't imagine."

"Dearie, you can experience heartbreak without being broken. Losing Fifi prepared me for greater losses in life."

"I'm so sorry. No wonder you've bounced back after all that happened to you," Beatrice said.

"Yet I vowed I will never leave any dog of mine behind again. And I never have."

Now Vlad understood why she had insisted he take care of Gaston, instead of Norm, although at the time he felt the handyman was more compatible to the mercurial dog. Norm might forget about the dog for days if he met up with an old drinking buddy. At least she could count on him to keep her pet safe and well-fed.

"You won't have to worry about anything like that happening to Gaston," Vlad said. *He's too overweight to dash anywhere,* he thought. Then he glanced at his watch.

"Oh yes. I learned to have all my dogs fixed after that."

"We really should be leaving. We're picking up the kids for Nicholas's birthday celebration." He slowly rose to his feet.

"We want to get there before the pizza parlor gets too crowded.

Saturdays can be crazy, especially with kids wanting to play the video games," said Beatrice, also rising.

"Wait! I have a little present for him. It's something from Howard's younger days, and I want Nicky to have it." She slowly rose to her feet and tottered across the room, disappearing into her bedroom. When she returned, she was carrying a gift clumsily wrapped in brown paper and adorned with black outlines of men's shirts and ties. A red bow reminiscent of Christmas was slapped in the center.

"I know it's not very festive, but this paper was all I had in the closet. It was on closeout sale for a good reason," she said apologetically.

"Nicholas cares more what's on the inside than how things look on the outside," Vlad said as he took the package from her.

"Just like my Howard used to be. Nicky reminds me so much of him. He and Katy are the grandchildren I never had."

More like great-great grandchildren, Vlad thought, but only said, "They feel that way about you, too."

"I'm sure going to miss them when I'm gone," Sandra said sadly.

"Don't think that way. You'll be around for a long time yet. You've got a lot of good years left before you pass," Vlad protested.

"Oh no, dearie. Not when I pass away. Goodness, no. I may be older than dirt, but I'm healthy as Old Dobbin," she laughed.

"Then what did you mean?" Beatrice asked.

"I meant, when I'm gone on the Rhine cruise. Norm says we can get tickets for the boat when you give Gaston half of the reward money for capturing that terrorist."

Chapter 3

THE THROB OF THE MUSIC BLASTED across the parking lot of the Pizza Lodge, causing Vlad to yearn for earplugs. As they stepped in the entry of the rustic log building, the pulsating beat combined with the shrieking kids and electronic noises from the video games to elevate the noise level to jet engine decibels. He and Beatrice had to shout just to converse. No one manned the waitress stand so they stood alone, waiting for someone to seat them. Beatrice carried the presents while Vlad held a bunch of helium birthday balloons.

"This doesn't seem like a place where Nicholas would want to come to celebrate his birthday," Beatrice said, surveying the chaos.

"Maria insisted Nicholas come here and invite a friend. She said Gordy always brought his kids here for parties. No mess to clean up after at home." Since Maria had started dating Gordy, she constantly deferred to his opinion on childrearing matters as well as his professional advice on selling real estate. Vlad almost felt nostalgia for Al, the bowling alley manager, whose secret love precipitated the demise of their marriage. Al apparently didn't have many opinions beyond how to throw a strike and not to start drinking until the second frame.

"It's like being inside a pinball game," said Beatrice, dodging two children chasing each other around a foosball table. The laughing boy held aloft a pink baseball cap, obviously snatched from the girl screaming, "Give that back or I'm telling Mom."

Vlad peeked at the dining room. "They're not here yet so we'll grab a table and wait." He grabbed a frazzled waiter. "Can we just seat ourselves?"

"Go ahead. Wherever you can find a table."

Luckily, one of the large tables with benches on both sides was available. Vlad anchored the balloons with the foil-covered weight he'd bought at the dollar store.

"No backs on the benches. Probably designed to be uncomfortable so you eat fast and clear out," he commented.

"Or because they're inexpensive to maintain," Beatrice said. "This is quite the happening place."

Teenagers crowded in the booths that lined the sides. A fiberglass moose with a toothy grin stood in the center of the game room, surrounded by various video games. Cut-outs of bears and moose lined the log cabin-like wall, alternating with signs advertising soft drinks and greasy, deep-fried snacks such as cheese curds, jalapeño poppers, and chicken wings. Gamers could participate in virtual car races, hunting safaris, or military expeditions. Yelling, pushing, and shoving seemed to be the behavior norm while parents guzzled pitchers of beer oblivious to the noise.

Finally, Maria and the kids entered. Vlad let out a sigh of relief when he saw Gordy was absent. However, it was just Nicholas and the girls—no school friends in tow. Erin, his 16-year-old daughter, carrying the cake, saw them first. Almost fully recovered from her broken ankle, a casualty from the protest march gone awry, she limped over to the table and gently slid the cake next to the balloon bouquet, exclaiming, "This place is crazy busy! You can't get near the video games. The players are three deep. Insane."

Kaitlyn, her effervescent four-year-old self, ran full tilt to Vlad. "Daddy! Mommy said I can play video games today because it's Nicholas's birthday party. I'm going to drive a car. Zoom, zoom." She darted toward the virtual car, but Vlad caught the edge of her jacket and held on tightly before she disappeared into the crowd of youngsters.

"Leggo! Leggo! I want to drive the car."

"Just a minute, young lady. We want to order food first," Vlad said as he reeled her back to the table and deposited her on his lap.

Maria came bearing gifts while Nicholas lagged behind. She gave a perfunctory nod to Vlad and Beatrice and a curt hello, then sat down as far away from the two of them as possible.

"Hello, Birthday Boy!" Beatrice said as she stood up and hugged the unsmiling boy. "How does it feel to be a year older?"

As Nicholas mumbled something unintelligible, Vlad extended his hand toward the boy. "High five, Buddy! Fist bump!" Nicholas lamely slapped his hand and made a fist. Still no smile. "What's the matter?"

Maria answered, "He's bummed because his friend John couldn't come today. His grandma came down with pneumonia and had to be hospitalized so they're driving to Beloit to see her."

"That's just an excuse," Nicholas said gloomily. "He probably didn't want to come."

"That's nonsense. Look around. Any kid would be thrilled to be here. Gordy says his kids begged to come even when it wasn't their birthday. He'd give them each twenty bucks and wouldn't see them again until the money ran out. Plus, the beer is cold and the pizza piping hot."

"Speaking of pizza, let's flag down a waitress and put in our order," Vlad said. "Then I'll take Kaitlyn over to the game room."

A fresh-faced young girl wearing a plaid shirt and lumberjack cap sidled up. "Welcome to the Pizza Lodge. May I take your order?"

Vlad turned to Nicholas. "We'll have a pitcher of soda. Our birthday boy gets to pick out the flavor."

"I suppose root beer is ok," Nicholas said in a monotone voice.

"Can I have a diet cola?" Erin said. "I don't want the extra calories."

"And I'd like a beer. Whatever you have in light on tap," Maria said. "And make it your largest glass."

"Is root beer ok with the rest of you?" Vlad looked at Beatrice and gave Kaitlyn a squeeze as they both said yes.

"We'd like to order two large pizzas right away. Nicholas, is pepperoni OK for one? That still your favorite?" Nicholas gave a gloomy nod. "And the second one, make half veggie and half sausage and mushrooms."

"I'll put your order in and bring you your drinks." The waitress sauntered away.

"Should we open presents first or wait until after the food arrives?" Vlad asked.

"I don't care. Whatever." Nicholas shrugged, then slouched down on the bench.

"Open presents," ordered Kaitlyn. "Erin and I got you something good. Open ours first." She squirmed out of Vlad's arms, grabbed the clumsily wrapped package, and thrust it at Nicholas. "I helped Erin wrap it."

Nicholas fumbled with the heavily taped box, tore off the paper, and then saw the printing on the side of the box. "It's a magic kit! I can learn to do tricks!" The first smile of the day appeared on his face. "Thanks." He lifted it up for all to see. "It's awesome!"

"Now you can have your own act," Erin said. "You don't have to depend on Gaston if you want to get in show biz."

"And I can be your 'sistant." Kaitlyn said. "I can wear my show biz dress again." She did a pirouette around the table to demonstrate her skill at performing on stage. "Aunty Sandra showed me how to dance like this."

"This one's from Aunty Sandra," Vlad said. "She said it was Howard's but she wanted you to have it."

"That's strange wrapping paper for a child," Maria said drily. "It looks more like a recycled grocery bag with scribbles."

"I'm not a child. I'm almost in middle school, and I kinda like the colors. They're more sophisticated," Nicholas said, carefully sliding his finger under the tape so as not to rip the paper.

Nicholas lifted a cast iron mechanical bank from the box. A circus clown stood in the middle holding a hoop. A little black dog with a gaping mouth for coins sat on the right of him while a barrel with a slot on the top stood on the left.

"Wow! I've never seen anything like this." His voice filled with wonder. "Is it an old-fashioned bank?"

"It's a mechanical bank. You put money in the dog's mouth, I think, and something moves." Beatrice said. "I've seen them in antique stores."

"Make it work, Daddy. Give Nicky a penny!" Kaitlyn shouted.

Vlad did just that. He handed a penny to Nick to put in the dog's open mouth. The clown lowered the hoop and then the dog jerked over to the barrel and threw the coin through the hoop into the slot.

Kaitlyn clapped and exclaimed, "Do it again!"

Even Erin approved, "Wow, Nicholas. That is so amazing."

"I can't wait to tell Aunty Sandra thank you,' he said, his face brighter.

"If that's an antique, it's much too valuable for a child," sniffed Maria.

"We'll discuss it later," Vlad said. "After all it is a birthday gift. Now I'd like Nick to open my present. Beatrice helped pick it out." He slid the box toward Nicholas.

He ripped off the paper to reveal a set of books featuring a vintage photo of a strangely dressed little girl that appeared to be floating in air.

"I guess we were thinking the same thoughts, that you liked magic." Beatrice said. "Only this magic is in a book."

"Thanks, Dad and Aunty Bea. I saw this set in a book order at school and wanted to read them." The gloom completely disappeared from his face. "This birthday is getting better."

"Well, we saved the best for last," said Maria. "This is from Gordy and me." She pushed the last present in a bright gift bag toward him. "Check it out."

Nicholas pushed aside the tissue paper and dug out a baseball glove with a large softball in its center. A gamut of emotions flickered across his face, first dismay, then annoyance, and finally a tight smile. "Thank you, Mom."

"Gordy will teach you how to pitch and field a ball. Look, it's signed by Ryan Braun! Isn't that cool?" Maria gushed as Nicholas silently nodded his head.

The waitress appeared with their drinks. "Looks like somebody got some special presents," she said as she placed the glasses and pitcher of soda on the table. "Aren't you a lucky boy?"

"Let's play games now," yelled Kaitlyn. "I want to drive the car."

"There's a pretty long line for that," said Erin. "Let's play foosball instead. Come on, Nick. I challenge you and Kaitlyn to a game." She gave him a gentle punch in the shoulder.

He replied, "All right. We'll whip your butt."

"Here you are." Vlad handed her some money, and the kids disappeared into the game room.

"I don't approve of Nicholas accepting such a valuable gift from that old lady. She's not even family," Maria said with a sour look on her face.

"She doesn't have anyone left. I don't see any harm in her acting like a grandmother to the kids," Vlad argued. "She's really a terrific lady."

"Well, you should know since you take care of her and her nasty dog."

"A very smart dog that's going to share in the reward money," Beatrice blurted out.

"Reward money?" Maria knotted her eyebrows together. "What reward money?"

"Waco fire bombed Drake University two years ago, then disappeared. They had a reward for any information leading to his arrest," Vlad explained. "Since Gaston attacked him first, I only felt it was fair that Mrs. Tooksbury and he share in the reward money."

"Do you have plans for this money? The kids could use some new summer clothes," Maria said.

"Yes, I do have plans. I'm taking a trip to Germany—a river cruise along the Rhine. I'm leaving at the end of the spring semester."

"How nice that you're able to travel now that we're divorced!" Maria's voice dripped with sarcasm. Vlad bit his inner lip, holding back the reminder that she was the one who had sent him to the used husband lot. No sense in spoiling Nicholas's birthday party with accusations.

"And I'm traveling with him, but I'm paying for my own room," Beatrice added. "We're hoping you won't mind keeping the kids the weekends Vlad will miss. And we'll return the favor someday if you want to take a special trip."

"I suppose…if it's just two weekends," she said grudgingly. "And when were you planning to tell the children?"

Just then the three of them appeared at the table. "Tell us what?" Erin asked as she flopped down on the bench.

"Your father is going to be gone again. He's taking a river cruise on the Rhine with Beatrice," Maria said smugly.

"You're missing my swim class again?" Kaitlyn cried, stamping her feet. "You said you'd take me this time."

"And you promised this year you'd take me to College for Kids!" Nicholas protested. "You promised we'd eat lunch together at the Union."

"And I will keep my promise. I'll take you to the Aqua Kids lessons, too, Kaitlyn. I'll be here almost all summer. We're just going for ten days in May." Vlad said. "There was a reward for the capture of Waco, and I decided to use it to travel on the Rhine—something I've always wanted to do."

"And Beatrice is going along?" Erin said. "That's kinda cool. Is it on one of those really long ships like we see in commercials?"

"Yes, it's a smaller cruise ship—only several hundred people. Mostly grown-ups, older grown-ups like in the commercials. Beatrice has always wanted to visit Germany, too."

"Will you bring us back a present?" Kaitlyn asked. "I don't got anything from Germany."

"I don't HAVE anything from Germany," Maria corrected her.

"Mommy doesn't got anything either," Kaitlyn said. "Will you bring her something, too?"

"We'll bring back souvenirs for everyone. Especially your mom because she's making it possible for your dad to leave you so we can go on this special trip," Beatrice smiled graciously at Maria. "We'll take over whenever she would like to take a special trip."

"Gordy and I just might take you up on that offer."

Just then the waitress brought a pile of plates and two wire pizza stands. "Your birthday dinner is almost ready," she said to Nicholas. "Are you having fun?"

"I beat my sister at foosball, and I got some cool presents," Nicholas said. "My birthday turned out OK."

"Our daddy is bringing us a present from Germany. He got a reward for capturing a terrorist with Gaston," Kaitlyn informed the server.

"Are you the guy who was on the news last fall?" the waitress said. "I saw you and the dog on TV. Thank you for keeping us safe."

"I couldn't have done it without Gaston," Vlad said.

"Is he going to Germany, too?" Nicholas asked.

"I seriously hope not! This is supposed to be a vacation, not a disaster."

Chapter 4

STANDING BEHIND A LONG LINE OF PASSENGERS waiting to board the ship, Vlad's feeling of exhaustion lifted. He clutched his black carry-on. In addition to a spare shirt and a set of clean underwear, it held his most precious possession—the sleek gold ring with the tiny diamond.

"I can't believe we're in Switzerland, three feet away from the Rhine," he said.

About the width of the Wisconsin River, the river flowed sluggishly past the ship. On the opposite shore, the narrow, four-story buildings, all gleaming white with small dormer windows jutting out from black roofs, indicated they weren't in the States anymore. Even the air had a different scent, not fishy but fresh and woodsy.

Beatrice grasped his hand and gently squeezed it. "This is better than I imagined."

Yes, it was. And certainly better than the flight to Europe had been—at least for Vlad. Sleeping on the overnight flight had been next to impossible in the narrow seats, which reclined only inches—comfortable enough for dwarfs and toddlers. He'd tried to fold his long legs in the small space so he wouldn't bump the seat ahead of him. He'd encouraged Beatrice to push up the armrest between them and lean her head on his shoulder. She'd curled up as best she could, her feet propped up on her smaller carry-on, and soon her head slid down into his lap so he gave her his pillow. His right leg had become numb with the weight, but he would have rather cut it off than disturb her much-needed rest. Every time he started to nod off, his head jerked forward, waking him with a start. The doughnut-shaped pillow purchased at the airport was useless for sleeping but at least his neck stayed warm. Vlad had gently rested his arm on her back, happy just to be flying with her despite his discomfort.

"Too bad the cruise was all sold out when Sandra and Norm tried to make their reservation," Beatrice said now, as they waited to board. "I know they were so disappointed they couldn't come with us."

"Yes, most unfortunate. Apparently, the last few openings filled quickly."

Vlad had feigned disappointment when he heard the news from Norm but it was all he could do to keep from doing his happy dance. Now they were about to board the cruise ship and spend ten glorious days (and nights) together without work and family obligations. At home, every time Vlad worked up the courage to talk about his feelings for her, his kids called or her parents appeared or her cellphone dinged. The moment quickly passed, and he could never seem to get it back. Life flowed on, their friendship along with it, like twigs drifting on the river, however much he longed to grasp it with both hands and just hold on forever. Hopefully, the ring would cement their forever.

When the tour bus dropped them off at the dock, the driver stacked their suitcases next to the gangplank. The riverboat gleamed in the morning sunlight, the top deck awash with blue sun umbrellas, deck chairs, and a long blue and yellow striped awning down the middle. Vlad observed three levels of rooms: The top tier, ending in a large open-air café, had individual balconies with two chairs and a small table. The second tier had just a patio type door opening to a railing and the bottom tier just small round windows overlooking the river. Unfortunately, these were the only rooms left when he called to book the cruise.

"Those will be our rooms with just the window." He gestured toward the bottom tier.

"It's fine," Beatrice said. "We'll be gone on excursions so much of the time we really only need our rooms for sleeping."

He hadn't even been able to book a room next to hers—but perhaps they wouldn't be too far apart. By the end of the trip, he hoped they would be sharing a room.

"We're on a ship called *The Haven*. How perfect! Look at the lobby. Isn't it beautiful?" Beatrice exclaimed. She peeked over the rail into the ship and saw a stained glass mosaic of a castle on the water on one wall of the lobby, stairs wound up to the next level on either side. Sunlight flooded the atrium from the large skylight.

"It's amazing!" he agreed, and craned to see more of the ship's insides.

A monitor showing their position on the river faced the mosaic; a TV screen with their first scheduled excursion described a walking tour of Basel at 1 p.m. and 3 p.m. with the Captain's Welcome Dinner at 7 p.m. A large mahogany reception desk faced the entrance, and a small concierge desk was off to the side. Three people were hustling at reception, handing out keys and small maps of the ship. Glassed-in shelves held ship related souvenirs available for purchase, none of which would appeal to his children.

Despite the three crewmembers all working at an accelerated pace, the line moved slowly. An elderly man, either hard of hearing or with short-term memory loss, kept repeating, "What was that again?" The tall blonde in her crisp blue uniform patiently repeated, "A buffet luncheon is now available both in the restaurant on this level and on the open-air café upstairs."

"So my room is this way?" he said, heading toward the large dining room sign, moving fairly quickly for an old man with a cane.

"No, no, sir! That's the restaurant. Rooms are in the opposite direction." She stepped from behind the desk and intercepted him. "Let me call a bellboy to help you." She nabbed a white uniformed mate passing by. "Please show Mr. Kerwin to his room and get him settled." She handed the folder and key to the crewmember, who gently took the man by his elbow and headed him in the opposite direction.

Just then a middle-aged man stepped out of the men's room, brushing his hair back into a pompadour, the split in his sports jacket revealing a rear too big for his skinny jeans. "This is my father," he said to the attendant. "I'll take over from here. Your room is this way, Dad."

He turned to the blonde. "I'm so sorry. I thought he'd be all right for a few minutes on his own."

"Don't worry, sir. He just got a little mixed up with the directions."

Finally, Vlad and Beatrice made it to the reception desk. The blonde woman glanced at their bright blue name tags and looked in the file box for their room assignments.

"Let's see—Beatrice Krup."

Bea looked at Vlad and smiled, eyes sparkling excitedly.

Before she could hand Beatrice her key, loud voices were heard from the gangplank. Vlad couldn't quite make out what the male voice was saying but he did hear a dog yipping. He stifled a shudder. Annoying dogs could be found the world over. At least he could walk into a room without dreading sharp little teeth sinking into his ankle. Maybe the twitch he'd developed since living with Sandra and Gaston would disappear after ten glorious days away on a magical cruise ship—just the two of them, Beatrice swept up in the moment and into his arms. A newly purchased silk dressing gown was folded in his suitcase—very sexy and sophisticated. Too bad he didn't smoke a pipe to complete the picture.

The voices outside grew louder, and the people behind him drifted over to the entrance. A crowd started to form, squeezing into the doorway to observe the altercation at the gangplank. Vlad still couldn't quite make out the words of the argument.

"I wonder what the commotion is?" said Beatrice, drifting over with the crowd to see. Standing behind her taller shipmates, unable to peer over their shoulders, she stood on her tiptoes and craned her neck from side to side, trying to catch a glimpse of the action.

Vlad followed, not wanting to lose her in the throng at the door. Curious, too, over what was attracting all the attention, he joined the press of bodies.

"What is that crazy old lady trying to do?" a voice said.

"It looks like she's trying to bring a dog on board. A fat little poodle on a leash."

"It couldn't be!" Vlad exclaimed, and he pushed himself into the crowd. But it was.

Below him, Sandra Tooksbury in the aged flesh pointed to the crumpled vest adorning Gaston with bold lettering. The overweight poodle with the dingy white fur wagged his tail but showed no sign of retreating from the gangplank.

"Can't you read, young man? It says 'Service Dog' on his harness. This dog is a highly trained service dog. MY service dog," she declared. "He accompanies me wherever I go because of my disability."

The attendant grew flushed but said firmly, "Like I said, madam, no dogs are allowed on board the ship."

"I was told by the young man who made my reservation that

service dogs were allowed on board ship."

"That dog doesn't look like any service dog I've ever seen," sneered the older crewmember manning the gangplank. "He looks like a clown dog escaped from the circus."

"Rejected from the circus, more like it," said a voice in the crowd.

"I'll have you know, young man, I'm prone to having seizures, and this service dog warns me and my traveling companion when I'm about to lose consciousness," Sandra said indignantly.

"Your traveling companion? Who might that be?" asked the crewmember.

Vlad groaned as Norm pushed his way through the throng bottlenecked at the gangplank and planted himself next to Sandra, resting his fists on his hips.

"I'm her traveling companion. I'm trained in first aid procedures, and I know what to do when her service dog gives the warning," he declared.

"If that fat mongrel is a service dog, then I'm Angela Merkel," snorted the older man.

"You don't know who you're dealing with, sir. I've long retired from show business but I still have friends in high places. You don't want to tangle with talk show stars. They'll smear your cruise line all over the Internet," Sandra threatened. "Check me out on YouTube. My dog and I are celebrities."

Sandra opened her purse and began rummaging through its contents, scattering used tissues, a half-eaten Mars bar, and several restaurant receipts on the ground. "Here it is. The headline story from *The New York Times*. 'Dog Brings Down Terrorist.'"

She thrust the *Crawford Daily Gazette* in the crewmember's face.

"Madam, this is not *The New York Times*," he said. "It's some small-town paper."

"Don't you get smart with me. The New York paper ran the story, too. It was all over the country. My dog is famous."

"I don't dispute that, madam, but famous or not, I can't go against the ship's policy." said the man, running a meaty hand through his thinning hair. "I could lose my job."

"Then I demand to talk to your captain. You can check with Laurant who made the reservation. He told me my service dog was allowed on board with me."

Just then Vlad felt a burly man in an immaculate white uniform push past him, captain insignia gleaming.

"What seems to be the problem, Seaman Klaus?" he growled.

"This elderly lady wants to bring her dog on board, and I told her that's not possible," his voice rose to a whine.

"He's a service dog, Captain. I need him to warn Norm here when I'm about to have a seizure. I was informed service dogs are allowed." Sandra thrust out her chin defiantly.

The captain scratched his head before he spoke. "Yes, they are allowed in certain cases, but we have to be notified beforehand so special accommodations can be made."

"There was a last-minute cancellation. I just made the reservation yesterday, and your representative Laurant assured me the necessary paperwork had been filed with you."

"I'll check with headquarters, madam, if you'll just step aside and let the other guests through." He looked at the disgruntled passengers behind her and Norm.

Vlad saw Sandra flick her index finger at Gaston. Immediately, he began to bark loudly. Not just loud but frenzied barking, so extreme that his body shook, belly fat undulating like waves on the nearby river. He jumped on Norm, grabbing his pant leg with his teeth and dragging him close to Sandra.

As if on cue, Sandra emitted a loud moan. She jerked her head backwards, and her body went rigid. She toppled like a Northern Pine felled by a lumberjack straight into Norm's outstretched arms.

"She's having one of her attacks!" Norm shouted. "Stand back. Give her some air." He gently lowered her onto the grassy bank alongside the ship and began wildly waving his Green Bay Packers cap in front of her face.

A lady shrieked, "Is there a doctor here?"

Gaston's barks turned into pitiful howls as he sat on his haunches next to her.

"I'm her guardian! Let me through!" Vlad exclaimed as he pushed through the crowd and rushed down the gangplank. He knelt beside her and reached for her wrist. He could see the blue veins standing out in her frail arm, a tangled network, and felt for her artery with his fingertips. Her pulse felt strong, and he let out a sigh of relief.

"She's had a mild heart attack before, but her pulse seems all right." he said to the captain standing nearby.

The man's forehead furrowed with concern as he also knelt down beside them.

Sandra let out another little moan, and her eyes fluttered open. "Where am I?" she mumbled. "What happened?" Then she closed them again.

"Ya had another one of yer spells," Norm said. "But yer all right. Gaston let me know just in time to catch you." The dog's howls changed to a whine as he stuck his head under her limp hand.

Another moan and then her blue eyes opened wide. "My goodness, Vlad, is that you?" She struggled to sit up.

Vlad put his arm around her to support her to a sitting position. Beatrice glided to his side with a cold glass of water in hand.

"What are you doing here? The last thing I remember is some rude fellow arguing with me about boarding the ship. Then everything went dark. I must have had a seizure."

Every eye in the gathering crowd now turned to the reddening crewmember and glared at him.

"For shame. Giving the poor old lady a heart attack," an angry voice in the crowd spoke up.

"She told you the service dog was trained," said another.

"Let her on board so the rest of us can sign in, for heaven's sake," an irate lady next in line said.

The crowd picked up the chant. "Let her on board. Let the dog on."

Gaston stopped whining and began licking her hand. Beatrice knelt down and laid her hand against Sandra's forehead. Her eyelids fluttered again, and her moans grew louder.

"Here, Sandra, have a sip of water."

She took a small sip and stage-whispered, "Thank you, dearie. That cleared my head."

Beatrice's eyes appealed to the captain, her lips knitted into a worried line. "She seems very weak."

The young crewmember, wringing his hands, turned to the captain as he slowly rose to his feet and began stroking his well-trimmed mustache.

"What now, Captain?"

The captain stared for a moment at the pathetic tableau before him, brow furrowed with concentration, and then at the tense crowd growing more fractious by the second. He sighed.

"If she says it's a service dog, then it's a service dog and they can both get on board."

Vlad and Norm bent down on either side of Sandra and helped her to her feet. Like a heavily blooming delphinium in a windstorm, she swayed precariously between them. Then she leaned heavily on Norm and weakly said, "Thank you, Captain."

"Let her go to the head of the line," another voice said. "We don't mind if she skips ahead."

"Are you able to walk to the registration desk?" The captain asked solicitously. "I think we have a wheelchair in the first aid room if you need assistance."

"Norm is all the help I need, thank you. As long as I have my service dog by my side, I'll be fine."

"A little snooze and she'll be good as new," Norm said. "Don't ya worry. She's a tough old gal."

Norm and Sandra slowly made their way up the gangplank, Gaston somberly trotting at their side, followed by the captain, Vlad, and Beatrice.

The tall blonde at the registration desk looked through the file box. "I don't see a Sandra Tooksbury or Norm Clodfelder here."

Then she searched her computer screen. Her eyes widened as she exclaimed, "My goodness, it says here you have a verandah suite!"

"Lucky for us, there was a cancellation and we were ready to go at the drop of a dime," Sandra said.

"We'll give you the keys to the suite and change the names on the guest list. One of the attendants will show you to your room. We're sorry for the incident at the gangplank. We'll make sure the rest of your trip is special."

"Don't worry, dearie. Anyone can make a mistake. Luckily, my service dog is on top of things."

Vlad swore she gave him a sly wink as she passed by.

To: erinflamethrower@gmail.com
From: Chomskyv@crawford.edu
Subject: Arrival
Hi, Erin,

Please let your mom know we've arrived safely. Our ship is *The Haven,* and it's amazing. An open-air café and a top viewing deck that looks like a park, complete with potted trees and boxes of flowers and herbs. Beatrice sends her love, too, and hugs to you kids.

We had a surprise—Auntie Sandra and Uncle Norm joined us with Gaston in tow. Did you know he was a service dog? Neither did I. But Auntie Sandra convinced the captain and crew that he was. Guess how? Gaston started barking in the midst of the argument with the crew. She fell down with a seizure, right into Uncle Norm's waiting arms. The bystanders grew so ugly the captain didn't dare kick him off the ship.

Our flight was long, and I'm very tired but not too tired to miss our first tour. We'll be walking around Basel, Switzerland, which is supposedly a well-preserved city, never destroyed by wars. I'll try to send pictures with my phone.

Give Nicholas and Kaitlyn a hug from me.

Love,
Dad

From: erinflamethrower@gmail.com
To: Chomskyv@crawford.edu

Got the news about Uncle Norm and Auntie Sandra. Too bad you didn't pack Nicholas's soccer pads as protection from Gaston. lol

Nick's acting weird. Went right to his room—no whining to use the computer. I told him I made some nachos, and he told me to go away. You know he loves nachos. He didn't come out of his room when Mom came home with Kaitlyn. She was busy fixing supper and yakking on the phone with Gordy. Nick came down to eat, but he hardly said anything. Kaitlyn yakked about some dumb field trip to the fire station. Then Gordy came over so I couldn't get Mom alone.

What should I do? Nicky always talks to you when you have him trapped in the car. Maybe tomorrow I'll just trap him in his room and make him talk.

Chapter 5

VLAD DIDN'T DISCOVER HIS MISSING suitcase until he went back to his stateroom to dress for the Captain's Welcome Dinner. He stood for a moment in the compact but well-appointed room, scarcely believing that he was actually on a European cruise. His carry-on was still on the bed where he had dropped it before hurrying off to lunch and a walking tour of this charming Swiss city, with its tall narrow buildings and green crisscross tiled roofs. Of course, the first thing he did upon entering was take the ring out and flip open the case to admire it. Then he locked it in the safe with his passport and gold watch. Beatrice suggested an espresso when they returned in the open-air shipboard café—just the two of them, no sign of Norm and Sandra. While sipping coffee, Beatrice smiled and reached for his hand. His heart grew so full he felt his chest expanding, barely able to contain his joy, but his tongue froze, refused to move and, try as he might, it lay impotent. All he could do was smile weakly.

And now, no suitcase.

First, he checked the narrow closet, in case the crewmember had placed it there to make enough room for him to walk over to the bed. Nothing. Then he looked under the bed. Nothing, not even dust bunnies. The room was so compact; no corner nooks could hide a large suitcase.

Maybe it was mistakenly delivered to Beatrice's room. Vlad walked down the hall to her door and lightly knocked.

"Just a minute," she called.

He could hear the shower being turned off and her swooshing about the room. She looked a bit surprised as she opened the door dressed in an oversized terrycloth bathrobe.

"I thought you were changing for the Captain's Welcome Dinner. I'm not anywhere near being dressed." She stepped aside to let him enter.

"My suitcase has disappeared. It didn't by any chance show up in your room?" He glanced about her tiny room, but all he observed was her open suitcase on the bed and her carry-on tucked under the desk.

"No. The last time I remember seeing it was when the driver stacked bags on the dolly. It was next to mine, I swear, because I was glad we had tied the hot pink ribbons on the handles."

"That's the last time I saw it, too. I just assumed the ship's crew would deliver everything right to our rooms."

"Mine showed up. I've even unpacked. I hung some of my outfits in the closet." When she gestured toward the clothes hanging before him, the robe slipped open. Vlad tried not to look, but he couldn't help but notice how dewy and pink her nipple was after stepping out from the shower. She caught his glance and self-consciously pulled the bathrobe closer together. "What on earth will you do?"

Vlad stepped closer, wanting to take her in his arms, slowly remove the bathrobe, and kiss every part as he leisurely exposed it, but he remembered his missing suitcase. Making love to Beatrice wouldn't produce his evening clothes. Besides, she hadn't exactly flung off her robe and ravished him. She took their pledge to take things slow seriously. Vlad would never do anything to make her regret this trip. Instead, he just inhaled the clean soapy smell of her and sighed. "I'll walk down to the front desk and inquire if anyone had an extra suitcase show up in their room. Thank goodness I packed clean underwear and a change of clothes in my carry-on, just in case of an emergency like this."

"Would you like me to get dressed and come with you for moral support?"

"No, that's all right. You just finish unpacking and continue to make yourself even more beautiful for dinner," he said as he kissed her quickly on her lips. 'I'll pick you up in an hour."

"Good luck," she said as he left the room.

Vlad trudged down the hallway, listening to all the muffled chattering as he passed by the occupied rooms, everyone happy in anticipation of the Captain's Dinner and upcoming excursions. Perhaps the mistake with his bag was already discovered so he would soon be joining the happy chorus. Determined to make the best of the situation, Vlad climbed the stairs to the lobby, humming his favorite aria from *La Bohéme*.

The tall blonde was still at the desk. She shook her head after Vlad explained his problem and said, "I'm sorry, sir. We have had no word from any guest finding an extra bag in their room. We will contact the driving services and the airline. We will do all we can to find your missing bag. We have complimentary toiletries and a laundry service, should you need them."

"Thank you. I'll contact you when I need clothes laundered. If my bag fails to appear, I assume I can purchase clothes in the cities we'll be touring."

"Of course. And keep your receipts for reimbursement. You did take our travel insurance, correct?"

Vlad sadly shook his head. "We were trying to minimize our expenses."

"Still keep your receipts. You can always try to claim your loss from your homeowner's insurance if we determine your bag was stolen."

Vlad trudged even more slowly back to his room. A shower and a shave seemed in order. Then clean underwear and a clean shirt. He'd only packed shorts in his carry-on so he would need to have his slacks laundered tomorrow and wear shorts on the excursion. Hopefully, the weather would cooperate, and they would find time for shopping.

AN ATTRACTIVE YOUNG LADY with sleek black hair pulled into a ponytail and wearing the ubiquitous white shirt with gold buttons and blue skirt seen on all the wait staff handed them a glass of champagne as they entered the lounge. Vlad had shaved, trimmed his mustache, and combed his still wet hair into the usual side part, then selected the most formal shirt of the two in his carry-on—a plain turquoise tee bought last summer in Greece. He wore the rumpled slacks he'd put on fresh twenty-four hours ago—dressier than cargo shorts. Of course, Beatrice looked lovely in a summery green dress with layers of ruffles cascading to the hem and a short matching sweater with crystal buttons.

"No luck finding your suitcase?" she said, kissing his cheek. "You're still the most handsome man in the room, even if you're not wearing a suit."

She slipped her arm through his, and they walked harmoniously into the crowded room just as an ear-splitting whistle reverberated through the lounge.

"Doc! Beatrice! Over here!"

No mistaking the source of the whistle or the gravelly voice shouting their names. Norm was standing and waving wildly at them. Sandra was ensconced in a lounge chair in the company of the old man from the lobby and his son, the ever-present Gaston crouched under her chair. Two empty chairs stood around the small table for them.

Vlad gave a wave, and they slowly maneuvered through the crowd until they reached the seats. He felt as if every eye in the place followed them as they made their way across the room. Norm picked up a bottle from the table and held it overhead.

"Look, Doc. Complimentary champagne. An apology from the captain for the incident at the gangplank. We're waiting on you to open it."

The cork exploded from the bottle with a loud POP, causing the startled couple at the next table to spill their drinks.

Vlad and Beatrice slouched into the empty chairs and took a sip of their champagne. Before either could speak, Sandra said, "I'd like you to meet our new friends. Clarence Kerwin and his son, Douglas."

"Not so formal," said the younger of the two. "My friends call me Dougie."

Vlad plastered on what he hoped was a friendly smile at the two strangers and held out his hand.

"Vlad Chomsky. Pleased to meet you. And this is my friend Beatrice Krup."

He couldn't help but notice the three rings on the younger man's hand and the expensive-looking watch as he vigorously shook his hand. He also reeked of some musky cologne. The old man barely nodded at them; his eyes fixed on Sandra in her fuchsia cocktail dress with the cut-out shoulders. Gaston growled a greeting. On his back he sported a handwritten sign: "Don't talk to me. I'm working."

Vlad sat next to him but shifted his feet out of the dog's reach. "We're from Wisconsin, a small college town called Crawford. Where are you from?"

"Pennsylvania—just outside of Pittsburgh. My sister was going to take Dad on this trip, but she fell and broke her leg. Since I'm newly retired, I stepped in so Dad could cross this off his bucket list." Dougie said. "I'm used to a little more action on a cruise. Massage rooms, swimming pools, night clubbing, lots of single ladies." He winked at them. The top of his shirt was unbuttoned, exposing gray chest hair and a string of gold chains that almost blinded Vlad. A diamond pinky ring glittered in the overhead light. Yet he wore a sports jacket as did most of the men at the event—except for Norm, who wore a clean Green Bay Packers polo shirt and new matching cap.

"Yer dressed down a little tonight, Doc," Norm commented.

"My luggage is lost. This is all I had."

"Tough break. Ya can always borrow something from me. I brought my best duds."

"Thanks. Hopefully, it will turn up. I'm planning on buying something tomorrow if it doesn't."

"Here's to the loveliest woman in the room: Lillian," the old man interrupted and lifted his glass to Sandra.

"I'm Sandra, remember? If you think I'm hot now, you should have seen me in my show biz days." Sandra giggled as she clinked her glass against his, and they both took a drink. "I had a vaudeville act with my trained dogs. Gaston's great-great grandparents."

Gaston gave a happy yip at the mention of his name.

"You're still an eyeful," he declared. "I bet a fellow would have a hard time keeping up with you. I'd sure like to find out."

"Now, Dad, remember what your doctor said. You can't overexert yourself," Dougie said with a frown. "If anything happens to you on this trip, Janie will kill me."

"You kids are always nagging. I can keep up with you any day, with your beer gut and your big lard ass." He poked Dougie in the aforementioned gut with his cane. "Mind your own business. It's not every day I meet a beautiful former star of the stage and screen."

"I mentioned our appearance on that talk show," Sandra said to Vlad. "Told him to catch it on YouTube when he gets back home."

Just then the captain's voice came over the speaker. "Welcome on board *The Haven*. I'm Captain Schultz, and I'd like to introduce our crew tonight. Their goal is to make this trip the most enjoyable ever."

After a whole line up of crewmembers took a bow, the Captain turned to the steward. "This is Lutz, our program director, and he will tell you what's in store for tomorrow."

"We will take a trip into the countryside," said Lutz. "You'll see the breadbasket of Germany with many family farms that date back to the fifteenth century. Our destination is the Black Forest where we will view the mountains and take a hike into the foothills. At our stop in the village you will view artisans at work blowing glass and carving wood, including creating the finest cuckoo clocks in the world. And don't forget to have a piece of the delicious Black Forest Cherry Cake."

"Unless they sell wearable art, Doc, yer kinda screwed," Norm said.

As they rose to shift to the dining room, Vlad overheard a snooty voice say, "If I'd known they allowed such riffraff on this cruise line, I'd have booked this trip with another company."

Out of the corner of his eye, Vlad noticed an imposing sixtyish lady in a dark blue silk dress with a plunging neckline highlighting a diamond and sapphire necklace so extravagant Vlad doubted it could be real. Diamonds dripped from her ears, and as she gestured, a diamond bracelet flashed in the track lighting. Her male companion was one of the few men sporting a cream dinner jacket and black bow tie. Both looked as if they had just stepped off the cover of *Vogue* for an evening in Paris or London. Few cruise patrons were as elaborately dressed, making Vlad feel like a cockroach in comparison. A good couple to avoid at all costs.

"Won't you join us for dinner?" Dougie said mostly to Beatrice. "My father so enjoys your friend's company. I'll push on ahead and save us a table if you bring up the rear with Dad and Sandra."

"I'll go with ya, Dude." Norm was already steamrolling through the throng as he turned and shouted over his shoulder. "Doc, maybe you'd better take the elevator to the dining room. It's kinda tricky on the stairs."

The doors opened to a miniscule elevator. At least the growling Gaston kept the other passengers at bay. No one wanted to get too close to a working dog. Vlad was almost happy to have him as a bodyguard until he nipped him on the ankle as the doors closed.

Chapter 6

MOST OF THE TABLES WERE FILLED by the time Vlad and Beatrice ushered Sandra and Clarence into the dining room. Waiters were pouring wine and handing out the evening's menu. Small shrimp puffs enticed diners at each place setting, and most were enjoying their hors d'oeuvres by the time they reached the table commandeered by Dougie and Norm. Vlad first pulled the chair out for Sandra, then Beatrice, as Clarence settled in the seat next to his son.

Their waiter, a slim, energetic Pacific Island youth, handed them the menu. "Good evening, ladies and gentlemen. I hope you enjoyed your welcome drink. My name is Sam, and I'll be your waiter tonight."

"You don't look German," Beatrice said to him.

"I'm not. I'm from the Philippines. I'm earning money for school and to send home to my family," he said with a charming smile. "And to practice my English."

Just then a young woman appeared with two bottles of wine—white and red—and asked which they'd prefer. "I've already had more champagne tonight than on ten New Year's Eves. I better not indulge in anymore, thank you," Vlad said.

"But, Doc, it's free. Ya never pass up a free drink," Norm told him. "He'll have the red like me. More of a man's drink."

The young lady poured them both a full glass.

"To an enchanting trip with the two most enchanting ladies on board this ship." Dougie lifted his glass in a toast, and they all clanged their wine glasses together.

Two empty seats remained at their table and, to Vlad's dismay, the overdressed couple from the lounge paused beside their table and surveyed the room.

"Plenty of room at our table. Feel free to park it here." Norm gestured at the empty chairs.

The woman frantically searched the crowded room. Finding nothing else open, she frowned and muttered something under her breath. Vlad swore she said, "Beggars can't be choosers." She gave her husband a withering look, saying, "You had to order that extra Manhattan," then seated herself at the table. Her husband slid in next to her and gave them an uncertain smile.

"I'm Warren Beaumont, and this is my wife, Katherine."

"Welcome to our table," Beatrice said and introduced them all. Katherine gave them each a perfunctory nod as she said their names while Warren plastered on an expression as if he'd just been introduced to the WWE women's Champion and offered a ringside seat. Beatrice bravely continued, "Where do you hail from? Vlad and I are from Wisconsin, and these folks here are from Pennsylvania."

"We have a home in Boston, but we winter in Naples. Katherine can't stand the cold. If our children want to celebrate Christmas with us, it's Florida style," Warren said.

"Our winter home is right on the Gulf, clear blue water, golden sandy beach, a lanai with a pool. We stay there six months and one week, to be able to claim it as our main residence."

"No sense paying Boston taxes if we can avoid it," Warren added with the first genuine smile of the evening. "But we still prefer the East Coast in the summer."

The girl came back with the wine, but Katherine waved her away. "Tell your wine steward we are premier travelers. We'll choose from the special wine list."

"What a beautiful bracelet!" Beatrice said as Katherine's wrist flashed in front of her. "All your jewelry is exquisite! I've never seen anything like it."

"Sapphires and diamonds. Actually, the earrings are blue diamonds. We found them while traveling in India. They are fairly rare, but the bracelet has diamonds almost as valuable."

"I don't know why you insisted on bringing them along. They should be home in our safe where they belong." Warren scowled as he spoke.

"You know very well, darling, that I'm hoping to find a ring to match my earrings when we reach Amsterdam. Amsterdam is the diamond capital of the world. Gassan makes the finest diamond jewelry. You can't find anything like it in America."

The wine steward stood quietly waiting with the premier list.

Katherine looked it over, wrinkling her nose. "I suppose the Cabernet will do," she said. "I was really hoping for something better. I do so appreciate a fine wine."

"Me, too," Norm said. "I was so bummed when they stopped making Ripple."

"I've never been on a river cruise before or any cruise, for that matter," Beatrice said. "Have you done this before?"

"Oh, yes. Last year we took a trip through France's Bordeaux region called Chateaux, Rivers, and Wine. We went to the Sauternes wine region—even created our own blend of cognac at the famous Camus distillery. It was glorious," she said as she took a sip of her wine. She pressed her lips together with a sour expression. "The wine was so much better than this red."

"We hunted for truffles with our host at a private chateau. He prepared a dish for us: pan-fried foie gras with Périgueux sauce. You can't imagine how delicious," added her husband.

"When I'm hungry for truffles, I usually just buy them at the candy store," Sandra said. "I like the truffles with hazelnut filling."

"Ruffles have ridges," cackled Clarence. "Love that commercial."

"Ya know, my lady friend and I did some traveling, too. Went to San Antonio on a road trip. Wisconsin doesn't get hot like Texas—especially in May when we went." Norm said, smiling broadly at the Beaumonts.

"Weather in Wisconsin can be unseasonable in May. We've even experienced a late winter storm. I have pictures of my tulips buried in snow," Beatrice said.

"San Antonio is really hot in May," said Norm. "I splurged and coughed up the dough for a fancy hotel with good air conditioning. My old lady was pretty impressed—king-size bed, fancy little couch, chocolates on the pillow."

"If I ever found chocolates on the pillow in the dives I stayed in when I did the burlesque route, I knew the traveler before me ate candy in bed." Sandra chortled, and Clarence joined in her laughter.

"We went upstairs to the rooftop spa and took a dip in the hot tub, but my old lady said it was too hot," said Norm. "She just wanted to catch some rays so she could show off her tan when we got back home."

"Too much sun can be bad for your skin," Dougie said. "I hope she used sunscreen."

"She was tough as a pit bull—didn't worry about no sunscreen," said Norm. "We seen a spot that was kinda private—fenced off—but that didn't stop us. Just climbed over the fence and laid down. It was the tallest building around—like we had our own special place up in the sky. No one else could see us. She looked pretty hot in her bikini. Pretty soon we both were hot so we went back to the room to cool off, if ya catch my drift." He elbowed Warren and winked.

"My word! How common!" huffed Katherine as she looked at her husband, who grimaced in distaste.

But Norm ignored their gaze. "Next day she wants to go back up again so we sneak over the little fence and spread our towels. Only this time she sez, 'I'm gonna sunbathe nude. Nobody can see us up here. I'm gonna get an all-over tan.' So she strips off her suit. I don't want burnt balls so I keep mine on. But I'm admiring the view. Pretty soon we hear thump-thump-thump. Footsteps. Someone's coming."

Katherine began waving her arm, bracelet glittering, and flagged down the Filipino youth. "Waiter, how long before we get our food? The other tables are being served."

"Soon, madam. I must serve in a certain order. Your food will be coming up shortly." He bowed his head as he scurried away.

"No hurry, Sam. I'm not done with my story," Norm said.

"Once Norm gets going, there's no stopping him," Vlad said to the Beaumonts, sympathetically shaking his head.

"Anyhoo, we see a guy from hotel security step over the fence. My old lady sits up, grabs her towel. The guy sez, 'I'm sorry but you aren't allowed over here.' 'I don't see why not,' she sez snotty-like. 'We're not hurting anything—just catching a few rays. Nobody can see us.' He sez, 'Because, madam, you are sitting on the skylight over our restaurant.'"

Norm laughed uproariously. Vlad couldn't help but join in, but he could see by the disgusted look that Katherine was not amused.

Just then Sam brought the entrées—plates of Parmesan scallops and risotto. Conversation stopped as everyone began to eat. When it resumed, it was at a more formal level—sharing information about occupations and family members. Every time Norm started another story, Vlad directed the conversation back to mundane topics: Packers football, Great Lakes shipping, unusual weather—safer that way. Sam brought dessert—tiramisu—and more wine. Warren and Katherine didn't even wait for after-dinner coffee. They bolted down their desserts, all the while scanning the dining room.

"There's that nice couple from the plane," she said. "Warren, we must go and say hello." She gave a Princess Di wave to a well-dressed couple and, without another word, headed across the room, dragging Warren behind her. Vlad sighed in relief at their departure.

"Ya want to head to the lounge for a nightcap?" Norm asked.

"I'm afraid my age is catching up with me," Sandra said. "Even with our afternoon nap, I still feel exhausted. Tomorrow is a full day. Can't wait for Black Forest Cake." She yawned and creakily rose. "I've got to hit the hay."

Clarence's chin was resting on his chest, and his eyes were closed. Dougie gestured toward him as he said, "The old boy's already fallen asleep. I've got to get him in bed."

"I didn't have a nap so I'm retiring right now. Couldn't really sleep on the plane." Vlad felt the words stumble out of his mouth, a combination of exhaustion and wine. "I'll see you in the morning."

"Me, too." Beatrice said. "Vlad, would you accompany me to my room?" She offered him her arm, and they made their way out of the dining room, across the lobby, and down the hall to her room.

Grateful for her steadying presence, he staggered a bit as he spoke, "If we eat like that every night, I'll need Spandex pants. And all the wine! Not used to drinking and dining."

"Dinner was delicious, but I'm too tired to say another word. What time should we meet for breakfast?"

Before Vlad could even finish saying seven o'clock, she kissed him on the cheek and floated into her room. He stared at the closed door for a moment. The walls were starting to move. Maybe he was feeling a touch of seasickness, but the ship wasn't due to set sail until two a.m. Vlad staggered to his room down the hall. The attendant had efficiently turned down his bed, and he found a toothbrush and toothpaste in his bathroom, courtesy of the receptionist. When he checked his e-mail, the message from Erin was worrisome but unfortunately, he couldn't make his fingers find the right little keys on his phone to form a coherent reply. He deleted the gobbledygook, tossed off his clothes, and slid into bed. When he closed his eyes, the room swirled even more. The toilet was just a few steps away, and he knew he'd feel better if he vomited. But he was too tired for even that. He fell into an uneasy sleep, dreaming he was on a huge raft, careening down a turbulent river.

Chapter 7

WAS THE POUNDING IN HIS HEAD GETTING LOUDER? The noise was deafening. Vlad swore he would never overindulge in that much champagne and wine again. Did anyone at the lobby desk have aspirin? It really should be mandatory to include complimentary aspirin with the complimentary champagne. The aspirin amenity would be more useful than free cookies and cappuccinos. Vlad opened his eyes. The room stopped spinning but the agitation moved to his stomach. Suddenly, the thought of Parmesan and garlic made his stomach contract. The pounding continued even more frantically.

"Doc! Doc! It's me. Open up!" Unmistakably, Norm's voice. Was that Gaston yipping in unison?

Vlad reached over to the bedside light and turned it on. He brushed aside his shirt, which covered the glowing alarm clock— 2:30—in the morning. What the hell was Norm doing pounding on his door at this time? The ship was really moving now, and as he lurched to his feet he felt the gentle motion. He grabbed his pants from the floor, pulled them on, and moved toward the door on unsteady feet.

"Just a second. I'm coming. Do you want to wake up the whole ship?' he hissed. He barely turned the lock as Norm barged in, smelling of cigarettes, stale wine, and a deodorant failure—Gaston in tow on his leash.

Alarm was etched all over Norm's face as he spoke. "Doc, ya gotta come quick. You're not gonna believe this!"

Vlad grappled with the zipper on his pants and reached for the tee shirt flung over the nightstand. "Is something wrong with Sandra? Did you call the ship's medical number?" He slid into his shirt, not caring that it was inside out. "Why did you leave her alone?"

"Naw, it ain't Sandra. It's something worse!"

At the mention of Sandra's name, Gaston started yipping again and lunged toward Vlad. He hastily backed away from the little dog's flashing teeth. Norm jerked on the leash, and the animal immediately heeled, quieting down to a low rumble in his throat.

"If it's not a medical emergency, then why aren't you in bed like the rest of us?" Vlad gave him the best glare he could muster.

"I told ya, it's something worse. There's criminals on board this ship. Thieves! They're gonna pull a heist, and it's gonna be a big one." Norm's voice grew louder as he paced around the stateroom.

Gaston's little legs had to work overtime to keep up.

"What have you been smoking? I warned you to be careful. I don't want to have to bail you out of a German jail. I don't even speak the language."

Norm abruptly halted, moving so close Vlad could see where he'd missed a patch shaving. He said excitedly, "I ain't been smoking nothing. I just overheard somebody talking outside on their balcony, only they were below me so I couldn't see them. But it's gonna be big—no small potatoes."

Vlad raised his palm toward him, "Hold on. Slow down. What on earth are you doing outside someone's balcony at this time of night?"

"I was above it, not outside it. The little fella had to take a whiz. He ain't on European time yet. Sandra was out cold. She needs her rest, ya know, so I decided to take him out. Only the ship was moving, and I couldn't take him down the gangplank onto the grass. So I took him to the next best thing—the upper deck."

"Where did you find a dog relief section on the upper deck?" Vlad brushed his hair back in exasperation. "This ship wasn't built to accommodate dogs."

"There's some big potted plants up there. Close enough to a fire hydrant. So Gaston and I sneak up the back steps, away from the captain's wheelhouse, and we go by the big plants." He bent down, picked up the chubby poodle, and began stroking his head. Gaston reached up and licked his face.

"He does his job so we're getting ready to go back to the suite when I hear voices. Sounds like they're arguing so I stop to listen. I really couldn't help overhearing."

"What did they say?" Vlad backed away, wishing he had a breath mint or two to offer up.

"One was talkin' about that rich lady that ate with us tonight— the one that ain't got no sense of humor. Called her posh—especially with her diamonds. Be a cushy job to snatch her diamonds. Come up with me and listen for yerself. They might still be talking."

Vlad didn't even bother with socks—just slid his bare feet into his shoes and grabbed his room card off the nightstand. His stomach was doing flip-flops, his head still throbbing. Norm already had the door open, shifting Gaston over his shoulder as he pushed into the hallway. The dog gave him a sneer. Vlad swiveled his head around to check out his surroundings. No movement in the dimly lit hallway as they made their way silently to the back stairway. Norm whispered hoarsely as they climbed up the three flights to the top deck.

"They started talking about a bigger heist. That gassy place the rich dame was going on and on about. The diamond capitol of Amsterdam."

"The Gassan? I'm sure they have armed guards. You don't just walk in and steal a few diamonds."

"Seems that they got someone on the inside that's gonna help them. One said she's a bit of a clumpy dumplet, but she's shagadelic—whatever that means?"

"Are you sure you heard right? You're sounding like Dr. Seuss."

"I'm just trying to repeat what the one with the gravelly voice said—sounded like nonsense, but my memory might not be so good."

"It's good enough. Go on. Anything else?"

"They talked about mingling on the ship with the tourists—sorta blending in so nobody gets suspicious when we get to Amsterdam. The smooth talker's already been to the diamond place. Pretended to be a buyer. The weird one wants to hit the rich lady first. We got to stop them."

As they reached the top, a ghostly silence loomed over them. Shreds of clouds drifted across the half-moon; an occasional star pierced the thick cover. Like monsters lying in wait, the outlines of the recliners and deck chairs took on strange shapes in the darkness. Vlad had to shake his head to chase the sleepy fog away as they crept past the awning into the open area where the huge potted plants stood guard. He clutched Norm's arm and brought him to an abrupt halt.

"I can't hear anything. Are you sure you heard real voices? Maybe someone had their TV turned up loud with the window open."

"They were real. I heard them moving around. Sounded like one was bossing the other around, I told ya—they was arguing."

Vlad tapped the side of his cheek with his forefinger. "Do you think you can locate the balcony? If we can figure out which room it is, maybe we can turn them in."

"I'll show you where Gaston did his job, and maybe you can help me figure it out." Norm led him over to the large containers of plants.

"Which one was Gaston using?" Vlad whispered.

"I can't tell. They all look alike in the dark. Maybe you could drop down on your hands and knees and sniff—see which one smells like dog pee," Norm suggested.

"Maybe YOU could drop down and sniff. Or maybe you could check with your hand—feel which one is still wet," Vlad muttered furiously.

"That's a no-go, Doc. One of the crewmembers came through and watered all the plants before we turned in. I saw him busy at work when I was scouting out an alternative spot for a doggy break, just in case we couldn't get on shore." Norm put Gaston on the deck and said, "Go, Little Buddy. Show us where you took a whiz."

Just then a bird perched on the railing on the opposite side of the deck, and Gaston darted toward it, barking furiously.

"Shut that dog up!" Vlad hissed. "He'll wake someone up or the wheelhouse will notice we're up here."

Norm took off after the dog, whispering loudly, "Come back, Little Buddy. Stop barking. It's only a bird."

The bird flew off, and Gaston stood growling at the empty spot on the railing. Norm caught up and scooped him into his arms. He held his mouth shut and crooned softly. "It's OK, Gaston. Sh-h-h-h! Ya seen birds before."

Vlad marveled at how near to the dog's teeth Norm placed his hands without receiving even a scratch.

"Settle down, fella. It's all right." Then Norm began caressing his head in slow circles. The dog quieted down immediately and squirmed to be free. As soon as his little legs hit the ground, he scurried back to the potted plants and made a deposit next to a plant in the middle.

"That must be the one." Vlad said. "Let's lean over the railing and count how many balconies from the end to this plant. Then we can figure out which room and tell the captain."

"Naw, it ain't the one." Norm shook his head emphatically. "It was closer to the end. Didn't want nobody in the wheelhouse to notice what we was up to."

"Let's go down to the end and count balconies," he suggested.

"But I'm not sure. I was too afraid to look over the railing—in case they saw me and rubbed me out or something."

By now Vlad was beginning to wonder if Norm really overheard jewel thieves plotting a crime. "How much did you have to drink in the lounge?" he asked suspiciously.

"Just a nightcap. That Dougie dude never made it, and I felt weird drinking alone." Norm held up two fingers in a V. "Scout's honor. I'm cold sober—especially after hearing them guys talking."

"What did they sound like? Could you tell if they were American?"

"No, one had that British accent like Dr. Who on TV."

Vlad shrugged his shoulders. "That narrows it down to half the people on the ship. Did you notice anything else?"

"One said that gobbledygook that didn't make no sense. I was trying so hard to keep the little guy quiet that I couldn't think of nothing 'cept to get you."

"Let's sneak down the corridor and at least jot down the room numbers of the possible thieves. We'll note who's staying from the very end to the middle and then try to strike up a conversation with them—see if you recognize the voices."

"Great idea, Doc. I knew I could count on you. Look how you caught that terrorist. A jewel thief should be a snap."

"I just got lucky that night. I wasn't intending to capture Waco. Gaston tripped him, and I struck him with the lamp. Just instinct. Survival of the fittest."

"But once ya done it, it gets easier the next time. Like riding a bike, I betcha. Ya already come up with a good plan to narrow down the suspects. Maybe we should keep a close eye on the rich lady, too, to stop them in their tracks if they make a move."

"I suppose you're right. We'd better get going before the crew starts waking up." Vlad turned toward the back stairs.

"Oh, Doc, one more thing. I forgot to bring a plastic bag for poop. Could ya please take one of those big leaves from that plant and use it to scoop up the little guy's business? We don't want him to get in trouble. Thanks." And Norm disappeared down the stairway before Vlad could say a word in protest.

Chapter 8

"UNSEASONABLY HOT FOR MAY," said Lutz, the program director, wiping his forehead with a handkerchief as they filed onto the bus. "Note the bus number because you need to return on the same bus."

Earlier that morning Vlad had woken up with his head still pounding and his mouth feeling like little centipedes in combat boots were marching back and forth over his tongue. The middle of the night adventure with Norm seemed like a crazy dream except for the giant leaf wrapped around dog doodoo resting in his bathroom trashcan.

Before breakfast he handed off his clothes for laundering to the cabin attendant vacuuming the hallway. The huge buffet with every type of breakfast food imaginable turned his stomach—he was barely able to finish a piece of dry toast and black coffee. Luckily, the day was hot enough to wear his shorts; many of the men were similarly clad. Beatrice sat next to him on the bus, looking pert in her coral top and tan capris. Norm and Sandra had ensconced themselves in the row ahead of them. Norm, uncharacteristically quiet, popped up to scan the fellow travelers but Sandra happily chattered about seeing the Black Forest. Gaston quietly sat on her lap as the bus pulled away, nestling his head into the crook of her arm for a quick snooze.

Soon they were traveling down the autobahn, cars and trucks zooming past at high speeds. The wide silver freeway curved into deeply forested valleys until they veered off on a narrower road. Beatrice reached over, slid her hand into Vlad's hand, and smiled. He returned her smile halfheartedly, the lack of sleep and wine hangover spoiling the happy moment.

"Look to the right," Lutz said. "See the rows of newly planted wheat. This is why the area is called the breadbasket of Germany."

Row after row of neatly planted crops were patterned in

geometric perfection—wheat seedlings, grapes vines tied to stakes, round bales of hay. No weed would dare show its face in such fields. The bus passed by immaculate farm complexes perched on the fertile green valleys, outlined by dark trees on the hilltops. Freshly painted houses, sheds, and barns, little private chapels, and fruit trees of all varieties could be seen in abundance. Goats peacefully grazed in a meadow. Almost all of the small farmhouses had solar panels on their roofs. Lutz told them, "Seven percent of Germany's electricity comes from solar energy with wind providing another twenty percent. By the end of the decade, we hope to have sixty percent of our energy coming from renewable sources."

Vlad would have been impressed if his head weren't pounding so. Every little bump made it worse, and he was trying hard not to upchuck. As they drove into the mountainous region, little mountain streams started to appear. The hillsides were covered with dark evergreen trees. All he could think about was the path to the restroom and would it be free when he needed to puke?

"I'm feeling a little queasy," Beatrice said. "I'm not used to drinking wine." She wrinkled her nose in distaste. "Pretty nasty the day after. You feeling that way, too?"

"Yes, but it's not just the aftereffects of the wine. When we get back to the ship, I'll tell you at dinner. Something hard to believe. I'm not sure I believe it myself," he whispered to her.

"Something concerning Norm?" she whispered back. "He's acting strangely, even for Norm."

Vlad nodded, swallowing hard to eliminate the taste of bile in his throat. Thankfully, Beatrice didn't pursue their conversation, content to listen to Lutz share the history of the region.

A short time later the bus pulled up at its first stop, and a sweet-faced young woman wearing a lime green dirndl with a pink apron greeted them as they exited. Her long hair was pulled back with a small clip adorned with a flower garland, long pink and green ribbons trailing down her back.

"Please follow me for a short walk into the Black Forest. I will point out some of the unique flora and fauna as we enter. The trail is a little steep in places and very uneven. So if you have mobility issues, you may want to visit the shops and restaurant instead. We don't have a gentle version of this excursion."

"That's me," Sandra declared. "Mobility issues. My service dog and I will hit the shops. How about joining us, Clarence?"

The old man stood nearby with Dougie, cane in hand. "Do you mind going by yourself, son? I'm going to stay behind with this charming lady."

"No problem, Dad. I'll find you in the restaurant."

Norm was already mingling in the crowd. Vlad surmised he was eavesdropping on conversations in search of his potential jewel thieves. He hovered near a cluster of tourists, tilting his head as near to the speaker as he dared, inching closer as the conversation shifted to someone else.

Vlad and Beatrice followed the line of tourists over the sunny knoll and into the shade of the forest, the temperature dropping by at least ten degrees as they entered the gloom. A murmuring brook meandered alongside the path, its soothing sounds overpowering the guide's memorized patter. Huge rocks and exposed roots from trees caused Vlad to stumble several times, each jolt making his headache worse. Dougie suddenly appeared next to Beatrice. "Isn't this just like being in a story from Grimms' Fairy Tales?"

"You mean the original Grimm Brothers stories? Not the ones sanitized by Disney," she said.

"Yes. My oldest kid came home with an illustrated book close to the original. Every drawing all dark and grotesque. No happy endings." He gestured to the surrounding forest. "You can almost imagine an ugly troll jumping out from behind that tree." He pointed to a crazily tilted tree, dead limbs catching on the tall tree nearby, trying to pull it down to the rocky ground.

"Spooky-looking, I agree,' she said with a slight shiver.

The path narrowed, and Vlad found himself trailing the two of them. Dougie chattered away, recounting plots from his favorite detective shows, which all featured a macabre element. Vlad wished he had taken the bottle of water with him from the bus; he was developing a giant-size thirst as the trail grew steeper and more challenging. When he stopped to catch his breath, the few people straggling behind him passed by. His heart thumped so loudly it felt as if it was popping out of his chest.

"I've had enough of this," he said to no one in particular. He could see Beatrice looking back for him, hesitating on the path while Dougie tugged on her arm. Vlad waved her on and pointed back down the trail they had just covered. She nodded and waved back, moving on with the group. He slowly retraced his steps down the path. Thick tree branches blotted out the sky. The only sound disturbing the gloomy quiet was the buzz of some sort of insect near his face. He trudged on back into the sunlight, losing the gnats to the darkness, and made his way toward the restaurant.

As he entered, he spied Sandra and Clarence sitting at a table with large slices of a cake layered with cherries, whipped cream, and chocolate. Gaston lay at Sandra's feet. He noticed her slipping a gob of whipped cream to the dog's waiting mouth.

"May I join you?" he asked.

"Of course, dearie. We're just having a little nibble and a cup of coffee. This is self-serve so you have to get in that line." She gestured with a tilt of her head to a small cluster of people. "In a few minutes the chef is going to give a talk on how to make Black Forest Cake at home. Think I might try it someday. Maybe Gaston would like a break from Cheese Danish. He loves the cherries and whipped cream, but no chocolate for you, sweet-ums." She popped a cherry into Gaston's mouth.

Vlad looked at the whipped cream smeared on the dog's jaw and the eager gleam in his eyes. "He certainly is enjoying his treat."

Clarence tried to take Sandra's hand under the table but Gaston emitted a low growl so he hastily withdrew it. Vlad thought, *Poor smitten fool. You have no idea what that beast is capable of.*

"There's a wonderful souvenir shop above us—full of stuffed animals, all adorable. I'm sure Katy would love one," Sandra suggested.

"As soon as I get something to drink, I'll check it out."

"This lovely lady and I were enjoying the cake by ourselves. You know what they say about 'two's company...'" Clarence said pointedly. "You might want to go upstairs now before it gets crowded. When the hikers return, it'll be packed."

"Good idea. I'll leave you two. Thanks for the heads-up." Vlad went to the check out and purchased a Coke Lite, then drifted up the stairs.

A virtual zoo of well-crafted stuffed animals covered one whole wall of the shop. Vlad looked at a lion in a band uniform holding a tiny trumpet, a puppy so realistic he half-expected it to lick his hand, bears in every shape and size, elephants, giraffes, kangaroos. He settled on a grey striped cat, soft and pliable. Kaitlyn begged for a kitten of her own, and this was as close to real as he'd ever seen. He handed his credit card to the cashier.

As she returned with his card and the kitten tucked in a bright green bag, Vlad heard loud haggling from the other end of the shop where every cuckoo clock imaginable was displayed. Some depicted hunting scenes, complete with carved stags and foxes, a crossed set of rifles arching over the cuckoo opening. Others showed tranquil rural scenes with cottages, flowers, and evergreen trees. A parade of brightly painted folk art figures marched past the cuckoo bird as it squawked the time.

The Beaumonts were arguing with a salesman over the largest standing clock in the store—a finely carved bear stalked on top dominating layers of evergreen trees. Below the bear, bright hunters marched out of their homes in a circle on the hour. Two bear cubs cavorted under the clock face. No other clock in the shop featured this ursine theme.

"This price is outrageous. I'm sure when we shop in a real town we can get a better price." Katherine snorted.

"But madam, each piece is hand-carved by our finest craftsman. It took him months to complete. This clock is totally unique. You won't find one like it in all of Bavaria."

"I've seen Black Forest clocks on Amazon at a better price— maybe not with bears, but…" She let her voice fade into skepticism.

'I guarantee you won't see one like this. The sale price is the best we can do. We're a small business. We only sell here in this shop. Our clockmakers are all artisans from the surrounding countryside."

Warren touched the top of the clock with his index finger and held it under the salesman's face. "Look at the dust. This clock has been here a long time, I wager. I'd think as a good businessman you'd want to move it."

"Sir, madam, look at the fine workmanship…"

"Sad, so sad. Terrible maintenance." Warren frowned.

"You'd think the tour would choose higher quality shopping establishments." Katherine tossed her head. "I'm going to write a letter to complain."

"I'll throw in the shipping. That's the very best I can offer," said the frazzled man.

"What do you think, dear?" Warren said to Katherine.

She pursed her lips in a disgusted expression, then reluctantly said, "I suppose. I did want it for a birthday gift for Mother."

The clerk ushered them to the cash register and began filling out the paperwork. Vlad went back downstairs to watch the cooking demonstration. Sandra stood up front at the head of the gathering crowd, Gaston at her heels. Clarence sat alone at the table, sipping his coffee and watching her with a lovestruck expression. Vlad eyed the door, hoping for Beatrice to appear.

Warren and Katherine came down the stairs gleefully clutching a sales receipt. They sidled next to Vlad and waved it in his face.

"Did you see what we just bought? That beautiful cuckoo clock and only fifteen hundred dollars. You'd never get it for that price in America," Katherine crowed. "You just have to know how to bargain with these people—show them who's boss."

"I knew how to close the deal!" Warren boasted.

Vlad couldn't help but see the price as the bill was thrust into his face.

"Are you sure you're talking about dollars? See—here's a comma where we would normally see a period in America. I think you're talking euros so, with the exchange rate, the cost was more like twenty-two hundred dollars."

Both Katherine and Warren examined the bill more closely. "Darling, I do believe he's right. And it clearly says all sales final," Katherine said.

"These foreigners." Warren sighed. "You just can't trust them."

Using all of his willpower not to roll his eyes, Vlad walked away, leaving them to their complaints. The May sunshine beckoned; the diet cola eased his headache somewhat. He pushed open the door, inhaled the fresh spring air, and waited in silence for Beatrice to emerge from the forest. Sometimes when he didn't want to cause a commotion, he found it best to say nothing. His father always said, "Say nothing and you'll be thought the fool. Open your mouth and you'll prove it."

Chapter 9

AS SOON AS THEY BOARDED THE SHIP, Beatrice steered Vlad toward his stateroom by loudly announcing, "I'm exhausted by all the hiking. I need to take a break and rest for a while. How about you, Vlad?"

Before Dougie could offer his services, she took Vlad's arm and split from the group, most of which were happily enjoying the fruit smoothies the crew handed to them as they disembarked the bus. Instead of her room, however, she ordered him to open his door when they reached it.

Closing it firmly behind her, she poked him in the chest with her forefinger and said, "Will you please tell me exactly what is going on? Norm is acting like a human surveillance drone, and you look like death warmed over. You barely spoke on the bus ride, and I was stuck listening to Dougie recall episodes of his favorite TV shows while you went shopping."

'You're not going to believe this. I find it farfetched myself, but Norm swears it's the truth," he said, hugging the bag with the stuffed animal for protection from her glare.

"Spill it, Buster. And it better be good. I've got a bit of a hangover, and I'm in no mood for BS." She crossed her arms over her chest and waited.

He took a deep breath, sat down on the edge of the bed, and began. "Norm was walking Gaston on the top deck late last night and overheard some thieves talking on their balcony—planning a diamond heist in Amsterdam."

Her eyes widened and her voice rose with incredulity. "A diamond heist in the diamond capitol of the world? Norm's been watching too many *Miami Vice* reruns on cable television!"

"I thought the same thing, only I thought he might have been smoking something stronger than cigarettes. But he repeated the conversation. Walked me through the scenario. It seemed plausible."

"Plausible?" She plopped down on the bed beside him. "This is Norm we're discussing. The guy who sunbathes on a skylight over a fancy hotel's restaurant!"

Vlad waved his palms in the air. "I know. I know. But sometimes he has good advice. He helped me with my divorce."

"Why didn't you tell the captain? YOU at least have some common sense. He could alert the authorities and have the thieves investigated." She wagged her finger at him.

"There's a slight problem. He doesn't know which balcony. He can't remember where they were standing. Besides, I'm sure the captain won't be too happy to learn Gaston relieved himself on the potted plants."

"The ship's not that big. Gaston's a little dog. There's only so many places he can relieve himself on the top deck." She rolled her eyes. "I can't believe I'm even having this conversation with you."

"We came up with a plan. We know what side of the ship the thieves are on, and Norm's trying to identify the voices he heard. He's going to loiter in the hall outside the possible rooms until he pinpoints the voices."

She snorted. "Hmmph. And that's not going to look a little obvious?"

"His other plan is to stand guard over the Beaumonts because the thieves might hit her diamonds first."

"Won't robbing the Beaumonts tip the police off that there are thieves on board the ship? They can't be that stupid."

"They let Norm overhear their plot.'

"I guess they can be that stupid!"

Just then the object of their discussion pounded on the door.

"Lemme in, Doc! Lemme in!"

The urgency in his voice made Vlad hurry to the door. A wild-eyed Norm pushed past him into the room and removed his Packers cap, waving it in frustration.

"It's no good, Doc. All them Brits sound alike, even the women. Now I'm more mixed up than ever. I'm just gonna have to station myself in the hallway and reconnoiter the rooms. Ya think one of the crewmembers would let me borrow a uniform? Maybe I could steal one?"

Beatrice stared wide-eyed and said, "I don't think stealing a uniform is the answer…"

"Guess not. So I'll just have to pretend I'm waiting for a friend. Keep checking my watch like they're late. Maybe I'll see somebody who looks suspicious." Norm started pacing around the small room while Vlad and Beatrice dodged his movements.

"I highly doubt they'll be wearing all black or a mask or gloves," Beatrice said drily.

"But maybe they'll act shifty—ya know—nervous-like, watching for the heat. Crooks always are looking out for cops." To reinforce his point, Norm aimed the cap brim at her.

Against his better judgment, Vlad gave him a nod. "Give it a try tomorrow but try not to act conspicuous. You don't want to draw attention to yourself."

Norm shook his head. "Naw, I'll be careful. Don't want to tip them off I'm on to them, whoever them is. I'll be on it first thing in the morning."

"What if this doesn't work?" Beatrice asked.

Norm firmly placed both fists on his hips and said, "I go to plan B, but I'm gonna try this one first."

All three headed for the dining room, stopping first to pick up Sandra.

"She wanted to freshen up a bit," Norm said. "She really likes this Clarence guy, even if he's an old codger."

"He seems like a nice man, just a tad forgetful," said Beatrice.

"And he seems quite taken with her. Just don't try to join them when they are having a *tête-à-tête* over Black Forest Cake. He is almost as surly as Gaston," Vlad commented ruefully.

Norm knocked before using his key card. "It's just us, Sandra. Are you ready for dinner?"

She flounced across the room in her midnight blue cocktail dress with the lace bodice and satin skirt. "You'd never know I found this at the thrift store for five bucks. It has a little stain, but if I keep my arms down, you don't even notice it," she confided. She wore blue crystal chandelier earrings dangling down to her shoulders and a three-strand crystal necklace to match. Even Gaston wore a rhinestone-studded collar. "And these were only four bucks for the set. I was lucky I got there when the gal put them out. I snatched them up before anybody else got the chance."

Norm whistled. "Wow! You're hot stuff tonight, baby!"

"Are you planning to go dancing in the lounge after dinner?" Vlad asked.

"You betcha, honey. I haven't gone out with a man who was still breathing without an oxygen tank in years. I'm going to take advantage when I've got a live one. Why don't you two join us?" she said to Vlad.

"I'm still trying to recover from last night," he said. "I'm afraid I had a little too much to drink. And then Norm stopped in…" He gave Norm a look, unsure of how much to reveal about the late-night stakeout.

Norm frowned and gave a quick shake of his head.

"Dancing sounds so romantic. Maybe we should join them for a nightcap?" Beatrice said, turning to Vlad. "Just for a song or two. I don't often get to enjoy live music."

Norm chimed in. "You go ahead, Doc. Have some fun. You don't get out much at home, what with your work and the kids. You deserve a night out with your lady."

Vlad hesitated but couldn't resist Beatrice's shining eyes. "I guess I could remain awake for a song or two."

"That's the stuff, Doc. I'm hitting the sack early so it will be just you lovebirds out on the town, the ship, whatever." Norm winked. "And I'll take care of the pooch and give him his midnight constitutional."

"It'll be a double date, just the four of us," Sandra said.

Singing *There'll Be a Hot Time in the Old Town Tonight* only slightly off-key, Sandra grabbed Vlad's arm and started swaying back and forth as they walked down the hall. When she sang, "All join round as sweetly you must sing," he remembered seeing an old *Steamboat Willie* cartoon on Disney when he was a kid and hearing the same song. The music was so infectious, soon he found himself humming along. Beatrice laughed at the two of them sashaying down the hall.

"I doubt if we'll hear that tonight in the lounge," she said. "But you two certainly are a sight."

"Hope you can keep up with the Hoochie Coochie Girl there," Norm said.

They headed straight toward the table where Clarence and Dougie were waiting for them.

Vlad floated on a happiness bubble throughout dinner. He sat across from Beatrice and caught her smiling at him several times during the meal. When Sandra exclaimed after dessert, "Let's take this party to the lounge!" he felt some of the tiredness slip away. Beatrice leaned into him as the crossed the room, and he felt the warmth of her as he slipped her arm into his. The verbena scent of her hair mixed with the spicy smell of her perfume made him want to linger in the hall to keep this moment all to himself. Maybe tonight would be the night, the chance he was waiting for. He felt his throat constrict around the words he longed to say aloud.

Unfortunately, no one informed Dougie of the romantic plan because he followed close behind them. "A drink in the lounge sounds like just the thing. I had a few at lunch but my buzz wore off with all the walking around and all the chitchatting."

"No need to stay up. I'll see to your dad," Vlad volunteered. "I'll make sure he gets safely to his room."

"No, that's all right. I'm wide awake and full of energy. I'll join you in a nightcap."

The lounge act was already playing when they found seating. The same piano player from the previous night tickled the keyboard but this time a lovely young woman in a slinky black sheathe crooned pop songs from the sixties and seventies. She finished the last verse of *It's Not Unusual* as the waitress came around.

"Just ginger ale for me," Vlad said.

"Me, too," Beatrice added. "Tomorrow is the Alsace region. I can't wait to see Strasbourg."

"And a winery with a traditional treat in the afternoon. I wonder what the specialty will be," Dougie said.

"Something that goes with champagne, maybe. Lutz said they make their own version of sparkling wine," Vlad said.

Just then the woman started singing *Close to You*. Several couples were already dancing.

"I didn't get this dolled up for nothing," Sandra said. "Gaston, you sit and be a good boy. Handsome and I are hitting the dance floor."

She grabbed Clarence's hand and hauled him to his feet. "You can lean on me. Leave the cane behind."

"Let's show these youngsters how to swing it," he said, and they tottered onto the floor, holding each other up. They took slow-motion steps to the music, his arm firmly around her waist with an occasional slip to her derriere. Handholding in the air soon turned into her hand resting on his chest as he put both arms around her for support. She nuzzled into his neck, her eyes half-shut, a slight smile on her face.

"I'd like to take a swing on the dance floor myself," Dougie said, turning to Beatrice. "I can't let my old man have one up me. How about a dance, fair lady?"

Before she could refuse, he snatched her hand and dragged her out on the floor. She started to protest but he swirled her into the midst of the swaying dancers. He pulled her closer, and she backed away. But he seemed to have her in some sort of death grip. She shook her head after he whispered something in her ear.

Just then the waitress came with the drinks, and Vlad had to sign his name and cabin number. The happy bubble popped, and Vlad narrowed his eyes as he watched Beatrice and Dougie dance. Gaston sat up on his haunches, too, intently following every move Sandra made on the dance floor. Vlad heard a low rumble in his throat.

"I don't like it very much either, boy. My idea of a romantic evening isn't sharing a ginger ale with a bad-tempered dog while some jerk dances with my lady. I wish I could bite him and get away with it like you can."

Beatrice gave a helpless glance his way as Gaston emitted a small bark.

"I know. I know. I should just cut in on the two of them. Push that idiot over the railing or something. But with jewel thieves on the loose, I need to keep a low profile."

To his surprise, Gaston stood on his hind legs and thrust his paws on his upper leg. He made a lunge toward the hand resting on his knee. Vlad braced himself for a nip from his sharp little teeth but, to his surprise, the dog licked his hand. Then he settled back on his haunches at Vlad's feet and intently watched for Sandra's return.

To: erinflamethrower@gmail.com
From: Chomskyv@crawford.edu

Trapping Nicholas in his room might work. Sometimes he gets stubborn and shuts down. You could try giving him the computer and playing a game with him. He might open up if he's distracted. E-mail me tomorrow and let me know if it works.

I sent a picture of the Black Forest. I can see why Grimms' Fairy Tales are so dark if they lived in this creepy forest full of roots and gnarled branches that look like witches' hands.

Tell your brother and sister I love them.

Dad

Chapter 10

AT BREAKFAST, NORM STRAGGLED IN LATE. Vlad and Beatrice had visited the buffet and were enjoying their second cup of coffee when he finally appeared. Beatrice draped her sweater over a chair to save him a place, even turning a clean cup upside down for his coffee. Vlad hadn't seen him with such a downcast expression since the Green Bay Packers fumbled the football during the last seconds of the play-offs, losing the big game.

"How'd it go?" Vlad asked.

"Not so good," Norm answered. "Some cruise guy was vacuuming the hallway while I was spying. Had to pretend I lost a contact and dropped to my hands and knees to look for it. He turned off the vacuum and got down to help me. Asked what color it was. I said brown cuz my eyes are brown. Two guys left while we were searching the carpet, but I didn't get a good look. Then Clarence came out. One room was his. Had to leave when we got to the end of the hall. The poor guy apologized for not finding it and went back to his vacuum."

"Then what did you do?" Beatrice said.

"Stood in the stairwell and tried to listen for doors opening. Heard one and jumped out, but it was just some lady. I guess I startled the cruise guy cuz he tripped over the vacuum cord, crashed into the wall, and gave me the snake eyes. My stomach started growling so I left and came here."

"If you hang out in that hall too much the crew will start to think you're a pervert." Vlad said, pouring coffee from the urn into his cup. "Not such a good idea."

Sandra and Clarence wandered past their table so deeply engrossed in their conversation they didn't stop to say hi. She was dressed in her lavender Easter bunny outfit, but Clarence was wearing a Mediterranean blue shirt that hung loosely on him, a cotton button-down with "Santorini" emblazoned over the pocket.

"That's my shirt!" Vlad exclaimed. "Clarence is wearing my shirt!"

"Yer right, Doc. That does look like your fruity shirt."

"It's obviously too big for him," Beatrice said. "Just hangs on him like a tent."

"That old fart has my shirt. My suitcase's probably in his room," Vlad sputtered. "How do I get it back?"

"Talk to Dougie. He checks in on him morning and night—makes sure he's taking his medication, wearing pants, things like that," Beatrice said.

"I'm on it. I'd appreciate getting my clothes back and not having to buy a new wardrobe."

"See, Doc. One case solved. The mystery of the stolen suitcase. I told ya—yer a detective, all right."

"Where's Dougie? I'm getting tired of wearing the same clothes." Vlad abruptly pushed away from the table and stood up. "Excuse me while I try to find him."

Dougie was standing in line waiting for an omelet at the egg station when Vlad caught up with him.

Dougie greeted him warmly. "Where are you sitting? I'll join you. Dad and Sandra decided to have croissants and coffee in the lounge instead of waiting for service here. Apparently, Gaston likes their Cherry Danish."

Vlad's response was anything but warm.

"Have you noticed what your dad is wearing today? A shirt from Greece. I think that's my shirt—from my missing suitcase."

"I thought it didn't fit him properly, but when I asked, he said it was a new shirt. Got it out of his suitcase."

"My suitcase!"

"I'm terribly sorry, bro. Dad's not at the top of his game lately. I have his key. After I eat, we can check out his room—see if we can find your missing suitcase."

"Thanks a lot. These clothes are starting to stand on their own. I was going to go wardrobe shopping in Strasbourg today instead of the winery excursion. I'm that desperate."

When they checked out the old man's room, they found the

suitcase under the bed, with a red ship tag prominently displayed. Vlad lifted the suitcase on the bed and discovered it only half-filled with clothes. Thankfully, his underwear and socks were still untouched, but some of his shirts and trousers were hanging in the closet along with his silky new robe. He tossed the clothes from the closet into his bag, then slammed the lid shut.

All the while Dougie blithered away, "I'm so sorry. My dad is getting so forgetful—even starting to misplace things. I put fifty euros on the desk while I went to the bathroom. When I came out, it was gone. He put it in a safe place but couldn't remember where. I swear, I was only gone a minute. I had to tear the whole stateroom apart trying to find it."

"Did you?" Vlad said as he headed for the door.

"It was in his shaving kit. Why he put it there I'll never know. But that's how forgetful he is. He doesn't mean to take things that aren't his. Just doesn't remember. I'm sorry for the inconvenience."

"Me, too."

THE BUS WAS ALREADY LOADED by the time Vlad stowed the suitcase in his room and dashed down the gangplank. No time to even brush his teeth. He popped a breath mint on the walk down the aisle and hoped no one got too close. Luckily, Beatrice saved him a spot while Norm sat with Dougie directly behind them. Grateful to have recovered his suitcase, he decided to be charitable toward Dougie, even though his blond Elvis toupee and shiny purple shirt irritated him. Anyone with good sense would wear a looser shirt to hide their love handles, but not Dougie. The manly hairs on his chest couldn't distract from the marshmallow puffs around his belt.

Lutz spoke into the mic as the bus pulled away. "Today Alsace is a part of France. But control of this region on the Rhine has gone back and forth between Germany and France, so both countries have influenced their culture. First, our bus will tour Strasbourg, driving past the home of the European Parliament, the legislative center of the European Union."

Huge, elegant buildings and broad, tree-lined avenues all flashed by. Vlad tried to focus on Lutz's talk, but Beatrice's soft hand rested on the seat between them, occasionally brushing against his thigh. He longed for her touch on his bare flesh. He shook the image of her glimpsed breast out of his mind and grabbed the offending hand, cradling it as he smiled at her. Could she feel the heat rising as he did or was it just the unseasonably hot weather?

Lutz pointed out all the white stork nests as they passed them, perched precariously on steep rooftops. "It's considered good luck if a stork builds a nest on your rooftop. Storks migrate in the winter. Then the male arrives early in spring and repairs the nest for his spouse; the nest can grow almost large enough to hold a refrigerator. When the nest is comfortable and sturdy, the female returns to mate."

"Male storks have the right idea, doing all the housework. You men could take a page from their playbook," Beatrice quipped, and Vlad squeezed her hand.

"I'd like to see some storks mating. That's a sight for YouTube," Dougie said. "I wonder if they do it in their big ass nest or screw in flight."

Beatrice rolled her eyes skyward, and Vlad gave a barely noticeable headshake.

Finally, the bus stopped in the oldest part of the city known as Petite France where their walking tour host greeted them. The aging Englishman with badly dyed black hair and sagging jowls looked like a man on the last day of a seven-day bender. Scuffed slip-on shoes, no socks. His faded pink oxford shirt looked slept in as did his rumpled grey pants.

"Ladies and gents, we will be taking our stroll today along the river of this World Heritage Site of Grande Île. Before we start our journey, you may want to use the loo—your last chance for public accommodations until we end our tour."

Norm whispered, "Come with me to the can. I got an idea." He wore the ubiquitous Green Bay Packers cap and aviator sunglasses, peering at Vlad over the rim, willing him to follow. As they stood in line in the dank restroom, he drew close and continued in a low voice, "I'm going to shadow the rich lady today. If you notice, she's wearing her fancy bracelet. Easy for a thief to brush up against her and undo the clasp. She's so busy yapping to her hubby, she prob'ly wouldn't feel a thing."

Vlad took a step back. "You're on to Plan B?"

"Yep. Gonna watch her like a hawk. Catch the thief in the act."

Norm started humming *Goldfinger* and sauntered over to the urinal. He kept his head straight, but shifted his eyes all around as though the thief might be taking a whiz next to him. Vlad couldn't wait to get back into the sunshine next to Beatrice, and away from Double O Three and a Half.

Alas, that was not to be. Standing next to her was Dougie, already sweating profusely in his glossy shirt. All the earlier gratitude seeped away like a balloon not properly tied off—with only limp annoyance remaining. As Vlad shuffled over to her other side, she glanced and smiled at him.

But Dougie blabbered on. "Didn't know it would be this hot in May. Might have to buy a few tee shirts. Left all my wife beaters at home. Ha-ha."

Thankfully, the English guide signaled for their attention and they were on their way. First, they saw a huge dam with water flowing through brick arches topped by a long fortress-like building. If attacked, soldiers could raise the level of the river and flood the lands south of the city. Inside they wandered through the ex-fortress, now a museum with classical statues and a flock of gargoyles.

"That gargoyle looks like my ex-wife," Dougie said. "Put some lipstick on it and it's a dead ringer."

"Too bad we don't have time to visit the museum that has the originals of these sculptures," Vlad said to Beatrice. "I know how you love art."

"Maybe someday we'll have a chance to return and spend more time here." Beatrice whispered to him. "Just the two of us."

They followed the river past medieval buildings and down cobblestone streets, some so narrow not even a Smart car could drive down it. Flower boxes adorned each half-timbered house, and more flowers grew in planters outside. Vlad noticed the rooftops had many dormer-like structures, stacked in rows on top of each other.

"What are those?"

"Well, gent, to have enough food when enemies laid siege, people built storerooms in attics and had screened windows to better circulate air and preserve the grain. Those are windows to the former storerooms."

'This is like a walk into the past," Beatrice said. "Look at the signs hanging above the shops. I could imagine tanners and shoemakers and craftsman having their symbols on them."

Vlad looked back to check on Norm. He saw Katherine right

away, with a bright blue straw hat, oversized shirt, and matching blue capris. She had pulled a small iPad out of her voluminous flowered purse and was snapping pictures of the buildings as they strolled past, bracelet glinting in the spring sun. Slouching behind her was Norm, baseball hat pulled low, the brim touching his sunglasses, hiding behind a planter whenever she paused to snap a photo. Warren trudged on ahead, listening to the guide and ignoring his wife as Norm slunk behind them, moving from shadow to shadow.

SUDDENLY, THE NARROW STREET emptied onto the most magnificent cathedral Vlad had ever seen, made of pink sandstone with flying buttresses looking ready for flight. The stonework was carved so intricately it resembled lace. A multitude of thin, stone spires so fragile-looking you'd swear a strong wind could snap them in two pointed heavenward. Incredibly, according to the Englishman, it was the tallest tower in the world until 1874. A circle of stained glass rose above the entrance, massive double doors with a delicate statue of Mary and Baby Jesus between them. The twelve apostles flanked the walls on either side, and highlights from the life of Jesus depicted in stone relief formed a collage above the door.

"Ladies and gents, this is where I leave you. You have an hour to visit the church and wander around the square nearby. Lutz will meet you by the large carousel on the square—Gutenbergplatz—can't miss his statue—at noon. On to the ship for lunch, then the winery tour in the afternoon. Ta-ta. It's been a pleasure." With a wave of his hand, he disappeared down the narrow street.

Every alcove in the cathedral was filled with relics from saints or stone-carved crypts containing the remains of a ruler or holy man; since in the Middle Ages the two were sometimes synonymous. The tourists entered with hushed tones. Even though Vlad wasn't Catholic, he still felt the power of the faithful who built the church. Beatrice knelt down on the kneeler in front of Mary's statue, made the sign of the cross, and bowed her head. He stood silently beside her, admiring the gilded pulpit that rose toward the ceiling, recalling how the English guide told them the guilds of Strasbourg embraced the Reformation so they wouldn't have to pay indulgences to the Catholic priests. As Alsace changed hands between France and Germany, so did the cathedral, switching between Catholic and Protestant.

Beatrice rose to her feet and whispered to Vlad, "My mother

always says, 'Sorrow looks down. Worry looks around. Faith looks up.' I wish she could see this. Everything inside here makes you look heavenward."

The Gothic arches pointed toward the gilded ceiling, a promise to the faithful.

He wandered into a side room with the immense astronomical clock. Before the guide departed, he warned them not to miss seeing this wonder, which not only tells the time but tells the day of the week, month, year, the sign of the zodiac, the phase of the moon, and the position of several planets. As the clock struck the hour, intricately carved figures depicting the Four Ages of Man traveled before Death. How many men and women had stood before this clock since 1842 when it was built and watched Death win over Man? But Jesus vanquishes Death at noon, according to the guide, when a winged angel blows into a horn and, on the upper tier, the twelve Apostles travel before Jesus as He raises His hand to bless each one, but turns His back on Judas. Unfortunately, by that time, they'd be on the way to the ship.

Beatrice drifted next to him and said, "The guide over there told her group the priests blinded the creator of this clock so he couldn't reproduce it for another church. Can you believe their cruelty?"

"Unfortunately, I can. Look at the Spanish Inquisition. The Crusades. Joan of Arc. So many atrocities in the name of religion! All by so-called believers who wanted to impose their version of the Kingdom of God on others."

"Seems like some of that is still going on today with extremists of all religions." She gave a little shiver. "I'm catching a chill in here. Let's find an outdoor café and relax in the sunshine with a cup of coffee."

"Yes, let's. The stench of mortality fills these walls. I had enough gloom yesterday in the Black Forest."

At the nearby café, Sandra and Clarence were already seated. She waved for Vlad and Beatrice to join them. As they sat down, Vlad notice Clarence had dribbled coffee on his shirt; oblivious to the spreading splotches, the shirt was beginning to look like a Jackson Pollock canvas. Gaston was contentedly munching on a French pastry, cherry-filled by the looks of the stains on his fur.

"We're skipping the afternoon excursion," Sandra said.

"Too much walking on bumpy streets," Clarence grumbled. "Don't know why they don't pave them with concrete like we do in the States. Just a nuisance. And a health hazard."

"He almost fell, even with his walker. It got stuck in a rut, and he pitched forward. Luckily, he stumbled into a nice gentleman with quick reflexes. Unfortunately, his straw hat flew into the river. It probably floated to Switzerland by now," Sandra said.

"Better the hat than Clarence," Beatrice said.

"If we were in America, I'd have sued their pants off. That was my favorite hat. Damn rocky streets. Made me tear my new shirt when I fell."

He pointed to his side where a flap of Greek cotton dangled under a triangular tear.

"Damn shame it tore. Most comfortable shirt I own."

THE DANK COOLNESS OF THE WINE CELLAR was a sharp contrast to the bright sunshine of Obernai, the Alsace city. After miles and miles of passing Riesling vineyards in their neat rows of grape vines, the walk to the winery was a short-lived pleasure. On the bus ride, Lutz talked about the American connection.

"Years ago a blight attacked the grapes, and it seemed as if the wine industry in this area was doomed. Because grape plants used to start the California wine industry came from Alsace, growers were hoping healthy plants from California could be grafted onto the ailing ones to develop a crossbreed that would be blight-resistant. It worked! The new plants were healthy, and the wine industry once again flourished."

The owner, a dapper man with a neatly trimmed mustache, crisp pleated pants, and shiny oxfords, welcomed them to his establishment. "My family has been making wine since the 1600s. All the wine is made naturally—no sulfites. We make some of the finest wines in all Alsace."

The first stop was the wine cellar. As they walked down the narrow dimly lit steps, Vlad was startled to hear Norm whisper in his ear, "Doc, this would be a perfect spot for a robbery. Close quarters, bad lighting, people bumping into each other. I'm going to stick to that Katherine dame like glue. Nothing gets past me."

He brushed past and waited at the bottom of the stairs for Warren and Katherine to appear, hanging in the shadows of the giant casks, carved wooden behemoths as large as a Ford Focus. Flipping his sunglasses to the top of his baseball cap, he struck the threatening pose of a *Mission Impossible* poster.

Vlad noticed the intricate carvings on the outside of the casks—curving grape vines and flying birds; one with a rural scene of a farmhouse dated back to 1700. It was hard to pay attention to the vintner with Norm ducking behind them and constantly swiveling his head from side to side, standing on the balls of his feet, ready to spring into action. They walked into an area where workers were hosing down giant gaskets with a pressurized hose. Beatrice started to cough and wheeze.

"Fungi from the fermenting process is being washed out," their host explained. Soon they all were coughing. "Perhaps it's time to visit the tasting room," he said, and they followed him up a different set of stairs into a long room with bottles of wine completely covering one wall.

He directed them to the seating area of long tables surrounded with wooden stools. Vlad managed to steer Beatrice toward Katherine and Warren. He slid on the stool next to Katherine. Thankfully, her diamond bracelet was still attached to her arm. She fanned herself with her bright blue hat and cleared her throat several times before she spoke.

"It's hard to catch my breath after that unpleasant experience. This wine better be worth it."

Norm sat at the table directly behind her and flashed Vlad a thumbs-up sign. He moved his stool to their side and nudged toward Katherine, almost touching her oversized bag with his foot.

"Can you imagine inheriting a business that's been in the family for four hundred years?" Beatrice said. "You get a whole different concept of time over here."

"Wonder what kind of capital gains taxes they have," Warren said. "Must not be as high as ours."

A pretty woman in a puffy sleeved dress wearing a white cap with wings that curled on both sides poured them a glass of wine. "This is the Riesling," she said.

To Vlad, it tasted perfect. A fruity taste, not too sweet, not too dry. He sipped it slowly, savoring the cool liquid on his tongue. "This is wonderful—so smooth." Katherine just sniffed. Behind him, Norm declared, "Best wine I've had in years—sure beats Mogen David."

Next came a Gewürztraminer, a bit sweeter and fuller bodied, but still delicious to Vlad who had never tasted such wine before.

"What do you think of this one?" he asked Katherine.

"Better than the Riesling. I've had wines from the Columbia Valley that were just as good. Perhaps America has better growing conditions for the grapes. I'm a bit disappointed, I must say," she sniffed.

The last bottle was the winery's version of champagne, a sparkling wine that frothed in the glass. Vlad remembered his hangover from the first night and gingerly took a sip. He shuddered and pushed it aside. Behind him, he heard Norm gulping his and said, "If yer not gonna drink that, I'll take it, Doc."

The waitress brought them a pastry with fluted sides that resembled an upside-down muffin, the top decorated with a circle of almonds and a light dusting of powdered sugar.

"This is called a kouglof—a traditional pastry of Alsace made with yeast and raisins."

Vlad bit into the delicious buttery, yeasty cake, bread-like in texture with a hint of orange flavor, not sugary at all. "I could get addicted to this," he said.

"Too dry," Katherine said as she slid it over to Warren. "Would you like to finish this?"

"No thanks, one is enough," he said, wrinkling his nose.

"Ya really don't want that?" Norm said, picking up the plate with the pastry. "I'll take it. No sense letting perfectly good food go to waste."

Katherine shot him a look like he was covered in excrement, then abruptly rose to her feet and went into the buying room, Warren in tow.

Norm took her place next to Vlad. "No jewel thieves yet." he said. "But at least I won't starve waiting for them.

Chapter 11

WHEN VLAD SET FOOT ON THE COBBLESTONES of Heidelberg, he felt as if he had arrived home somehow. Perhaps it was the knowledge that Heidelberg University had once been the home of Hegel, his favorite philosopher, who said: "Education is the art of making man ethical," an ideal Vlad aspired to in his teaching. He almost felt Hegel walking beside him with his scraggly thinning hair and wire-rimmed glasses sliding down his nose. Many times during the past year as he struggled to create a new life for himself, he mulled over another Hegel quote: "Nothing great in the world has ever been accomplished without passion." Unfortunately, Vlad's brief affair with the sexy co-ed Britney had had lots of passion but only accomplished regrets, nothing great for sure.

The tourists followed Lutz to the Old Bridge, guarded at the entrance by two white towers bookending a raised sentinel building. Beatrice smiled as Vlad snapped her picture on the ancient bridge, the Neckar River winding in the background. The old historical side contained narrow streets and side-by-side houses in styles ranging from Romanesque to Baroque. Opposite the Old Town he viewed beautiful Art Nouveau houses of the wealthy, stacked along the rolling hillside like a fairy village. Looming over it all stood the gigantic ruins of Heidelberg Castle, the scene of some epic battles between the forces of princes and clergy that ravaged Europe for centuries until it was utterly destroyed in the 1660s by King Louis XIV of France.

Fortunately for Sandra and Clarence (and Gaston), Lutz had arranged a motorized vehicle to take them to the castle ruins. Dougie rode with his father, and Norm continued his surveillance of the Beaumonts. Vlad finally had Beatrice all to himself. As Lutz guided the rest of them past a garden gate dedicated to the English princess

Elizabeth Stuart, who was married to the German prince to form an alliance, she reached over to hold his hand as they were walking.

"Isn't this castle a warning of the price of arrogance?" she mused. "If the Germans hadn't built a palace walk upon the hillside to view the gardens below, the French wouldn't have been able to so easily position their cannons upon that same hill and wipe them out."

The gate opened into a central courtyard—one side was the only part of the castle that had been renovated. The rest was an empty shell, like the false front of a movie set, adorned with row upon row of classical Greek-like statues strung across its face. Lutz explained who they were as he gestured toward the seven virtues, the nine planets, and the German Palatine electors and generals.

As he snapped pictures of the ruins, Vlad considered his own mortality. Once these feudal lords were among the most powerful of Germany—kings and popes deferred to them—but now they moldered in their graves for hundreds of years.

What would he leave behind to posterity? No published work, certainly no statue, maybe a brief obit in the newspaper? A few photographs that his great-grandchildren would laugh at and then toss into the trash? Hegel would be disappointed, already leaving him behind in a legacy in Heidelberg as he rose to greater academic glory in Berlin.

Lutz herded them through a passageway onto a terrace with magnificent views of the Old Town and the river—the red rooftops, the tiny houses, the beautiful garden, the ivy-covered ruins.

"Can you imagine waking up and eating your breakfast out here every day?" Beatrice said. "You certainly would feel you were part of a magical world. I can feel the enchantment just being here in the sunshine."

Vlad wouldn't trade this morning with her for fleeting power and fame. Death seemed like an illusion when she smiled, and her eyes shone.

They wandered into the Friedrich Building, restored in the 1890s. By this time, Sandra and Clarence had joined them with Gaston obediently trotting beside her as though he realized he needed to be on his best behavior. No nipping at a stranger's ankles or lifting his leg to an ancient sculpture. The *"Don't talk to me, I'm working"* sign protected innocent victims.

"This is even prettier than the Palace Theater," Sandra gushed as they walked through a gilded hallway lit by crystal chandeliers. Red velvet curtains pulled back by gold ties, delicate golden benches, and paintings of beautiful ladies in idyllic gardens spoke of a previous vitality.

"So much opulence!" Vlad said. "No wonder wars were fought for this wealth."

Suddenly, they entered a dark room and crowded together on a platform, overlooking a room-size wooden cask smelling of moldy earth and long-ago fermented wine. A brightly painted statue of a comical-looking man with long flowing hair and a neatly trimmed beard stood on a high pedestal. Broadly smiling, his upraised arm held a goblet lifted into a toast.

Lutz explained, "This is the royal wine cellar. The cask was made from one hundred and thirty oak trees during the reign of Elector Karl Theodor. It furnished the palace with wine all winter. The painted statue is Perkeo, the dwarf, his Italian wine steward, the prince's favorite. Whenever anyone called for wine, he said 'Perke no?' Why not? That's how he got his name."

"Now there's a guy I can relate to. Why not have a drink?" Dougie said, suddenly appearing at Beatrice's elbow. "He'd be a lot more fun than those stiffs on the front of the building."

They slowly made their way down the stairs. Vlad took care to make sure Sandra was close behind him, ready to catch her if she stumbled. She held on tightly to the railing, carefully taking one step at a time, while Gaston hopped step by step. Dougie pushed ahead with Beatrice, leaving Clarence to bring up the rear, and slowly inching his four-pronged cane down the well-worn steps. When they both reached the bottom, Vlad heaved a sigh of relief. Now he could focus on the tour. Unfortunately, the group was mulling in front of the gift shop.

"You have twenty minutes to look over the souvenirs and use the restrooms before we move on to the cathedral," Lutz said.

Castle-themed books and mugs, postcards, flags, and toys abounded. Beatrice brought over a large book on castles and knights in English. "I think Nicholas might like this," she said. "Look. Each double-page spread has a different illustration of castle life while the small drawings in the margins explain what each figure is doing. It's pretty informative without overwhelming."

"I like it,' Vlad said. 'How much?"

She turned it over to look for the price sticker.

Before she could answer him, Dougie waved a miniature catapult in his face. "Look what I found for my ten-year-old grandson over there. I had a tough time choosing between this and a life-size mace." He gestures toward a counter filled with models of medieval weapons. "This really shoots rocks or marbles for a distance of ten feet." He pulled back an elastic sling on the two-foot long contraption that twanged loudly when he let go. "Don't you have a son around his age?"

"Yes, but I'm thinking of getting him this book. It has excellent illustrations—lots of fascinating information." Vlad held up the book on castles.

"That's a sissy gift. How old is he—five? Maybe he likes little kiddie stuff. But kids my grandson's age like stuff that does something. Gotta compete with the video games, you know. I can see him chasing the cat around with this baby!" Dougie took aim at an imaginary feline.

"Nicholas prefers books," Beatrice said. "He's always reading."

Dougie snorted. "Reading! Sounds boring."

"He likes fantasy—epic battles between good and evil forces. But I think he'll like to learn about castles." Vlad tucked the book under his arm and glanced around for the check-out counter.

"Then he'll like this weapon. Bet they have shit like this in his books. You can always get a book from the library. But where can you get a catapult or a mace? They have smaller sizes if you think this one is too powerful for the kid to handle."

Beatrice frowned and said, "You don't know Nicholas. His interests are different from most boys his age."

"I know kids. I raised enough boys of my own to be somewhat of an expert. Three of my boys played rugby; no sissy stuff for them. The other one went right into the family business with me. Didn't get that smart from a book."

"Nicholas isn't much interested in sports. He did play soccer last year for a bit," Vlad said.

"And confided to me that he hated it!" Beatrice said, her voice rising.

Dougie drew down the corners of his mouth and shrugged his shoulders. "Just steering you in the direction of what's popular with kids. They like a bit of danger and excitement. Don't want your kid to look like a pussy."

"He wasn't very excited about the softball and glove from his mother. What makes you think he'll like a mace or a catapult?" she said, her eyes widening in disbelief.

"Let me see that thing for a minute," Vlad said as he set the book down on a counter and held out his hand for the device. The catapult did look like something from one of the Lord of the Rings battles. Nicholas had a lot of books. Maybe he would like something different. As he pulled back on the elastic, he remembered a slingshot he had when he was a young boy, the feel of it as he stretched the sling and pulled back, the twang as he let go shooting rocks at tin cans set on a fence post. He felt like a Superhero then, like Spiderman sending out his web to thwart the villain. Maybe this would make Nick feel like a hero in one of his books.

"Where did you find this?" Vlad said as he handed it back to Dougie.

"Over here, Sport. And it's only 29 euros."

He left her staring at the rejected book while he and Dougie compared features of the various catapults at the toy counter.

BEATRICE DIDN'T SPEAK TO HIM at all as they made their way through the Old Town to the square with the next pink sandstone cathedral. He carried the bulky package, wishing he had a small backpack like Dougie to place it in. Whenever he glanced her way, her face resembled the frozen look of the statues they had just observed at the castle. Lutz pointed out the wall built by the Romans hundreds of years ago, still in use today, the ancient stones exposed for the tourists' benefit.

"I'd like the name of that contractor," Dougie joked. "Never have to worry about wear and tear if the walls last for centuries. Slap a coat of paint on it, and it's good as new."

He elbowed Vlad, who managed a grimace that could be taken for a smile. Beatrice's downturned mouth and knotted brows couldn't be mistaken for anything but annoyance.

"I'm going to skip the cathedral and do some shopping. We've seen so many they are all starting to look alike," she said. "I'll meet you back at the bus." And she disappeared before Vlad could volunteer to accompany her.

"Wonder what pissed her off?" Dougie said. "She's kinda moody today. Maybe it's that time of the month."

With Norm busy shadowing the Beaumonts and the elderly lovebirds toddling slowly down the cobblestones, Vlad was stuck with Dougie. When he suggested visiting an interesting gift shop filled with locally made items, Dougie proclaimed, "Arts and crap! What do you need that junk for? Just a waste of money."

"There's a candy store—lots of those Kinder things and gummy animals. Your grandkids might enjoy a treat from Germany." Vlad looked at the colorful window display of jellied bears, dogs, cats, and various zoo animals.

"We got better candy in the good old USA. No thanks."

Suddenly a scruffy-looking man in skinny jeans and a faded David Beckham tee shirt grabbed Dougie's arm, "Alf, mate, is that you? What the bugger are you doing in Germany?"

"Sorry, bro, you must be mistaken. Name's Dougie. Douglas Kerwin from Pittsburgh, Pennsylvania."

"I could've sworn you were Alf Pearce, my old mate from Liverpool. I heard you moved up in the world. Struck it rich after a few capers. Word on the street your old man retired and you were taking over."

"Not me, I'm afraid. They say you have a double somewhere. This Alf guy must be mine."

"Sorry to have bothered you. You do look a lot like the other bloke. Give you darker hair and a mustache and Alf could be your twin. Oh, well. Cheers!"

As the man disappeared into the crowd of shoppers, Vlad shook his head and said, "What was that all about?"

"Mistaken identity. Happens to me all the time. I just have one of those faces, I guess. Most of the time people think I'm a young Wayne Newton with my Vegas clothes."

"Should we stop for a drink somewhere? I see a beer garden in the next block."

The outdoor tables spilled onto the street while the welcoming scent of hops and lager drifted their way.

Dougie gave him a playful punch in the arm. "First good idea you've had all day, pal. Let's grab a table."

They sat in the shade of an awning, sipped foamy warm beer,

and nibbled on giant pretzels. Sausages sizzling on the grill evoked a response like Pavlov's dogs, but Vlad contented himself with the pretzels, ignoring his rumbling stomach. He watched the passing crowd closely, hoping for a glimpse of Beatrice.

"I wasn't too thrilled about this trip, but at least the beer is good," Dougie said. "If Dad wasn't so set on crossing this off his bucket list, I'd have bailed. But Sis insisted on me taking over. Hell, if I wanted to look at a bunch of old shits, I'd have gone to my ex-wife's family reunion."

"I teach archaeology and ancient history at Crawford University so this is the trip of a lifetime for me. I can't imagine the thrill of finding the Roman structures underneath the plaster, still standing after all those years. Who knows what could be buried under these city streets?" Vlad ran his finger around the cold rim of his beer glass as he spoke. "A veritable treasure trove of artifacts!"

"Yada, yada. More old broken shit." Dougie gulped his beer. "So tell me about your lady friend Beatrice. You two a hot item?"

"I'm just divorced after twenty-some years of marriage. Dating is all new to me. This is the first time we've traveled together."

'Wait til you've been free for a couple of years. Your attitude will change. There are lots of single women out there looking for someone. I usually have no problems finding a babe temporarily. Too bad this trip is filled with couples or geriatrics. Speaking of which…"

He waved to Clarence. "Dad, over here!" He shouted and gestured to the two seats at their table. "Come join us."

Tap. Tap. Tap. Clarence made his way over the cobblestones with Sandra at his side and sank into the empty chair.

"I'm all in. Do you think you could help me find a bathroom in this place?"

"No problem, Dad. Do you want something to drink?"

"Just a lemonade."

"How about you, Sandra?"

"I'll have a Manhattan if they know how to make one here."

"I'll send a waitress over when I get Dad to the bathroom. You mind ordering for them?" he said to Vlad.

"Of course not."

As they watched the two men shuffle off, Sandra turned to Vlad and said, "I have a big favor to ask of you."

"Sure, anything."

"Could you please let Norm stay in your room tonight? I have big plans for me and Clarence."

"No problem. But are you sure he's up for something? He looks exhausted right now."

"He'll rest this afternoon. Besides, he told me he has Woody's Little Helper."

"I really don't need to know the details. I'll invite Norm to stay with me—but just for tonight! Remember I planned this trip to get to know Beatrice better. I'm hoping to stir up some romantic feelings," he said. "It's hard to plan romance when we're in Crawford surrounded by kids or her parents."

"Just for tonight. I got something special planned. Just you wait and see when we go dancing at the disco."

"I don't think it's a disco. It's just a restaurant with a live band."

"And I've got a live one with Clarence," she cackled. "You'll see."

Chapter 12

AFTER ENDURING THE SILENT TREATMENT on the bus ride back to the ship, Vlad followed Beatrice to her stateroom and closed the door behind them.

"May we talk about what happened today?" he said.

Her eyes flashed a warning, "Do you really want to go there?"

He took her hands into his and stared into her eyes. "Yes. I do want to go there. I want to fix whatever I did wrong. I know something upset you at the gift store."

She jerked her hands away in an explosion of anger.

"Why do you let that insufferable man push you around? I tolerate his self-centered drivel for Sandra's sake so she can be with Clarence, but really…you didn't need to let him bully you into buying that catapult!"

Vlad held his upturned hands toward her and said, "I wanted to buy it. I think Nicholas will like it. He has a collection of Star Wars action figures. He doesn't play with them much anymore but the catapult seems a good fit. Besides, it reminded me of when I was a boy."

"And you stormed the castle with your army? How many drawbridges did you knock down?" She glared at him, arms crossed.

"It's not like that. I didn't have a catapult, I had a slingshot. And my imagination. Pretended I was Spiderman. I'm hoping Nicholas will feel a bit of that magic. And I got the kit so we could build it together."

"Okay, now I get why it appealed to you. Maybe Nick will like it. I know he'll like doing something—just the two of you. But I'd still like to lose that obnoxious man and just be alone with you. We could enjoy a walk along the river, see some sights different from Crawford, Wisconsin. That has a certain magic, too."

Vlad grasped her hands again but this time she didn't jerk them away. "A stroll along the river sounds perfect. Maybe tonight…?"

"Yes, tonight."

He inched his face closer to hers as she half-closed her eyes and parted her lips, almost touching his. Her sweet verbena scent, her soft breasts pressed against his chest, a spark ignited as he tenderly kissed her.

BAM. BAM. BAM. Startled by the loud pounding on the door, they jumped apart like guilty teenagers and stood staring at each other.

"Hey, Doc! You in there? Just tried your room. Nobody's home." Norm's muffled voice seemed amplified by the closed door.

"Don't move," Beatrice hissed. "We'll pretend we're not here, and maybe he'll go away."

"Doc, open up. It's important!" Norm pounded even louder.

Vlad could imagine doors opening down the hallway as the other passengers looked to see what the racket was all about.

"I don't think we can hide from him. He'll just keep on beating on your door. The others deserve some peace and quiet," Vlad said regretfully.

"I suppose you're right." She moved slowly to the door and opened it a crack. "Yes, Norm. May I help you?"

He barged past her into the room and pulled the door shut behind him. "Doc, I'm not sure this plan is working. I watched Katherine like a hawk today but no sign of a thief. She may have noticed me following her when I tripped over the rack of postcards in a souvenir shop and they fell on her. The shop clerk gave me a dirty look when I started to pick them up. I apologized and tried to help but she scooted me away. By the time I picked up everything, she and the hubby were gone. I lost sight of them until we got on the bus. Luckily, she was still wearing the bracelet but I'm afraid my undercover was blown."

"Maybe this is all too complicated for you. You should just go to the captain and tell him what you overheard. Forewarned is forearmed," Beatrice suggested, a hint of a smile turning up the corners of her lips.

Vlad gave her an almost imperceptible shake of his head and assumed a serious expression. "Beatrice is right. You should go to the captain. I'll go with you if you'd like."

Norm paced up and down the narrow room. "And tell him what?

I overheard some thieves plotting a robbery while the dog was peeing on a planter? He'll think I'm some nut job. No. I don't want to go to him 'til I know who was talking. Maybe with some evidence."

Beatrice sat down in one of the chairs under the porthole and calmly folded her hands as she asked, "How do you plan on getting that evidence?"

Norm stood quietly for a moment scratching the side of his head. "Hm-m-m. Maybe I can ask Sam if I could borrow one of his uniforms. Tell him I want to play a prank, wake ya up early, pretending to be room service. I'd steal one from the laundry except they take all the dirty uniforms off the ship. I watched them haul everything off when we stopped in Strasbourg."

"Do you really want to involve Sam?" Vlad asked as he sank down in the other chair.

"He's a good kid. I always eat at his table, kidding around with him. He'll go along with the uniform thing. Then I'll knock on the two doors of the suspicious rooms early next morning, claim to be room service, and see if I can recognize the voice."

"I suppose it's a better plan than stalking the Beaumonts!" Vlad said.

"I still think you should turn it over to the captain. Even if he doesn't catch the thief, he can at least have the crew on the alert for potential trouble," Beatrice insisted.

"Naw, I'm gonna try this first. I'll talk to Sam right now. He probly won't need his uniform tonight anyway cuz we're going to the restaurant at Rüdesheim. I'll get it back to him tomorrow morning before the breakfast service begins."

"And tomorrow morning we sail through the Rhine Gorge so we're on the ship. Lutz is doing the commentary from the bridge," Vlad said as he turned to Beatrice and snapped his fingers. "He just might have a shot at catching the thief unawares."

Beatrice threw her hands up in the air. "I give up. Don't say I didn't try to tell you it's a bad idea." She rose from the armchair. "I'm going down to the lounge to watch the presentation on how to make Rüdesheimer Kaffee. I'm going to ask the chef for an extra shot of brandy. I need it after trying to deal with you two."

Later that evening Vlad and Beatrice milled about, waiting for the arrival of the mini-tram taking them to the restaurant along the river for their evening of authentic German food and dancing. Suddenly, he let out a loud wolf whistle.

"You weren't exaggerating when you said you had a surprise for this evening!" Vlad said as Sandra approached them.

She was wearing a white mini-skirt, topped with a zebra print boatneck shirt, along with black lace-up boots and diamond patterned black leggings. Dangly black earrings and a cluster of bangles on her wrist completed the ensemble. Even Gaston matched with an animal print scarf tied about his neck.

"When I read in the brochure about the dancing, I got myself a catchy new outfit. What do you think?" she said as she creakily turned in a circle to give them a complete view. She was a little wobbly on the heels. "It's been a while since I wore heels this high. I used to wear them all the time in my act. I figure dancing on them will come back to me—like riding a bike."

"You didn't bring any of your former costume along?" Vlad said warily. "I'm not sure how the Germans would view your G-string and pasties."

"Oh, no, dearie. Ever since I lost the Senior Center Beauty Pageant when they disqualified me for wearing them in the talent contest, I've hung up my burlesque duds. I know when to quit." She ran her fingers through her hair to make it look fuller. "You don't think I went overboard on the make-up?" She directed this question to Beatrice. "I put it on a little thicker tonight. I didn't want it to come off while we were dancing."

Two bright red spots of rouge complimented the brighter red lipstick, but it was all evenly applied. Beatrice kindly said, "No, it looks like it should hold up all night."

"I put on this purple shadow to bring out the blue of my eyes. I'm even wearing falsies."

Vlad gulped and glanced around to make sure no one overheard.

"I had a devil of a time putting them on. My hand isn't as steady as it once was. I could have ended up looking like Adolf Hitler, but I managed to rest my arm on the countertop. That close-up mirror was a big help, too. See how nice they look?" She batted her eyelashes at them a few times.

"You look unforgettable," Vlad said. 'Clarence will be blown away."

"I ordered a bottle of champagne chilling in the suite for later. Tonight's the night for romance. Don't forget out deal." She laughed lightheartedly and winked at Vlad. "Maybe I should include Gaston as part of the package."

"Maybe he's a deal breaker." A disdainful look from the poodle as he curled his upper lip to expose sharp little teeth prompted him to add, "No maybe about it. Gaston's a deal breaker."

"Oh, there's Clarence. Yoo-hoo!" She waved at the old man, snappily dressed in a white Key West shirt and dress slacks. "Over here, handsome."

He hobbled on his cane to her side, smelling of aftershave and lavender—the ship's signature body wash and shampoo.

"I didn't know I was going out with one Hot Mama!" he exclaimed. "It's going to be a good night. I hope I can keep up." He patted his pocket. "I brought my little blue helpers, just in case."

Lutz announced. "The train is here. Those of you who wish to ride please climb on board now. The rest of you, please follow me as we walk along the river to the Drosselgasse where our restaurant awaits. I'll point out some of the sights along the way."

The walk along the tree-lined promenade on a mild May evening beguiled both Vlad and Beatrice with the views of the river and the surrounding hillsides. Soon the park-like street turned into a market area with outdoor kiosks selling handmade toys, unusual jackets with large front pockets, ladies fashions, and the usual souvenir shot glasses and key chains. Charming cafes with inviting tables beckoned, but their restaurant was in the Old Town area.

Beatrice picked up an oversized white fisherman's sweater and held it up to her shoulders. "This will fit Erin perfectly. She'd look really cute in it."

"You're right. I'll get it for her now. The stalls might not be open later." He pulled out his credit card and handed it to the clerk while Beatrice kept her eyes riveted on their group.

"I wonder if Norm was able to connect with Sam," Beatrice said.

"I watched for him in the lobby, but I didn't see him. Hopefully, he'll catch up with us before we leave the promenade along the river."

They hurried to rejoin the group as Lutz narrated: "Rüdesheim is an historic city of winemaking dating back to Roman times. The grapes grown on the river valley produce the best Riesling in the world. The Drosselgasse, famous for its narrow, cobbled lanes, offers regional cuisine and live bands for every musical taste so you can dance the night away."

"I guess Sandra will get her wish to boogie on down," Beatrice said.

"Doc, Bea, wait up," Norm called from the back of the line. The narrow street made walking more than three abreast impossible as Lutz led them from the promenade to the lane. Intricate signs decorated with grape vines and wine bottles hung above on the various beer gardens and brightly lit restaurants emblazoned with the Drosselgasse name. Music blared as they passed by.

Vlad said, "Should we pretend we didn't hear him and just keep walking?"

"Let's ignore him," Beatrice whispered and grabbed his hand.

"I understand why they brought us here at night. All the music and lights, the beautiful signs hanging over the street," he said as he gently squeezed her hand.

"Look at that one, grape clusters in a circle, with the fancy lettering!"

Lutz pointed to the tram at the end of the climbing street. "That's the train. It leaves for the ship every half hour until midnight so you won't need to walk back."

"Excuse me. Excuse me." Norm's voice could be heard over the rumbling of the crowd as he pushed his way closer to them.

Beatrice sighed and rolled her eyes. "I guess there's just no losing him."

"Doc, ya musta not heard me. I did it. I got Sam to lend me his uniform, just until six tomorrow morning. Since I know Clarence isn't British, I'll check out the other two guys. So I'm gonna start at five and knock on those two doors. I thought I'd grab some towels from the bathroom and say, "Here's the extra towels you requested." That sounds legit, don't it?"

"It sounds plausible. You'd probably better shave and shower so you look as well-groomed as the staff. None of them sport any whiskers." Vlad gestured toward Norm's stubble.

"You're right. I didn't think of that. I should probably clean up my shoes, too. I don't think any of the staff wear Harley boots like these." He lifted up his pant leg to display a dirty motorcycle boot. "What size shoe do you wear?"

"Not your size. I just got my suitcase back with my spare shoes. I'm not planning on lending anything more out. Can't you just clean up your athletic shoes?"

"Do you really think at five in the morning anyone is going to notice what kind of shoes you are wearing before they slam the door in your face?" Beatrice pointed out.

"Ya got a good point there. And I asked the receptionist about the two guys and they're both British—a real tall fella named Ollie something and a fancy dresser she said was Nigel something. Now I just gotta hear them talk."

Lutz had stopped before one of the cafes resplendent in traditional German décor—painted scenes of forests and hunters with *Wellkommen* written in a cloud. A plump woman dressed in the ubiquitous dirndl and puffy sleeves greeted them at the door.

"Your dining room is waiting, if you will just follow me." She led them through the restaurant to an area at the back with long tables ready with place sittings. Dougie, Sandra, and Clarence were already seated at one. Dougie waved for them to come over, and Gaston barked a happy greeting at the sight of Norm.

Vlad held out the chair for Beatrice to sit down, then slid in beside her.

"Nothing like a little afternoon siesta to improve your mood," Dougie said, looking at Beatrice when he said the last three words.

"Oh, I didn't take a nap. I went to the presentation on how to make Rüdesheimer Kaffee. Believe me, whipped cream, dark chocolate, and brandy can do wonders for your mood, too. Especially if you have double shots of brandy." She smiled sweetly at him and said, "Maybe the restaurant will have it here after dinner. It's wonderful!"

Their waitress brought a cart to their table filled with wine. "Would you prefer white or red wine?" she asked.

"What do you recommend?" Vlad said.

"Winemakers here are famed for the Riesling so that's what I recommend. You won't find a better wine in all of Europe."

"Riesling it is." She poured glasses for Beatrice and himself, and placed the bottle between them.

"And you, sir?" she turned to Dougie.

"You mean I get a bottle, too?"

"Each couple gets a bottle. But if you and the gentleman," she nodded at Norm, "can't agree, then I'll see if I can round up another bottle.'

"I'm good with whatever..." Norm said.

"Then I'll go with the Riesling, too. When in Rome..."

"I thought we were in Rüdesheim?" Clarence interrupted. "It doesn't look like Rome. Not enough fountains and statues."

"A toast to a night of magic and dancing!" Sandra said as she lifted her glass.

"To magic and dancing!" Vlad repeated, gazing soulfully at Beatrice.

"Cheers!" shouted Clarence so loudly he woke up Gaston from his snooze at Sandra's feet and yipped. They took a sip.

"The wine is excellent!" Dougie said. "First rate!"

"Not Passion Pink Ripple, but not bad," Norm agreed as he drained his glass.

A second waitress had placed a plate of German food in front of them and explained what each dish was. "You have sauerbraten, red cabbage, and homemade spaetzle, the specialty of the house. Be sure to save room for the schaum torte for dessert."

Vlad had never eaten sauerbraten before so he just took a small bite. The sweet-sour flavor of the beef roast mingled with cloves, ginger, and other spices. He chewed slowly, then cut a larger bite, mixing its gravy over the herb flavored noodles.

"The wine is better than the food. The sauerbraten is dry, and the spaetzel is mushy but the wine more than makes up for it," Dougie said as he poured Norm and himself a second glass. "Have another glass, pal."

"I think the food's very good," protested Vlad.

"Obviously, you've never eaten at a good German restaurant. I thought you lived near Milwaukee."

"Crawford is mid-state. No German restaurants."

"But plenty of pizza and Mexican food, including my favorite Mexican restaurant Tequila Mockingbird," Norm said. "I like this— something different." He shoveled the food into his mouth and washed it down with a glass of wine.

Suddenly, two waiters carried a large plank with eight shot glasses permanently attached and stopped in the midst of their tables. The young lady who had just served them wielded a bottle of Jägermeister.

"Now we separate the men from the boys," one of the men loudly announced. "We challenge you to come up and drink a shot of Jägermeister without spilling a drop." They hoisted the plank above their heads so the entire restaurant could see. "Stand below your glass and we'll tilt the liquor into your mouth. Show us what you are made of."

Before he even finished, Dougie was out of his chair. He grabbed Norm by the shoulder. "Come on, bro. Let's show these pansies how to drink!"

"Remember Plan C! Tomorrow morning!" Vlad said, but Norm was already standing on the side of the plank with Dougie and a half dozen other males of various sizes and ages. The waiters lowered the plank, the waitress poured the Jägermeister into the shot glasses, and the men raised the plank just above their heads.

The head waiter said, "Give me the countdown. Three, two, one— Drink."

They tilted the board, and the men below opened their mouths wide to catch the booze. Some miscalculated and ended up wearing the liquor instead of swallowing it, but both Dougie and Norm achieved success. Laughingly, they sat down and high-fived each other, then a fist bump.

"Now it's your turn," Dougie said to Vlad, but he shook his head and held up his hands.

"I have nothing to prove!" he said, and Beatrice smiled in assent.

"How about showing what women are made of?" Sandra shouted. She stood up and made her way to the plank.

"She moves pretty fast for an old broad!" Doug said as Clarence shouted, "That's my girl! You show 'em, babe!"

Sandra took her place among the next group of men and waved back at their table, a tiny shriveled go-go dancer among the overweight tourists.

"She makes a mean martini. I'm sure she can drink half those guys under the table," Norm said.

The head waiter again began the countdown, and they all joined in. "Three-two-one-drink up!"

Sandra gulped it down without spilling a drop. As she faced the crowd with a triumphant smile, the waitress grabbed her hand and raised it high, declaring, "Here's the champ. Women rule." Whistles and cheers followed her as she returned to her seat.

"That was so much fun. You should really try it, dearie," she said to Beatrice. "Show those men who's got the right stuff."

"I also have nothing to prove," she answered, then winked at Vlad. Then she lifted her wine glass. "To a table filled with winners, on and off the drinking field."

"Here, here," Clarence responded, and they clinked their glasses together and took another drink.

Norm swirled the wine in his glass, then said, "This reminds me of the guy who went into a bar and sat down. Bartender looks at him and asks, 'What'll it be, buddy?' Guy says, 'Set me up with seven tequila shots.' The bartender does it and watches the guy slug one down, then the next and the next and so on until all seven are gone, just like that." Norm snapped his fingers.

"Bartender can't believe his eyes and asks why he's doing all the drinking. Guy says, 'You'd drink them this fast, too, if you had what I have.' Bartender says, 'Sorry, pal, what do you have?' The guy quickly replies, 'I have a dollar.'"

Sandra winked at him and said, "Are you sure that guy wasn't you? Sounds like something you'd do."

By this time the band in the corner was warming up. Two guitars, a drummer, and an accordion player. Since the drinking contest was over, the waitress resumed serving the meal. She cleared away their plates and brought them a foamy concoction covered in whipped cream and strawberries. "Here's the shaum torte," she declared as she set the little plates before them. "And an extra bottle of wine for the winner." One of the plank holders brandished a bottle of Reisling.

He bowed in front of Sandra and said, "The best of the house. Our finest bottle of Auslese just for you, madam. The grapes that made this wine were handpicked in December over twelve years."

"Picked that late?" Vlad asked.

"The wine is only made in certain years that are sufficiently warm in late autumn. An exceptional wine for an exceptional lady." He bowed again and uncorked the bottle.

"It's for our whole table. Didn't you hear my friend say—we're all winners?"

She gestured at them all. "Please pour them each a glass."

The wine tasted sweeter and richer—like the last days of golden summer captured in a bottle. Vlad savored his first sip as he said,

"Thank you so much, Sandra. This wine is delicious. Never had Auslese before."

"I never wore this outfit before. Lots of firsts today, I hope," she said as she gave Beatrice and Vlad a knowing look. "This trip is all about living life to the fullest. Now I hear the music starting, and Clarence promised me the dance."

She put her partly eaten schaum torte on the floor for Gaston and pulled Clarence to his feet. He picked up his cane with a flourish, but he still had problems making his way to the dance floor, limping along while the band played a polka version of The Commodores' *Brick House*. Sandra had no problem dancing her way to the band, snapping her fingers and stepping with a little butt shake every time the lead singer sang *"She's a brick house."* Then she stood in front of the speakers and began to rotate her shoulders from side to side, lifting her hands up in the opposite direction. Her derrière seemed to have a mind of its own, pulsing back and forth in time to the music while she pivoted her feet. Clarence managed to step from side to side as he leaned on his cane. She nearly knocked him over when the lead sang, *"Shake it down, shake it down, down,"* and she started to shimmy with her arms outstretched.

"I didn't know a lady that old could get it on like that," Dougie said. "I just hope nothing gets sprained or pulled."

"No worries. She was a burlesque dancer in her younger years. I don't think she ever forgot the moves," Vlad said.

"As long as she keeps her clothes on, she'll probably be all right. Old habits die hard," Norm said, rubbing his chin. "She had to sign a promise at the Senior Center to not strip before they let her come to the Senior Prom."

"She surely loves to dance. I don't think I ever saw her look so happy," laughed Beatrice. "Look at her wave her hands above her head."

"I just hope Dad can survive the excitement."

"Why don't we join them on the dance floor?" Vlad said to Beatrice.

"I'd love to. I can't dance like Sandra, though."

"Thank goodness. She's a loose cannon out there. Can't handle two wild women on the dance floor." Vlad held out his hand as she arose, and she took it, holding on through the crowd of dancers as they maneuvered to a quiet out-of-the-way corner. The tempo of the music slowed down to a romantic Elvis ballad, the lead crooning *"Wise men say, only fools rush in.*" She drifted into his arms and nestled her head on his chest, resting both her arms around his neck. Vlad inhaled the scent of her spicy perfume and felt the slow rise and fall of her breathing. She snuggled so close he matched her intake of air, and they seemed to become one entity, slowly shuffling from foot to foot in time to the music. They swayed into the darkest corner, and she turned her head to kiss him, all the while pressing against him in time to the music. Her mouth felt ripe and sweet, better than the glass of Auslese, better than the strawberries, so delicious he couldn't help thrusting his tongue inside. When the band stopped, she didn't pull away. Instead, she whispered, "Let's take the tram back to the ship and get away from this crowd. I'd like to just be alone with you."

He took a step back and gazed at her in amazement, thinking of the ring. *Was this finally his chance?* "I've been waiting for the right moment to get you alone, too. This whole trip was supposed to be about us."

"What are we waiting for? Let's not waste another minute!"

"Unfortunately, we have to go to your stateroom. I promised Sandra I'd take Norm in with me tonight."

"Give him your keycard when I grab my purse and your shopping bag. No one will even notice with Sandra providing the floor show."

Norm sat alone at the table with a third bottle of wine standing in front of Norm. He pointed to it and said, "The couple at the next table doesn't drink so they offered us their bottle. Want a refill?"

"No thanks. I'm exhausted so we're heading back to the ship." Vlad glanced around. "Where's Dougie?"

"He saw these two ladies sitting alone at the bar and went over to talk to them. See there?" Norm gestured to the spot where two middle-aged women, one frothy blonde and her red-haired companion, were deeply engaged in a conversation with Dougie, who noticed them looking and waved a come hither gesture to Norm, who just shook his head and picked up his glass.

"Here's the key to my room." Vlad dug into his back pocket and fished out his card. "Just make yourself at home. But don't get too comfortable. Remember you have to get up early tomorrow."

"I'm on it, Doc. I watched enough James Bond movies to copy all the right moves." He pushed the Green Bay Packers cap to the back of his head and grinned. "I may look handsome and de-boner, but I'm hardcore underneath. Jewel thieves, watch out!"

Chapter 13

THE TRAM DISGUISED AS A TRAIN moved slowly past the lighted restaurants with the faint bars of music floating into the spring night. Only one other couple chose to leave so early, and they sat right behind the driver, engaging him with questions about the city. *Is tourism bigger than winemaking? Would he recommend a castle to tour? Is it always this busy on a Wednesday night*? His muffled responses were lost in the motor's hum.

Vlad and Beatrice chose the last two seats, holding hands and smiling.

"This reminds me of when I was a child. Mom and Dad took my brother and me to the zoo. Our first time. We walked from animal to animal, but I really wanted to ride the train. Dad gave me a choice— have ice cream and soda or ride the train. Not enough money for both," she said with a faraway look in her eyes.

"So what did you choose?"

"The train, of course. My brother picked ice cream. Dad tried to get me to change my mind, but I was stubborn. The engineer blew the whistle at all the crosswalks, and the kids on the train waved. I wanted to be one of those kids. Mom said 'no, such foolishness,' and I started to cry."

"Then what happened?"

"Dad said we might not be back at the zoo for a long time. 'You're only young once,' so he bought the train tickets for him and me while Mom took Jerry to the refreshment stand."

"Your dad's like me—a firm believer in *carpe diem.*"

"It was a very hot day, and Dad could have been sitting in the shade, drinking a cold soda, but he stood in the long, dusty line so I could go on my first train ride. We crawled into the caboose, the train started, and we rode past all the places we'd just walked. I put my face to the window and felt the breeze. So cool. I waved to all the poor hot kids in the crosswalk. Like a magic carpet ride. I never forgot it." She smiled at the memory.

"Magical, like tonight? Riding past all the lights and music, leaving that commotion all behind, riding into the quiet darkness with you. Feels a little magical," he said, smiling broadly, enjoying the warmth of her hand nestled in his.

"Isn't it strange how you remember certain incidents from your childhood? Simple things, like how excited my brother and I would get when trucks from the canning factory drove by and a pea vine would fall off. We'd scoop it up and eat those raw peas like they were the finest chocolates," she laughed. "Mom could never get us to eat canned peas, but we'd fight over those pea pods."

"There's so much to find out about each other. I want to hear it all," he said, raising her hand to his lips and tenderly kissing it.

"And I want to learn all about you."

The tram drove down the dark river road that only a few hours ago they had walked along. The gleaming lights from the ship were reflected in the gently lapping waves as they pulled to a stop. The shadows of the arching trees in the parkway behind the road deepened the quietude. Vlad slid down from the car and held out his hands to Beatrice; her small warm hands grasped his as she hopped down. He felt his heart beat more furiously as they walked up the dimly lit gangplank. This was it—no turning back.

She slid her keycard into her door, and he followed her into her room. When she turned to face him, she had this look on her face, just a small smile. She didn't take her eyes off him as he reached for her. He looked back into her eyes and, for a brief second, he knew. She thought he was the most perfect man in the world. For that brief moment he felt whole. He felt like she loved him. Like it was safe for him to love her.

It was a slow, gentle thing. Slow, gentle kisses in the doorway. He was afraid to speak, to break the spell. What if he was wrong? What if the train ride was just a train ride in the night, nothing magical? But her kisses were so sweet, sweeter than watermelon on a hot summer day. He wanted the sweetness to linger so he kissed her so sweetly back. All that he felt in that fleeting instant in her eyes he wanted to feel forever. He put all that feeling into his kiss, his genuine affection, his—dare he think it—his love.

At first there was a gentle rap at the door, then a long pause. Vlad could almost convince himself it was just his imagination as their kiss lengthened and their hands began to explore each other's contours. But the knocking grew more persistent. Thud, thud, thud.

"Norm again? I thought we left him safely at the bar," Beatrice sighed, then reluctantly moved toward the door. Her sweet perfume left a lingering trail, making Vlad wish he could recapture the previous moment and bottle the scent in his memory.

"I gave him the key to my room. I hope the fool hasn't lost it already." He shook his head resignedly.

Now the knocking sounded as though a baseball bat was attacking the door. BAM. BAM. BAM.

"Just a minute. I'm coming as fast as I can," Beatrice snarled. "Have some patience, man!"

She flung open the door, only to find Sandra standing in the doorway with Clarence's cane poised to strike again. He was propped up against the wall in stocking feet, with his Florida shirt half unbuttoned. She was no longer wearing the white mini-skirt but a hot pink caftan was draped over her body, her boots replaced by feathery slippers.

Beatrice's eyes widened with surprise. "Sandra, you're the last person I expected to find here. You were having so much fun on the dance floor."

"We were, but then Clarence's little blue pill kicked in so we had to rush home. Got to strike while the iron's hot." She gave a nervous chuckle.

"And you knocked on the door just to tell us that?"

"We have a slight problem, and hopefully, you can help." She cast her eyes downward as she spoke in a rush. "You see, we started to make out hot and heavy on the tram ride home. We were primed for action. All the way Gaston kept acting a little weird, pushing his head between us and kinda clearing in his throat like a cat getting ready to cough up. He even sneezed a few times all over Clarence."

"Is he sick? Has he acted like this before?" Vlad joined Beatrice at the door, wondering where they would find a vet at this time of night.

"Dr. Chomsky, I'm so glad you're here. You're just the person we need. You know how Gaston can be." Sandra shrugged and smiled wanly.

"Unfortunately, I do," Vlad said grimly.

"He did his business on the riverbank and trotted up the gangplank, just like normal, but when we got into our room, it was like Dr. Jekyll and Mr. Hyde. He snarled at Clarence every time he tried to kiss me. He jumped on the bed and wouldn't let us even sit, much less do any hanky panky. Between snarling and sneezing, he totally wrecked the mood. But we still have hours left, and the love boat clock is ticking." She jerked her head toward Clarence, who gave a sheepish little wave.

"What do you want me to do about it?"

"You're a doctor. He might listen to you. Please come down to my room and see if you can calm him down," Sandra pleaded.

"Me? I'm not that kind of doctor. Besides, he doesn't even like me that much."

"Of course he does. He's bonded with you. You're his partner in fighting the bad guys. He respects you." She gave Vlad's arm a reassuring pat.

"Please come," Clarence said. "I may not have this chance again with a hottie like Sandra."

"Go ahead, Vlad. I'll be waiting. We have the whole night," Beatrice said sweetly.

Vlad gave a heavy sigh and said, "All right. Let's go see the monster dog."

Sandra handed Clarence back his cane, and they shuffled down the hallway, creaked up the two flights of stairs, and finally arrived at her suite. Just as promised, when they opened the door Gaston stood up and barked a warning from his spot on the bed, showing his sharp little teeth.

"That's definitely not a friendly greeting," Vlad said. He drew near to the pooch. "Hey, fellow, what seems to be the matter? Are you a little under the weather?"

The volume of the bark softened to a rumble at the back of his throat. He sat back on his haunches and gave a little whine as Vlad slowly, extremely slowly, reached his hand down and let him sniff it.

"Where's his stuffed monkey? Maybe he's missing his toy," he suggested.

"It's here inside the sofa." Sandra pulled out a sock monkey with stitched eyes and mouth and tossed it at Gaston. "Here, boy! Here's your widdle monkey wunky!"

The dog caught it in his mouth, jumped off the bed, and began shaking the stuffing out of the monkey. Then he went over to Sandra and dropped it at her feet. But when she bent to pick it up, he grabbed it before her fingertips touched the soggy cloth and ran away.

"Oh, look, he wants to play keep away. That's so cute! Vlad will play keep away with you, won't you, Vlad?" She blinked her false eyelashes coquettishly at him. "Uncle Vladdy will play with puppy wuppy."

Vlad took a step back with a doubtful look. "I don't know…"

"Please, Dr. Chomsky. Please play with the damn dog," Clarence pleaded.

"Bring the monkey here to Uncle Vlad," he said through gritted teeth. He crossed over to the pooch. "Give me the monkey." He reached his hand to the toy. The dog let him grasp the soggy mess, and then began to pull it away.

"Now Puppy Wuppy wants to play tug of war," Sandra said. "He wuvs his Uncle Vladdy."

Gaston snarled and continued to tug on the monkey, jerking Vlad's hand this way and that.

"I think that puppy wants to play with Aunt Beatrice, too, don't you, Puppy Wuvvy? I'll get his puppy treats and his leash and his collapsible water bowl for Uncle Vlad to take to her room to play." She scooped the items into a small backpack and hung it on Vlad's shoulder.

"If you just keep pulling on the monkey, he'll follow you to your room."

"I'm not so sure about this," Vlad said, still holding onto the monkey but keeping a sharp look out for the dog's teeth.

"I'm begging you, man. Just for tonight." Clarence lifted up his shirt to display the bulge in his pants.

Sandra appeared from the bathroom "Here's a towel. If he digs his heels, you can just wrap it around him and carry him."

She flung a bath towel over his shoulders like a shawl and nudged him to the door. "Don't forget his morning constitutional at six. He can't hold it much after that. You don't want him to make a mess on the carpet or the duvet."

As she shoved him out the door, he heard Clarence say, "Can you say more of that sexy baby talk, Luvy Wuvy? It really turns me on."

Vlad took Gaston on the top deck for one more pit stop. Gaston sauntered over to the little herbal garden in the containers and lifted his leg. Vlad jerked on his leash to try to direct him over to the flowers but it was too late.

"Remind me to tell Beatrice and Sandra to skip the Rosemary chicken tomorrow." Vlad said to the poodle as they descended the stairs.

To: Chomskyv@crawford.edu
From: erinflamethrower@gmail.com
I played dumb Minecraft for over an hour but Nick didn't say a word about what's bugging him. I had to beg him to come out of his room and bribe him with my lava lamp. But he still wouldn't talk.

From: Chomskyv@crawford.edu
To: erinflamethrower@gmail.com
I'm dog-sitting Gaston instead of spending alone time with Beatrice. I have all I can manage with this cursed dog.

Go to your mother and demand to talk privately. If Gordy's there, just say it's a female thing. He'll disappear fast—guaranteed.

Keep me posted.

Love, Dad

Chapter 14

"MY DIAMOND BRACELET IS MISSING! And my necklace! Someone stole my diamonds!" Katherine Beaumont's angry voice carried throughout the upper deck of happy tourists as she pushed through the door from the stairs leading to the first class staterooms.

THE JOURNEY DOWN THE RHINE GORGE meandered by an enchanting combination of little picturesque villages of pastel houses, tall towers of medieval churches, and castle after castle, each more magnificent than the last. Lutz narrated from the bridge as the ship drifted by countless sun-washed castles, the morning light tap dancing on the slow-moving water.

"The lord of the castle strung a barrier across the river, extracting a toll from each passing merchant ship. The ease of shipping goods up and down the river was offset by the number of tolls owners were forced to pay."

Beatrice shivered in the cold, windy breeze, snuggling next to Vlad for warmth. Despite the bright May sunshine turning the river into a thousand points of sparkling light, the weather on the upper deck was brisk. Vlad was glad he had packed his fleece jacket, only wishing he had added gloves. One hand in his pocket and the other tucked under Beatrice's waist, he stood on the prow, shifting away each time she pulled out her camera to take a picture, only to pull her close again after the scenic moment had passed. Not even the cold temperatures could dispel the warm afterglow of last night on the tram. Not Gaston hogging the bed nor Norm's snoring in the twin beside him, still under the effects of partying with Dougie. Vlad crept away in the morning, taking Gaston with him and depositing the dog at Sandra's doorstep before breakfast.

Unfortunately, now Katherine's hysterics drove away that loving feeling and replaced it with a sense of dread as she stormed onto the bridge. "There's a thief on board. Those diamonds are worth thousands. And genuine sapphires. You have to do something right now."

Katherine grabbed the captain's arm away from the ship's wheel and started pulling him toward the door. "Come and see for yourself."

"Calm down, madam. I can't just leave the ship to steer itself. Let me call my first mate and get him to take over." The captain reached for a nearby phone while the entire exchange went out over the loud speakers. "Are you sure your jewelry is really missing? Maybe it just fell behind something."

"I know it's missing. Don't you think my husband and I searched the room thoroughly before we came to you for help? It's gone, I tell you, gone. Stolen!"

Warren jabbed the captain in the chest with his forefinger and said, "See here, captain, we've looked everywhere in the room. It's nowhere to be found. Someone broke in while we were up here on deck. If we hadn't gone back for a warmer jacket, it would have been hours before we discovered the theft."

Beatrice turned to Vlad and muttered, "Where's Norm?"

"Probably still sleeping it off in my room. I have no idea how long he and Dougie partied last night."

She swept her eyes over the crowd, craning her neck to see the back of the ship.

"I don't see either of them on deck. You'd think no one would miss this—the whole point of the cruise is viewing the Rhine in all its glory today."

"Clarence and Sandra are bundled up with a blanket over there in the deck chairs. Let's ask if they saw them." He pointed to the lounge chairs under the bridge where the elderly couple sat holding hands. Clarence rubbed his nose against Sandra's, and they giggled like two middle school kids out on a first date, both oblivious to the commotion going on over their heads. Poor Gaston lay with his head on his front paws under her chair, strangely subdued by the cold and the crowd.

"You don't think Dougie and Norm hooked up with the women at the bar? They seemed very cozy when we left."

Vlad shrugged his shoulders and said, "Who knows what Norm will do when he starts drinking?" They made their way through the throng as quickly as possible. He knelt down to eye level with Sandra and asked, "Did you see Norm at breakfast this morning?" At the mention of Norm's name Gaston rose to a sitting posture and tilted his head.

"No, dearie. I thought he was with you. You promised he could spend the night in your stateroom."

"He did spend the night with me but he's not here now."

"You didn't lose him, did you? His head isn't always screwed on straight sometimes. Been like that since the war." Her eyebrows lifted in alarm, and she dropped Clarence's hand.

"What's wrong, love?" the old man said. "Do you have to use the ladies room again?"

Sandra shook her head, "No, I'm fine. It's Norm."

Beatrice touched Clarence on the shoulder and asked, "Did Dougie help you dress this morning?"

"I'm not a goddamned baby," Clarence snorted as he shrugged off her hand. "I got myself dressed after spending the night with this lovely lady, my dancing queen. I didn't need Dougie to hold my hand. I told him not to bother us."

"So you haven't seen Dougie? I'm going to check my room." Vlad rose to his feet. "Hopefully, Norm just overslept."

"I'll come with you." Sandra tossed aside the blanket and said to Clarence, "I'll be right back, lover. Keep my place warm."

"You don't need to come. This morning's cruise through the gorge is the highlight of the trip. It's a shame for you to miss it," Vlad said.

"Are you sure? If anything's happened to Norm…you know how alcohol affects him." Sandra sadly shook her head. "He's got a big heart but a small brain."

"I'm absolutely sure. You stay where you are. I'll be right back." Vlad grabbed the blanket and tucked it back around her. "If he's still sleeping it off in my room, I'll just roust him."

He turned to Beatrice. "You should stay here, too. Sailing through the Rhine Valley Gorge is a once-in-a-lifetime experience. I didn't mean for you to get involved in all this craziness."

"You're not getting rid of me that easily. A Romantic Rhine River Getaway implies two people. It's not very romantic if I'm by myself. I'm coming with you."

She slipped her hand into his as they started toward the stairway. Lutz continued the narration—the ship was passing a splendid rock formation, a huge outcropping at a bend in the river.

"The legend of the Lorelei stems from this steep, slate rock. Jilted by a faithless lover, Lorelei flung herself into the Rhine from this point. She returned as an enchantress who lured men to their death by singing her siren song high above the river, causing them to crash into the treacherous rocks. From the failure of love there is no more rescue."

They paused underneath the shadow of the gigantic rock as the ship sailed past, and Vlad said to Beatrice, "You rescued me last night from all my insecurities, the fiasco of my divorce, the false start with Britney." He raised her hand to his lips and tenderly kissed it. 'I could have crashed and drowned back in Crawford, but you lifted me up."

By this time, the first mate had arrived on the bridge. The captain ushered him into the wheelhouse while Katherine berated them both.

"If I had known the type of unsavory characters on board, I would have chosen a different cruise line. You are harboring a thief. I'm sure of it. And I have my suspicions who it is!"

"Now, now, madam. Let's make certain there actually is a theft before we point fingers." The captain patted the air, palms down, in a conciliatory gesture.

Warren raised his fist and shook it at the captain. "Don't take that condescending tone with my wife. We both know the diamonds are missing. We've seen it with our own eyes."

"I almost hope Norm did hook up with Dougie and those two women," Vlad said to Beatrice as they scurried down the steps. "Then he'll be clear of this mess. I can vouch for him finishing the night in my room. He doesn't need to reveal he's been trying to catch a thief on board ship."

"And that we've been encouraging him. I knew we should have told the captain up front. At least we'd be on record for trying to warn the crew."

"I just wasn't sure Norm hadn't hallucinated the whole thing." Vlad gave a halfhearted shrug. "I didn't want to create an incident."

"That train has left the station."

Vlad stood in front of his stateroom door and knocked loudly. He gave Beatrice a worried look as they waited a few minutes for a response. He knocked a second time, a bit louder. Still no sound from within the room.

"Guess I'll have to use my spare key."

As he swiped the keycard and pushed open the door, an unpleasant odor assailed his nostrils, reminiscent of rotten eggs and cooked cabbages. A sound similar to a chain saw downing a giant oak filled the room. In the dim light he could make out a still form lying under the duvet. He flicked on the light switch and entered his room, tripping over a pair of motorcycle boots.

"Are you all right?" Beatrice said from behind him.

"I'm fine, but I'm not sure about Norm. It smells like something died in here. You may want to stay out in the hall."

"I've smelled worse. My father likes sauerkraut and greasy sausages. Top that off with a few Pabst Blue Ribbons and you'd want to make yourself scarce the day after he had that for supper."

Norm was sprawled out on his back, still wearing last night's clothes. On the nightstand, the Green Bay Packers hat had been carelessly tossed over an empty bottle with a gold seal and the label GOLDSCHLÄGER. Shaking his head in dismay, Vlad reached down and jostled the sleeping man. "Norm, wake up. It's me, Vlad. You need to wake up. It's ten o'clock in the morning."

Norm pushed away his hand and turned away on his side, pulling a pillow over his head. He said in a muffled voice, "Go away. I need my beauty rest."

Vlad tried again, this time shaking more vigorously. "Get up, man! The jewel thief just struck."

"Wh-what did you say?" He rolled on his back, lay his head on the pillow, and opened one eye. "The jewel thief? Did you catch him?"

"Sit up, Norm, and listen."

Beatrice sat on the edge of the bed. Norm opened both eyes and raised himself on his elbows.

"Katherine Beaumont is missing her diamonds, and we think it must be your jewel thief," said Vlad. "What happened to your plan to knock on the suspects' doors?"

"A shooter called a Golden Elk—Jägermeister and gold something liqueur. Ya know that stuff has actual gold in it? Then Krystal and Joyce happened." He moaned and grasped his temple. "Oh, I think my head is breaking in half. Ya got any aspirin?"

"I have a bottle in my carry-on." Vlad went to the closet and opened the small suitcase perched on a shelf. After rummaging through the contents a few moments, he pulled out the aspirin. Meanwhile, Beatrice got a glass of water from the bathroom and held it out to Norm.

"Here, drink some of this," she said, urging him to take a drink.

Vlad handed him two pills, and he gulped then down.

"I didn't jump ship, Doc. I just flirted with Joyce, the one with the red hair, but I took the tram back. Dougie was still talking to Krystal at the bar when I left. Joyce gave me her phone number back in the States. She's a real nice lady, real classy—school secretary from Kansas. Kansas ain't that far from Wisconsin, is it?"

"So you met this woman last night. Then what happened?" Vlad folded his arms across his chest and peered down at him with a look very familiar to his children.

"Nothing. She and I talked. Didja know they have Packers fans in Missouri? She's one. Sez the Chiefs' fans are kinda stuck-up. She likes the Packers better."

"Anything else?" Vlad said through clenched lips.

"I knew I had to get up early so I was ready to call it a night. Dougie ordered some fancy shots with this gold shit—bartender gave me the bottle for a souvenir—so I had a shot or two to be sociable, then I came here."

"So you aborted your plan to get up early?" Beatrice asked.

"No, damn it all! I musta slept through the alarm." Norm hit himself on the forehead with the palm of his hand.

Vlad picked up the alarm clock and looked. No morning setting. "It looks like you forgot to set it."

"Why didn't you wake me up?"

"Sorry. I slept in with Gaston. A change in my plans, too." Vlad looked wistfully at Beatrice and the safe where the ring lay untouched.

"Damn it. I fergot to give Sam back his uniform for the morning service, too." He flung the duvet off and jumped to his feet. "I'm an idiot. A good-for-nothing drunk."

"No sense beating yourself up. Take a shower. Get dressed. We'll try to find out what happened to the Beaumonts," Beatrice said calmly.

Norm started pacing the small room. "I hope I didn't get Sam in trouble. I promised him I'd get his uniform back."

"He must have borrowed one from someone else because he had one on at breakfast. He didn't seem too put out. Now go to your suite, get some clean clothes on, and come up on deck when you're done. Beatrice and I are going back on top to catch what's left of the gorge tour."

Before he could move, there was a knock on the door. Vlad opened it to find the captain and a huge man wearing an armband marked security. The captain's face looked like judgment day had arrived.

"Dr. Chomsky, we're hoping you know the whereabouts of Norm Clodfelder. We have a few questions we'd like to ask him."

Chapter 15

THE CAPTAIN MADE AN IMPOSING FIGURE as he stood in the doorway wearing full regalia, including the hat. In addition, the burly security man seemed to fill the small room as he pounded a fist into his palm. Vlad felt as if they were sucking the very air out of the room; he found it hard to breathe. His voice squeaked when he spoke.

"Norm is right here. He's been here all morning."

'There's been a theft—some valuables are missing from another passenger's room." The captain moved closer to Norm and stared at him eye to eye. "The victim seems to think you were acting strangely all week. Every time she turned around, there you were. Almost like you were stalking her, waiting for the right moment to strike."

"I would never steal anything. I was just…just trying to help," Norm gulped.

"Help with what?" The captain narrowed his eyes as he stared blankly at Norm. "I don't understand."

"Hey, Captain Schultz, would you look at this?" The security man strode over to the counter and held up Sam's white uniform. "Doesn't this belong to one of the waiters?"

"Perhaps you'd care to explain what this is doing in your room, Dr. Chomsky?" The captain turned his cold eyes to Vlad. "Why would you need a waiter's uniform?"

"I didn't need it. It was Norm. He needed it. It was all part of the plan," Vlad answered nervously, twisting his hands together.

"The plan? What plan?"

Norm jumped in. "We had a plan to catch the jewel thieves, Cap. Ya see, at first I was following Katherine, hoping to catch them in the act. I have military training, ya know. Served in 'Nam."

"How did you know it was Mrs. Beaumont who was robbed? I didn't mention her name," the captain snarled.

Beatrice stepped forward. "Vlad and I were on deck when she came screaming onto the bridge. I'd wager the entire ship knows who the victim is, and probably half the countryside we were sailing past."

"Back to the plan. I had a plan to catch the thieves once I figured out who it was," Norm said. "That's why I needed Sam's uniform to disguise myself as a crewmember."

"You were going to disguise yourself as a crewmember?" Captain Schultz shook his head.

"So the thieves wouldn't get suspicious when I knocked on their door."

The captain looked heavenward and took a deep breath. "You were just going to knock on some jewel thieves' doors pretending to be a crewmember…and somehow get them to do what?"

"I wasn't gonna get them to do anything. I just wanted to hear them talk so I could identify them as the crooks I overheard that night. I wasn't sure which room they were in but I'd know their voices anywhere. One of them talked kinda funny," Norm said in a rush.

Vlad noticed the confused look on the captain's face and explained, "Norm heard a suspicious conversation while on the top deck, but he couldn't see who was speaking.'

"Ya see, Cap, it was late at night and too dark to get a good look. I didn't want them to see me either. But I knew which side of the ship they were on, and I knew who they were planning to rob."

The captain blew out a puff of air in exasperation. "You didn't think to inform me there was a possible thief on board my ship? We could have secured Mrs. Beaumont's diamonds in the ship's safe and prevented this mess. And, Dr. Chomsky, you went along with this so-called plan?"

Vlad carefully chose his next words. "Norm is my friend, but sometimes he's not the most reliable witness. I wasn't sure he actually overheard what he thought he heard. I didn't want to sound an alarm over a misunderstanding."

"He's right," said Norm. "Sometimes I get loaded and do crazy things—like losing my motorcycle in a cow pasture or accidentally crawling into the wrong house to sleep it off. But I swear I only had a coupla beers that night."

"Norm was going to impersonate room service and knock on the doors early in the morning in the hopes of finding the suspects,"

Beatrice said. "Then he was going to come to you with that information. Against my better judgment, I went along with his plan."

"Yeah, 'specially since my first plan of shadowing Katherine didn't seem to be going anywhere," Norm said.

"It did go somewhere," the captain said. "Katherine Beaumont thought you were stalking her, casing her room for the right moment to strike. Now she's accusing you of being a thief."

"She's got it all wrong. I was trying to be her bodyguard and catch the guy in the act."

"Be that as it may, I have no choice in the matter," Captain Schultz said as he folded his arms across his chest. "We've alerted *die kriminalpolizei*, and the detectives will board the ship at Koblenz. I know they will want to interview all of you. So perhaps you'll want to skip the excursion to make yourself available to them."

"You don't seriously think we're jewel thieves?" Beatrice exclaimed.

"It's not my job to accuse passengers of any crimes or determine the truth of your story."

"Some story!" snorted the security man. "I've heard better in a Disney movie."

The captain shot him a warning look. "No comments. I just turn the information I have over to the police; they will continue the investigation. Bring the evidence, please." He waved his hand toward Sam's uniform. "We'll add Sam Pempango's name to the list of witnesses. *Guten tag.*"

After a crisp nod to them, he and security swept out of the room.

"Evidence! Investigation! I can't believe he's even considering we may be suspects." Beatrice sank down unto the disheveled bed. "Luckily, there are plenty of witnesses to verify that we were on the top deck the whole time the robbery was committed." She lifted her bright eyes to Vlad's face. "Our alibi is rock solid."

"What about me? I got no one to verify I was here all morning." Norm settled beside her and put his hand to his forehead. "I can't believe the robbers got past me."

"You have nothing to fear. Once the police hear your story, they'll know you couldn't have possibly pulled off a robbery," Vlad said.

"I just wish I coulda found the real robbers," Norm said, looking downcast.

"Me, too, Norm. Me, too."

Chapter 16

"TOO BAD SANDRA AND CLARENCE couldn't join us. For once, I'd welcome their antics. I even miss Gaston's growling," Beatrice said as they boarded the excursion bus for the Marksburg Castle, their afternoon stop before Koblenz. After a sharp bend in the river, the huge white fortress popped into sight, its impregnable walls soaring over the steep, isolated hillside. A hodgepodge of towers, some round, some square, reached for the cloudless sky, reminding Vlad of some of the creations Nicholas built as a preschooler with his wooden blocks. Still, the edifice dominated its forested surroundings with a foreboding air.

"The 'strenuous' label scared them off. If we have to climb up this hillside, I'm not certain I'll be much better." Vlad craned his neck out the bus window to glimpse the end of the winding road that disappeared into the trees.

"Norm was in no shape to join us either," she said. "Being a suspect in a jewel heist has taken the wind out of his sails. I've never seen him so despondent."

"Hopefully, it's due to the hangover, not the captain's warning. He survived far worse situations during the Vietnam War. He's as tough as Gaston."

The gleaming white castle towered high above them as the bus parked. It loomed even larger than the initial view from the ship. Beatrice glanced up from the daily notes. "According to this, Marksburg Castle was never attacked during seven hundred years of warfare. I totally understand why." From where the bus stopped, all they could see was the sheer walls of the fortress and the rocky terrain. "Let's try to enjoy this tour. Trouble will be waiting for us at Koblenz. We'll get there soon enough. I've never been inside a real castle so I'm going to make the most of this moment."

She slipped her hand into Vlad's as they stepped off the bus, holding her head high and moving forward to hear Lutz speak.

"Marksburg Castle was built around 1117 and was never invaded, which is why it is in pristine condition. Built by the House of Epstein, it changed hands over the years, even once owned by Napoleon. Each noble rebuilt the castle constantly, adding the assorted towers and adapting the walls to hold artillery."

He led the way with a practiced step, gliding over the uneven slate slabs with deep ruts that led to the guardhouse. Vlad, however, stumbled several times, breaking his contact with Beatrice. Each time he landed he fervently hoped he wouldn't twist his ankle and have to be carried down the hillside. He imagined rolling down on a wheeled stretcher and crashing into a tree at the bottom. Beatrice merely grabbed his arm and held on tightly to him, like she would to a rambunctious toddler.

Banners from all the major houses of German nobility graced the ramparts. Huge cannons stationed in the narrow openings in the outer wall formed a formidable obstacle to any troops below hoping to storm the castle, *If Heidelberg had been built with outer walls like this, it would still be standing,* Vlad thought.

A young man in a medieval tunic and vest with flowing shoulder-length blond hair appeared, and Lutz turned them over to him. "If anyone feels unable to continue—we'll be climbing over eight hundred steps—please tell me now. We will have one stopping point where there is a shorter passage back down. You can end the tour there as well. It is extremely strenuous so listen to your body if it warns you to stop and catch your breath."

Beatrice elbowed him in his side and nodded toward a small cluster of shipmates standing in the ramparts near the cannon. In the center was Katherine Beaumont, holding out her wrist, minus the diamond bracelet, and angrily shaking her head. Then she turned, pointing her finger directly at him, and said loudly enough for him to hear, "I knew the first moment I laid eyes on that riffraff something was suspicious. Have you ever seen a stranger assortment of lowlifes?"

"Talk about vulgar!" Warren added.

"That old woman, dancing like a go-go girl in that outrageous outfit! And that thug following me everywhere, probably just waiting for the right moment to strike."

"Which was during the Rhine Gorge when we were all on the upper deck!" Warren angrily chimed in again.

"Exactly! Carte blanche for a thief," she said, tossing her head.

The young man stopped talking and pointedly stared at the couple, waiting for them to focus their attention back on his narration. Soon the rest of the tour group followed his gaze. Katherine snapped her mouth shut, folded her arms in a defiant pose, and gave Vlad a malevolent stare. She remained silent as the young man continued.

"First, we will visit the kitchen where cooks prepared meals for scores of noblemen and vassals. The types of meats, grains, and vegetables enjoyed by medieval diners have been researched and are displayed."

He slowly led them up steep stairs into a large stone-walled room where the butchered remains of a cow hung from rafters, as did shafts of wheat and colorful vegetables. Huge caldrons were suspended over logs in the massive fireplace, and a shovel-like tool for removing loaves of bread leaned against the wall.

Vlad should have been excited with the complete picture of medieval life that the castle offered. His lectures on the Middle Ages lacked authenticity, but now he had firsthand experience with their way of life. What good was any of it if he couldn't lift the cloud of suspicion over Norm? Katherine Beaumont wasn't making it easy to do that.

The guide led them outside to a battlement. He gestured to yet another set of uneven stairs that spiraled up a tower.

"Two hundred steps to go," he said. "We have a secret passage here that leads back down so if anyone feels fatigued, now's the time to turn back. The stairs in the keep are easier to navigate."

The cold wind muffled his words. Vlad looked at the steep stairs and then at the dark entryway where a young lady, also dressed in medieval clothes, hovered ready to take passengers back down the supposedly easy way.

Beatrice took his hand again. "I'm game to keep on going."

Vlad glanced over the parapet at the forest blanketed below. The ribbon of a road led to the river where the cruise ship tranquilly floated. He dreaded going back to whatever was Norm's fate. Better to keep climbing the twisted steps into the past, ignoring his aching calves and panting breath.

"Let's carry on," he agreed.

They entered the tower and the beautiful ladies bedroom inlaid with wooden walls for warmth and hung with still brilliant tapestries. A beautifully carved four-poster bed stood in the center. "If I were the lady of the castle, you'd visit me here every night," Beatrice whispered and smiled at him. But the sweetness of her being couldn't dispel the frustration of having to ignore the whispered insults from Katherine.

As they walked through the large dining hall, he imagined German noblemen planning attacks while seated at the massive table. A door to a closet-like room revealed the privy, a one-seater built for the lord, where he could literally shit on his enemies below and then return to his dining companions.

"And we thought indoor plumbing was a modern convenience," he joked to Beatrice.

"Definitely has a double function," she agreed as she peered through the window at the long drop to the forest below. "One way to get your enemy to retreat in a hurry."

Next, down many dark, winding steps to the torture room. Vlad wasn't sure which was worse: climbing up a hundred uneven stone steps or going down them? His heart was racing because of the extreme exertion. Finally, they entered a dank room where cruel medieval instruments of torture stood behind the innocuous rope.

"Is that a rack?" Beatrice pointed to a raised platform with a round winch on both ends.

"Yes, it is. The prisoner's arms were tied to one pole and feet to the other, and the winch was tightened as the suspect was pulled apart until he confessed," the guide explained.

A thick, wooden chair with straps hanging down from its arms, its seat covered with a multitude of small spikes, stood next to the rack.

"That doesn't look very comfy," a woman joked. "One way to get unwelcome dinner guests to leave."

"A prisoner strapped into the Iron Chair is pressed down into the spikes. They aren't large enough to hit a vital organ, but the pain would have been excruciating; infection and bleeding would result in death," the guide said matter-of-factly.

"What is that pyramid-shaped thing?" asked another tourist, pointing to a chair with a sharp triangular device in its center.

"It's called a Judas Chair. The victim is suspended over the point, and then his anus is slowly lowered onto it. Few could withstand the pain."

"That's horrible," Beatrice said. "I think I've heard enough." She exited into the next room where suits of armor were displayed.

As they left the exhibit, they heard Katherine mutter, "I can think of a hooligan I'd like to get to confess. He's lucky he wasn't living back then."

"That woman is awful. I'd like to smack her one," Beatrice muttered.

Vlad noticed her clenched fists held tautly at her sides and heard her sharp intake of air.

"Norm was just trying to help."

He reached down, took her hand into his, and gently massaged her palm with his thumb until he felt her fingers relax. She gave him a grateful look and bent her head to read the sign below the first set of armor, which resembled a mini-dress made of chain link, with three-quarter length sleeves and a mid-thigh tunic split from hem to crotch.

"This is called a hauberk from the fourteenth century. The split enables the knight to ride his horse," she read aloud. "I wouldn't want to wear that on a night on the town."

The next examples were full suits of plated armor, much like knights wore in the fifteenth century, with fully enclosed helmets. "Plate armor became cheaper than mail to produce because it required much less labor, and labor was more expensive after the Black Death," Vlad read.

"I could see Sir Lancelot wearing something like this," Beatrice said. "I think Norm is like those knights in a way. He wants to be a good guy riding in to save the day."

Vlad sadly shook his head and said, "Norm is living proof: No good deed goes unpunished."

Chapter 17

"THIS DOESN'T BODE WELL FOR NORM," Vlad said as they stood on the top deck watching the Koblenz dock come into view. Parked on the grassy riverbank, the afternoon sun glinted off the hood of a silver Audi with sky blue stripes and *Polizei* emblazoned on the sides and front. Standing next to the car were two uniformed policemen in dark blue jackets sporting ties and white hats. He observed they weren't carrying guns; hopefully, the theft of Katherine's jewelry wasn't considered a violent crime in Germany. But the sight of the police on shore caused Vlad's mouth to grow dry, and he swallowed hard, not daring to speak again.

"At least we're alone up here and don't have to tolerate Katherine and Warren's dagger eyes and false accusations," Beatrice said as she moved closer, resting her head on his shoulder and sliding her arm around his waist. The other passengers were enjoying a late lunch, but Vlad and Beatrice didn't feel like much like eating or mixing with the crowd after the bus trip back from Marksburg Castle. It seemed as if all eyes were on them as they walked down the aisle, and the half-heard words that stood out from the whispered comments that flew all around them were "thief" and "diamonds."

"I wish we could stay up here for the rest of the trip, just you and me, watching the shoreline go by," he said, brushing his chin against her soft hair, inhaling the clean smell of verbena.

"Me, too," she sighed, and squeezed his waist tighter.

Just then the captain stepped out of the wheelhouse and made his way to the stairs. As he glanced their way, his eyes narrowed and lips tightened. He paused for a minute, opening his mouth as though he wanted to say something to them, but instead, abruptly turned away and disappeared down the stairwell.

"I suppose we should check on Norm and give him some moral

support. I'm sure the captain will be coming to get him as soon as the police have listened to the Beaumonts and their wild accusations," he said as he disengaged himself from her and reluctantly headed toward the same set of stairs.

"We should check on Sandra and Clarence, too. Maybe we should offer to take Gaston for a quick walk along the river. He's been cooped up inside her room for most of the day."

"Let's see, Gaston or Katherine Beaumont. I can't say which one has a nastier disposition." Vlad scratched his head in a mocking gesture.

"Gaston can't spread vicious rumors so he's a prince of a dog compared to her." Beatrice wrinkled her nose and sniffed. "We should lock them both in a room and see which one comes out alive."

"I'd put my money on Gaston. Look what he did to the terrorist last year. Besides, he's smarter than he looks, probably smarter than both Beaumonts," Vlad said, reaching for her hand as they reached the bottom of the stairs. He led the way to Sandra's suite.

A downcast Norm answered the door, still wearing the wrinkled clothes from last night, and mumbled a brief greeting. The large screen TV was blaring with an *NCIS* rerun. Sandra sat alone on the sofa with Gaston stretched out on the cushion beside her, his head in her lap. He opened his eyes as they entered the room, then yawned and went back to sleep. She nervously stroked his head between his ears.

"What, no Clarence?" Vlad said, looking around the room.

"I sent him on the walking tour of Koblenz with Dougie after lunch," Sandra said. "No sense in getting him involved. I didn't go— couldn't let Norm wait all by himself."

"I'm innocent!" Norm declared. "My parents taught me never to lie. I just couldn't accuse anyone until I was sure. Sometimes ya don't find the rotten spot until ya peel the apple. I just wasn't sure which apple to go for."

"Don't worry. The police will sort it all out. It's their job, dearie. Just settle down and watch the end of your show." She patted the empty space beside her.

"I know. Just have a bad feeling whenever I see a cop. Years of riding with bikers. Getting pulled over for no reason. And then there was that disorderly bust in Beaver Dam at Beaver Fest." Norm's

Adam's apple bulged as he swallowed hard.

"Which one, dearie? It was an annual occurrence, springing you out of jail. More exciting than the crowning of Little Miss Beaver and the Water Ski Show," Sandra said, smiling at the memory.

Norm settled on the couch next to Gaston, propped his stocking feet on the end table, wiggling a bare toe through a hole in the sock, and gestured to the two empty armchairs. "Take a load off. How was the castle tour?"

"Cold and drafty, lots of treacherous steps," Vlad answered. "We got a good sense of castle life. Be glad you're living in today's world."

"Including a horrible room with all sorts of torture devices," Beatrice said, giving an involuntary shiver. "The castle was a bit of a letdown after viewing castles in the movies."

"Sounds like a good excursion to miss," Sandra said.

"Even I stumbled a time or two. Like walking over boulders after an avalanche," Vlad admitted. "You're better off peacefully drifting along in the ship."

Silently, they watched the NCIS agents follow up leads on a Navy corpsman's murder, skillfully questioning the witnesses, while advanced technology honed in on the culprit. Vlad hoped the German police were half as efficient in solving crimes.

The knock on the door made them all jump. Slowly, Norm made his way to the door, dragging his feet like Gaston going outside to do his "job" on a sub-zero morning. A second knock, louder and more insistent, rang through the suite. Vlad and Beatrice looked at each other with dread as Norm opened the door. At first the captain blocked their view of the hallway, until he faded away to admit the two policemen. A tall, solidly built woman briskly stepped into the room. Her broad shoulders put Vlad to shame as they nearly burst from the fitted jacket; only a hint of her breasts wrinkled the front. With her craggy facial features and her chestnut hair pulled back into ponytail, she could easily be mistaken for a man. Free of make-up, her skin was as florid as if she'd just finished a 5K. Her crisp white police hat shaded her unblemished forehead. Planting her feet firmly in the room, she surveyed them all with a disdainful stare.

"I'm Polizeimeister, I mean Police Master, Ashenbrenner. This is my partner, PM Griesbach." She gestured toward the second officer, a tall, lanky man who seemed to fade in her shadow. "We're looking for Norman Clodfelder. We'd like to interview him down at the Koblenz station."

"Interview me? I don't even remember applying for a job." He gave a nervous chuckle, then a wide smile.

"It's in connection with the recent robbery on board this ship," she said coldly. She gave him a flat stare, her brown eyes glinting dangerously.

"Just a little humor, Officer. I'm Norm Clodfelder," he said, holding his hand out for a shake, which she ignored. "Glad to help ya in any way I can. I have some important information about the thieves." He let his arm drop limply to his side as he flashed her a hopeful smile.

"Captain Schulz informed us when he spoke to you this morning that you claimed to be privy to some conversation between the thieves. He also discovered the unauthorized possession of a staff member's uniform." She knotted her brow in a quizzical look.

"Ya see, I was gonna go undercover, disguise myself as a crewmember and try to flush the crooks out."

PM Griesbach snorted and muttered, "Go undercover. Unbelievable."

"You'll need to come down to the police station to answer a few questions about the alleged theft. You understand, this is just a formality. You're not being charged with anything at this point." Her staccato voice punched out each word.

Sandra stood up and hobbled over to the police officer. She planted herself firmly in front of her and said, "Why would Norm be charged with anything? He didn't steal the jewelry. It's all a big misunderstanding, and when you hear what he has to say, you'll see. He'll set you on the trail of the real thief. My highly trained dog can assist you. He was there, too. Show them, boy." She made a circular motion with her index finger.

Gaston barked as he hopped down from the couch. He began sniffing around the room like a bloodhound in training, pausing first at Vlad, snuffing loudly, then pulling back his lips to expose his teeth in a vicious sneer, then abruptly turned from him to Beatrice. He greeted her with a friendly snuffle and put his paw out to shake. She reached her hand down in response and said, "Good boy. Look how smart he is!"

Gliding past Norm without pausing, Gaston stopped at the feet of the second officer and sat back, front paws down, back haunches high in the air, as he gave an ominous growl from the depth of his throat. Then he struck a pose like a water spaniel rousting out a duck from marshy shrubs and froze.

"He'll flush out the real thief just like that," Sandra declared, snapping her fingers, which Gaston took as a signal to begin frenzied barking. The lanky officer took a step back with a worried expression on his face as the little dog bared his teeth. His hand moved toward a device under his jacket that Vlad hoped was a Taser, but before he could draw it out, Sandra raised a finger in the air and made an abrupt motion downward. The poodle immediately stopped barking, trotted docilely over to her side, and plunked himself down with a canine smile at the officer.

"You see, highly trained. Descending from a line of famous show dogs. Can a German shepherd match that talent?" Sandra said proudly, tossing her head triumphantly.

PM Ashenbrenner frowned and folded her arms over her chest. "Yes, he's a smart little doggie, but we have a busy schedule. We need to go now. If you have information, perhaps you need to come along and we'll take your statement, too."

"Sandra wasn't there that night. Norm came to my room with the discovery of the planned heist." Vlad propelled himself next to Sandra. "I'm Doctor Vladimir Chomsky from Crawford University. I can confirm Norm's story from that night."

PM Ashenbrenner nodded toward the gaunt assistant. He pulled a small notepad out of his top pocket and opened a pen with a flick of his bony thumb. He flipped to a new page and began to take notes.

"Could you spell your name for me, sir?" he said, pausing expectantly.

Vlad carefully spelled it out letter by letter and added, "It's doctor of philosophy, PhD, not MD. A professor, not a physician."

"Thank you for clarifying that, Dr. Chomsky," he said. "Is there anyone else we should interview?" He arched an eyebrow and stared curiously at Beatrice.

"Nah, man. These ladies had nothin' to do with it," Norm said. "Detective work was totally our gig. Ya know, Doc here has some experience with capturing a terrorist, along with the dog." He turned to Sandra. "Ya still got the newspaper article. Show 'em." He nudged with his elbow.

"Of course, dearie. I carry it with me all the time. It's in my purse. Hold on a second while I fetch it. Or maybe I should show you how Gaston can fetch?" She bent down toward the dog, gesturing to the nightstand where her black purse lay. "Go fetch Mama's purse. Gaston, fetch!"

The fat poodle moved surprisingly fast for a dog of his size as he dashed across the room. He hopped up on his hind legs and grabbed the purse. Then he trotted proudly back to Sandra, waiting for her to remove the purse from his jaws before he went back to heeling.

She fumbled with the clasp and opened the bag stuffed with tissues, breath mints, lipsticks, and crumpled excursion agendas. "If you'll just give me a moment, I'm sure it's in here somewhere," she said as she attempted to sort through the detritus.

PM Ashenbrenner interrupted. "Thank you, madam, but that won't be necessary. We aren't questioning Professor Chomsky today. It seems there were many eyewitnesses that observed him on the top deck during the time of the robbery." PM Ashenbrenner nodded to the young officer, and he slipped the notepad back in his pocket. "We are only talking to Herr Clodfelder today."

She turned to Norm, "We'll return you to the ship as soon as we are finished. Hopefully, you will be back before the ship leaves Koblenz."

"I thought this was just a formality. I don't understand why you can't conduct the interview on board ship," Vlad protested.

"We don't have the proper video equipment here. We plan on recording your statement, Herr Clodfelder. We need to match it with the witness's statement," PM Ashenbrenner said gruffly.

"Witness? How could there be a witness? Everyone was on the top deck, enjoying the scenery."

"It seems we have a witness that's come forward, placing Herr Clodfelder in the vicinity of the crime scene. There's no physical evidence yet, but we do need to check out the veracity of his story," the skinny officer said. The large police woman frowned at him and gave a little shake of her head.

"It's nothing. German police protocol. If you'll come with us, Danke, Herr." She gestured with her ham-sized hand toward the door. "The sooner we get started, the sooner you can return to your friends."

"No problemo, Officer," Norm said as he pulled on his motorcycle boots, leaning on the arm of the couch as he wobbled on one foot at a time. Then he tucked in his flannel shirt and ran his fingers through the top of his thinning hair.

"Can I get my hat? I feel naked without it," he asked, reaching for the green and gold cap on the end table. He plunked it on at a jaunty angle, like he was heading to the stadium to watch a Packers game. As he followed the police officers into the hallway, he said, "The sooner you hear my testimony, the sooner you can catch the real thief."

Chapter 18

FIVE HOURS LATER, VLAD ENTERED the dining room and discovered Beatrice and Sandra sitting alone at a table meant for six in the back of the room, with Gaston perched on a chair next to Sandra.

"What—Norm's not back yet from his interview?" Vlad said in astonishment.

Beatrice said with a glum expression, "Not back and not a word from him."

He sat down across from Sandra and asked, "Where's Clarence and Dougie?"

"They must have decided to stay in Koblenz for supper. Dougie heard about some restaurant he wanted to try," she said as she gently stroked her dog's ears. At the sound of approaching footsteps, the dog hopped down from the chair and settled in at her feet. He gave Sam, the waiter, an innocent look.

An unsmiling Sam shoved the evening's menu at them and stood sullenly as they perused their options—the amiable chatter and chance to practice his English were replaced with silence and the chance to practice his dagger stare.

"How is the asparagus soup prepared?" Beatrice asked.

"How the chef always does," he sniffed. "He's been cooking for years."

"I'll have that for starters, the chicken for the main course, and *schaum torte* for dessert."

"I'll have the same," said Vlad. And then immediately regretted giving Sam the opportunity to spit in his soup.

"Make it three," said Sandra. "Would it be possible to have an extra *schuam torte* for Gaston?"

"Chef say no extras tonight for dog. Not good to eat human food," Sam said, gathering the menus. He turned abruptly and stomped away without signaling to the wine girl to bring their drinks.

"Do you think he got in trouble for lending Norm his uniform?" Beatrice said, watching him stalk off with a concerned look.

"I'd say that's a safe bet," Vlad answered as he waved his arm at one of the wine stewards. He watched as she filled their glasses and then lifted his to the two ladies. "Cheers! I hope you aren't too lonely tonight without Clarence."

"Dearie, it's just a shipboard romance. Enjoy it while it lasts. I don't think about the future. I'm just grateful for every day that I wake up above ground," Sandra said.

Sam brought their order, and Sandra attacked the cream of asparagus soup with gusto, slurping loudly and slipping pieces of her buttered roll to Gaston. "Besides, he can barely keep up with me. If I wanted a permanent relationship, I'd look closer to home."

Beatrice stirred her soup slowly, making little indentations in the thick cream. She lifted her spoon to her mouth and then set it back in the bowl. "Aren't you worried about Norm?"

"I've given up worrying about him years ago—maybe the first few times he was arrested for disorderly conduct but..."

"This is a little more serious than getting drunk in Crawford on Saturday night."

"You've got to understand, Norm has a secret weapon—his ability to make people laugh. If I learned one thing in all my years in Burlesque, nobody can withstand the assault of laughter. Norm's got the gift."

"Katherine Beaumont's not laughing away the loss of her diamonds worth thousands of dollars. AND we're in a foreign country. I wish I had your optimism," Vlad said.

"You can't look at all these castles and cathedrals and not think about all the people who built them hundreds of years ago. Where are they now? What did their worrying amount to in the long run? Norm will be fine. He's innocent."

"You know that, and I know that, but do the police know that?"

"They will when you and Gaston find the real thieves. You keep forgetting our Wonderdog is on the case." Sandra pushed her empty bowl away and fixed her bright blue eyes on his. "What's your plan for catching them? Now that Norm's a suspect, we'll have to get some skin in the game. No one will suspect a fragile old lady with a fat poodle and a doofus professor, much less a mousy librarian."

"Doofus! Mousy! Really?" Vlad glared at her, eyes blazing. "There's no need for insults."

"Wait a minute." Beatrice tapped her finger on her lip and said pensively, "She does have a point. We certainly don't look like detectives."

"Neither does Norm, and look where that got him."

"No. I think Sandra's onto something. Let's go back to her room after dinner and discuss this in private." She turned her attention back to the cream of asparagus. "By the way, this soup is delicious."

"How can you both calmly enjoy this soup while Norm's in trouble?" said Vlad. "Are you that insensitive?"

"We're just more practical, dearie. We can't hunt down jewel thieves if we don't keep up our strength. Now eat up." Sandra eyed the untouched butter horn on Vlad's bread plate and pointed her spoon at it. "If you're not going to eat that roll, Gaston would appreciate a second helping, since he's not getting *schaum torte*."

BACK IN HER SUITE, THE TWO LOVERS gathered on the couch. Sandra picked up a notepad and pen from the end table and handed it to Vlad. "I can't write anymore. My penmanship was never very good, and my right hand is shot to hell with arthritis." She held up her swollen knuckles. "Here you go, dearie."

She settled in the armchair with Gaston at her feet. He licked the butter off his jowls and then moved down to his back paws. He gnawed between the pads with a happy grunt, stretching his leg to his muzzle.

"What do we know about the thieves?" She focused her laser-sharp eyes at Vlad.

"Not much." He shook his head. "Only what little Norm told me."

"What was that? Try to remember as much as you can," she said intently.

"He claimed he heard two voices, both males, not American. Probably British from the way they sounded. But one man seemed to be talking gibberish."

"Gibberish? What do you mean by gibberish?" Beatrice said. "Why don't you let me write while you think?" She reached for the pad and pen.

"How did he put it?" Vlad bit his lip as he strained to remember. "I was a bit under the weather, and he woke me from a sound sleep, so I'm not sure I heard correctly,"

"Take a minute and do some relaxing breaths. Concentrate," Beatrice said, pen poised to write.

Vlad folded his hands on his lap, closed his eyes, and deeply inhaled. He held it for a second at the top of his breath, then slowly exhaled. Held it for a heartbeat again. He tried to chase the worrying images of Norm in jail away. He felt his diaphragm expand and contract again as he tried to recall Norm's exact words.

In a somnolent voice he uttered, "Posh. The thief said Katherine was posh. The theft would be cushy. Easy as shite."

"Posh is British slang for fancy. There was Posh, one of the Spice Girls," Beatrice said.

Sandra added, "Cushy sounds like tushy. Shite. Could be talking about an ass…"

"Some of what he said was pure nonsense. Shagalicous? Crumpy, crumples," Vlad continued. "Describing some woman on the inside, an employee of the Gasson."

"Is there anything else? Think hard. Take another cleansing breath," urged Beatrice.

Vlad relived his throbbing headache and churning stomach and the whirling room with Norm clutching his arm and babbling on. "The nicer speaking man, not the weird one, said he'd been to the Gasson, pretending to be a buyer."

"The Gasson wouldn't be fooled by a common thief. This guy would have to be pretty convincing that he was wealthy. So we're looking for someone who dresses well, acts sophisticated, like a diamond merchant," Beatrice said as she wrote quickly.

Vlad snapped his fingers. "That tall man comes to mind. Rugged-looking, expensive sport clothes, military bearing. Norm identified him. I've seen him at the table with the Beaumonts."

Sandra stabbed her finger at him. "Yeah, that hunky guy. Looks like Clark Gable. If I wasn't hooked up with Clarence, I'd have moved in on him. He could park his size thirteens under my bed anytime."

"What about the pretentious fellow who wears an ascot and silk shirts, like that Carly Simon song, 'like he's walking onto a yacht?'" Beatrice tapped the pen thoughtfully on the paper.

"You mean the man with the neatly trimmed mustache and perfect hair? Not even a hurricane could muss it up. Seems out of place from the rest of us. List him, too." Sandra ordered. "Anybody else?"

"They'll do for starts. Norm was suspicious of them both." Vlad rose to his feet and spoke. "Tomorrow, when we get to Cologne, we'll have to make sure we get on the same tour bus with each of them and watch for something suspicious."

"Gaston and I will take the hunky one! I'd like to strike up something with him." At the sound of his name, Gaston gave a little yip in agreement.

"What about Clarence? You can't just dump him," Beatrice said frowning.

"No problem. I'll hide his Viagra, and he'll waste time looking for it. He won't leave his room without it. Kinda like his version of an American Express card," Sandra chuckled.

"Beatrice and I will tackle Sir Ostentatious—figure some excuse to join him. We'll compare notes tomorrow night."

"How are we going to keep Norm out of this?" Beatrice asked.

"Don't worry. I'll think of something. He can stay behind to help Clarence, maybe. Or Gaston can have an accident on his pant leg." Gaston yipped again. "My Wonderdog can do anything on command!"

But there was no need to worry. Norm didn't come back that night.

Chapter 19

THE THOUGHT OF NORM AT THE KOBLENZ police station and the possibility of his own interview with the daunting police woman gnawed away at Vlad's slumber. Was their plan to infiltrate the suspects even feasible? He felt like he was the actor in a second rate sitcom; the specter of a bumbling Maxwell Smart flitted in and out of his consciousness. Hoping to form a comfortable headrest, he punched his pillow throughout the seemingly endless night, which resulted in a crick in his neck. When he finally dozed off, a loud knock on the door interrupted his uneasy slumber. He shot out of bed, surprised to find Beatrice and Sandra standing in the hallway with Gaston by her side.

"Norm never came home. Let's go talk to the captain. Surely, he knows when the police plan on returning with him," Sandra said. Her splashy flowered jacket festooned with sequins covered a low-cut shimmery fuchsia top with matching palazzo pants. His five-year-old Kaitlyn would have coveted her glittery pumps.

"Let me throw on some clothes. Won't you come inside while I get dressed?" He rubbed his eyes, still trying to absorb the sight of Sandra decked out in her finery.

"Oh, no, dearie. I don't want to embarrass you with Beatrice here. We'll wait out here," she said as she waved him away.

"Just come in. You don't want to attract unwarranted attention," he said.

Gaston bounded into the room, leash trailing behind him. He leapt onto the bed and began pawing at the misshapen pillow. Beatrice flashed Vlad a friendly smile and settled on the bed beside the dog, while Vlad scooped up his clothes in a hasty retreat to the bathroom. Gaston let out a happy whine as Beatrice patted him and murmured, "How's this good boy today?"

As he pulled on clean underwear and socks, Vlad could hear the two women talking.

"Do you think I look harmless enough in this outfit?" Sandra asked. "I picked something a little boring because I want to lull the suspect into thinking I'm just a doddering old lady."

"I wouldn't call anything you wear boring, but the silver slippers are a nice touch."

"Oh, these silly things? I was going to wear my flowered clogs but they seemed so practical. I'm going for the crazy old lady look. Totally disarming and innocuous. Checking with the captain before we go out to the buses. Got to get the scoop on Norm."

The two women were still deep in conversation when he came back into the room. Sandra carefully looked Beatrice up and down. "You're going to wear that sweater and skirt with those pumps? Undercover agents have to blend in, you know."

"I hadn't really thought much about it. I can change into something more comfortable for walking, like capris and my sneakers."

"Do you have anything sexy? Show a little cleavage. You want to keep the suspect off guard.''

Beatrice's forehead wrinkled with concentration. "Hm-m-m. Sexy? Let me think. I don't suppose what I wore to the Welcome Dinner would work?"

"Only if you're trying out for a role in June Cleaver's Wild Night at the PTA Meeting."

Beatrice let out an indignant humph. "I didn't think it was that dowdy."

"Honey, you can borrow something from me. I brought along a few outfits from the old days just in case."

Vlad heard the hesitation in Beatrice's voice. "I'm not sure. I really don't want to draw attention to myself. I thought we were going for mousy. You wouldn't catch Miss Marple in a bustier, would you?"

Sandra shrugged and said, "Guess not. Oh, well, to each his own," she said. Then she took in his choice of navy twills, his many pocketed vest, and pinstriped shirt with a cool appraising stare. "Apparently, you don't want to draw attention to yourself either."

"Isn't this doofus enough for you? Maybe I should check for my pocket protector?" he said. "We just want the suspect to let his guard down. This works for me. Now let's find the captain." He offered her his arm as they shuffled down the hallway with Gaston in tow.

They caught up with Captain Schultz in the wheelhouse, sitting alone on his tall swivel chair. A half-eaten croissant and a travel mug rested on a narrow ledge. A small computer screen tracked their progress along a map of the river. Electronic dials and buttons covered the dashboard. Looking down at the glistening water from the windows of this high perch, Vlad understood why he would want to eat breakfast away from all the hustle of the excited passengers. The calm of the early morning sun lit up the river in a special glow and affected him with the eternal feel of the ancient waters. No matter what happened in their fleeting lives, the river would roll on.

Sandra broke the silence. "Norm didn't come home last night. Have you had any word from the Koblenz police about his whereabouts?"

"Yes, they left a message. The interview went on later than planned. We had already left for our appointment through the first set of locks. PM Aschenbrenner will meet us in Cologne with him."

"What took so long? He didn't do anything wrong!"

"Of course not, madam. It just took longer to verify his story. They asked for our passenger list around midnight—just as we were pulling up the gangplank. I'm sure it was just a formality."

"Just a formality! Keeping our friend overnight with no lawyer to advise him!" she exploded. Gaston picked up on his mistress's agitation and began nudging her leg with his head. When she absentmindedly reached down to stroke him, he began to lick her hand.

"German police are very thorough. If your friend is innocent, they will confirm that. They want to be certain before he is released. It's very difficult to extradite suspects from foreign countries when a case comes to court."

"Are you saying you think he's guilty?" Sandra moved into Captain Schultz's personal space and gave him a frosty stare. He held her fierce gaze for a second, then looked away and held up his hands in surrender.

"No, madam. I would never presume to judge your friend. I'm just telling you how our police force operates, which may be different from law enforcement in America."

Vlad grabbed Sandra by her arm and dragged her toward the

door. "We should be heading down to breakfast. We don't want to miss the first bus for today's excursion. I hope you'll keep us informed if anything should change?"

"Of course. I expect your friend will catch up with you in Cologne by lunchtime."

"THERE'S MINE," SANDRA NUDGED VLAD as the passenger stood on the riverbank waiting for Lutz to lead them to the buses. The tall Englishman stood erect, head above the crowd, looking more like he was ready for a trek up the mountains rather than a stroll in a city. He wore hiking boots, plaid shirt, and khaki pants that could convert into shorts topped off by an Indiana Jones type expedition hat. His well-muscled arms were exposed by his rolled-up sleeves. Although some weight settled around his middle, he still looked like he could wrestle a grizzly to the ground without breaking a sweat.

"And there's yours."

Sandra directed their gaze at a slim man in a tailored shirt that fit his form perfectly, teal ascot jauntily tied about his neck. Pencil mustache and not a hair out of place, expensive camera equipment hung off his shoulder. He cocked his head at an angle in an apparent conversation with a blonde, middle-aged woman in a black strappy cold shoulder T-top, mini jean skirt, and oversized sunglasses. "You better move in on him before Blondie swoops down and snatches him up," she whispered.

She gave Beatrice a little shove in the man's direction. "Toodle-oo, dearie. Charlie's Angels are on the job." She formed a handgun shape with her fingers, took aim at the unsuspecting gentleman, and winked at Vlad. Tugging on Gaston's leash, she pulled her reluctant canine sidekick through the throng until she appeared at the elbow of the tall man.

They watched as Sandra began talking to him, fluttering her fake eyelashes at him, and tossing her head coyly as she looked directly into his waistband. He bent down to catch what she was saying. She laid her hand upon his arm and apparently, said something amusing because he laughed loudly.

"We'd better strike up a conversation with our fellow," Vlad said. "I'll try to steer Blondie to new prey. Where's Dougie? He'd be perfect. He's hard to shake off once he latches onto an attractive woman. And she certainly is attractive."

They both scanned the gathering crowd. No Dougie. Beatrice said, "He might be helping Clarence look for his pills?"

"Probably. We don't have time to waste wondering about Don Juan's whereabouts. I'll think of something to distract her while you focus on the Duke of Debonair."

Like a stealth drone, they honed in on the chatting couple. As Vlad sidled up to the blonde, he noticed the bit of grey peeking out from the part in her hair, and the fine line of wrinkles around her eyes. In comparison, Beatrice looked fresh and appealing, even though her soft coral tee shirt had no peepholes cut out and her capris were far from mini. The Englishman looked just as well-groomed close up as he had from across the reception room, just enough silver strands in his precision-cut hair, and the casually knotted ascot gave him an air of country manor living. Vlad almost expected him to shout "Talley ho" when they were loaded on the bus to leave.

He broke into the conversation. "What are you thinking of doing during our free afternoon in Cologne?"

The gentleman answered first. "There is an excellent modern art museum with a large collection of works by Picasso that I'm considering. Although climbing to the top of the cathedral holds a certain appeal. I imagine the view is fantastic."

Beatrice clapped her hands in delight. "An art museum! I love Cubism. Does it also have some of the German expressionists in the collection? I simply adore Franz Marc's Blue Horses!"

"I've heard the Fragrance Museum is very interesting. It's the birthplace of Eau de Cologne," Vlad said, hoping to entice the woman.

"Art? Perfume? Not for me," laughed the blonde. "My friend and I were hoping for beer and chocolate. We're going to try a glass of that Kölsch beer in a Brauhaus. Maybe several glasses. Then we're heading to the Chocolate Museum."

Where was Dougie? Here's a match made in heaven, Vlad thought as he joined in her laughter.

"Is your friend nearby? My name's Vlad, by the way, and this is my friend Beatrice," he said.

"I'm Sally. Pleased to meet you. My friend Jo-Lynn went to change her shoes. She came out in heels, foolish girl, and I reminded her of the horrible cobblestone streets. I'm sure she'll catch up with us." She turned her focus back to the mustached man. "And you are…?"

"Nigel, Nigel Hawkins. On my way to Amsterdam and I decided to take the scenic route."

"Are you traveling alone?" Beatrice asked him.

"Mixing pleasure with business, I'm afraid. Lived in Switzerland all this time and have never taken a trip on the Rhine. I decided this was an opportune moment to do a little traveling."

"Me, too. My colleague and I just finished the spring semester at Crawford University in Wisconsin and signed up for this river cruise to celebrate." She jerked her head toward Vlad and continued. "So relaxing after a hectic teaching schedule."

Before Vlad could say a word, Lutz began ushering them toward the waiting buses. Beatrice positioned herself tightly at Nigel's elbow as the crowd shuffled forward. Vlad volunteered to help Sally look for her friend while scanning the milling passengers for Dougie.

Suddenly, Sally screeched, "Jo-Lynn! Over here! Jo-Lynn!"

Vlad's muscles tightened at the unexpected scream, and he let out a little yelp. Sally gave him a quizzical look as Jo-Lynn, an athletic-looking brunette, now wearing sensible walking shoes, joined them. Before Vlad could introduce himself, she grabbed Sally by the arm and pulled her toward the bus, saying, "Hurry up! I don't want to get stuck in the seat near the toilet again." They disappeared in the flow of passengers like a twig in some rapids.

Good. Now I can focus on Nigel, Vlad thought, but when he tried to catch up with him and Beatrice it was impossible to push ahead. He noted which bus they entered and got in the queue to join them. Luckily, he was the last person allowed on, but the only seat left was in front of the door with a large WC emblazoned on it. The overpowering scent of disinfectant wafted down the aisle.

It could be worse, Vlad thought. Seconds later Dougie made his way toward him.

"Gotta use the shitter, bro. It's an emergency. Shouldn't have had all that sauerkraut and beer last night," he said as he ducked in the toilet.

Vlad tried to shut out the explosive noises and grunts coming from behind the closed door. Lutz was at the front, giving them a quick rundown of the day and explaining the options if they chose to stay on their own in Cologne. When the door opened a horrible smell emerged. Vlad pictured a cloud of poisonous gas seeping into the trenches. *Couldn't have been any worse than what Dougie left behind.*

"Hey, where's Dad's hot mama today? He couldn't find her after breakfast. Wanted to stay in his room looking for something. I couldn't convince him to join us. Is she staying on board, too? Figured they'd hook up. A little afternoon delight." He gave Vlad a lewd wink.

"She was looking for him. Must have been some miscommunication. I saw her get on the second bus."

"With Norm?"

"No, he was detained in Koblenz. He'll be joining us today, I'm sure."

"Tough break. That crazy rich bitch has him pegged as a thief. Just so you know, I don't buy it. He was with me most of the night before. He's not the type."

"Thank you. We know he's not capable of theft. But unfortunately, someone on board thinks he IS."

"Think the cops will figure out who? Saw them interviewing people. You gotta be careful around cops. They always want to pin it on the handiest suspect. Lazy assholes—just to say case closed."

Vlad thought for a moment: *Should I clue him into our plan? But he's so unreliable. First short skirt or cleavage showing and he'd be gone.* So he said nothing as he watched Dougie retreat up the aisle.

Chapter 20

A SLIGHTLY QUEASY FEELING ENVELOPED VLAD as he trudged down the aisle, the last person to step down from the bus. He sighted Beatrice, neatly sandwiched between Nigel and Dougie. Try as he might, he couldn't push his way to their side so he found himself an outcast from the excitedly chattering group. Beatrice gave him an intense look, slightly jerking her head toward Nigel and turning away from Dougie. Vlad shrugged and held up his hands in a helpless gesture.

Lutz led them all into a boxy building fashioned out of concrete slabs over a glassed-in entrance. A huge sign proclaimed it was *Römisch-Germanisches Museum*. A glimmer of excitement rose inside him despite the worry over Norm, because the Romano-Germanic Museum was world-renowned for its well-preserved collection of ancient Roman glassware. In the lobby area, as Lutz handed out listening devices, Vlad noticed Sandra giving him a thumbs-up as she put in her earbud and continued chatting with her tall companion, in contrast to the frown on Beatrice's face.

"I'd like to introduce you to your guide for this morning, Dr. Elke Sauer. Elke is the curator in the museum and the leading authority on Roman Art. We are so lucky she is joining us."

Vlad expected a dried-up, prune-faced academic, like most of the curators of ancient artifacts he'd met. After handling antique objects on a daily basis, they seemed to take on the veneer of the antiquities. He was pleasantly surprised when Lutz stepped aside to reveal a tall, blond Amazon with sharp features too angular to be pretty. Obviously braless, her nipples protruded under her pale brown linen tunic over flowing lavender pants. Gladiator sandals seemed a throwback to the ancient times she discussed, her concession to the present was the bright red toenail polish.

"I was telling you about this passenger," Lutz said as he led her over to Vlad. "He's a professor of archaeology and teacher at the university level. Elke, may I present Dr. Chomsky?"

With a surprisingly firm grip, the woman grabbed his hand and vigorously shook it. Her skin felt as if she'd laid bricks all her life without wearing gloves; calluses peppered her palm. Vlad ran his thumb along the rough edge, surprised at such a masculine touch, then caught himself and pulled away.

"I'm so pleased to meet you, Dr. Chomsky. I don't often have the opportunity to speak to a fellow archaeologist. I hope you'll enjoy the tour."

"I'm sure I will. I read about your collection last year in the *Journal of Archaeology*. The colors of the mosaic—incredible! Imagine building a museum around the discovery of such a floor. And the beauty of the fine glass!"

"So, you caught my little article? Glad you liked it. Perhaps we can talk more later." With a toss of her head, her fine, straight blond hair fell like a shimmery curtain to her shoulders. Brushing it back, she inserted the earbud and turned on the transmitter hanging from her neck. Vlad did the same, turning the volume control on his receiver just in time to hear her say, "Welcome, ladies and gentleman. You are about to embark upon a tour of the finest Roman artifacts found outside of Italy. Please follow me to the atrium."

She led them to a sunny area in the middle of the museum. Perched high above, they looked upon a beautiful mosaic stretching across a floor bigger than a high school gymnasium, the colors still vibrant after hundreds of years. An androgynous youth, naked with flowing cape, cavorted with lions, beautiful women, and bearded males. "This is the Dionysius mosaic, depicting scenes of the god of the grape harvest, winemaking, and drunken ecstasy. While digging for an air raid shelter in 1941, workers discovered this fine example of Roman art. They preserved it carefully, and in 1974 this museum was built around it."

Vlad heard audible gasps of astonishment from the crowd as they studied the scenes surrounded by a pattern of brightly colored tiles. "I can't believe the details, the lifelike bodies," the woman standing next to him said. "That girl—so graceful. Her hair flows like it's swept up by a breeze. What exquisite art!"

Marble staircases leading to the upper levels of the museum rose above them. Soon Elke led them to the next floor where beautiful sculptures in classic half nude poses were punctuated by a huge marble sepulcher, looking much like the entrance to a temple.

"Much of the artifacts in this museum were used in funerals and found in burial sites. Here is an example of a tomb where the elite were buried," she said, gesturing to the monument.

She kept them moving quickly past display after display of statues, exquisite jewelry, and richly decorated household items until Vlad felt totally overwhelmed. On the third floor she led them to the giant glass case holding the glass treasures from the magazine article.

"The rarities of Roman glass!" Vlad exclaimed.

Elke smiled at him. "Yes, these are rare examples of Roman craftsmanship. Some of the finest preserved works. Like the *conchylia* cup, one of four in the world, noted for the combination of clear and colored glass."

Vlad waited patiently for his turn to stand in front of the cup where tiny green fish swam forever through delicate multi-colored waves on a clear glass bowl. Next, he studied the cage cup, marveling at the smooth green circles like fine links of a chain encasing the clear glass bowl, the Greek inscription circling the rim: *Drink, Live well forever*. Another very rare find. Mesmerized by the multitude of richly colored glass—amethyst, crimson, sapphire—he didn't notice the tour had moved on.

The soft feel of a woman's breast grazed his shoulder. Startled, he turned his head, only to discover Elke standing close to him, staring at a finely made purple goblet in the glass case, her nipple stretching against the ecru cloth of her tunic, so near that the vanilla scent of her body wash drifted to his nostrils. Had she meant to stand this close? Averting his eyes from her breast, he glanced behind him to check for Beatrice, but no one was there. Vlad inched away as she prattled on, "I see you share my passion for Roman glassware. Such a rare collection. So beautiful it almost hurts to walk away." Her light blue eyes locked on his. "My theory is the glass blowers lived here in Cologne and created these exquisite pieces. That's why so many of them have been discovered here."

"I read your theory and, after seeing these, I can't help but agree," he said. "Perhaps one genius developed the technique that made these incredible combinations."

"We'll never know for certain. The answer is hidden for centuries beneath the layers of the city. Perhaps you would like to see some of our latest discoveries, though none so beautiful as these, Dr. Chomsky."

"Please call me Vlad. That would be amazing. Can't even imagine how exciting to observe archaeology in action. But this is only the first stop of our tour of Cologne. We're heading to the cathedral next."

"Haven't you seen enough cathedrals already? Every major city along the Rhine has their testament to God. Besides, this one is being refurbished so you'll mostly see scaffolding." She frowned and shook her head. "So disappointing."

"Don't you have to complete the tour of the museum?"

"This was the last stop. Lutz gave everyone twenty minutes to browse before he takes your group on a walking tour to see the remaining Roman towers. On to the Town Hall with the giant clock where couples must take their wedding vows. Lots of bridal parties and bouquets. You end with a tour of the cathedral, and then your free afternoon. You could skip all that and stay at the museum."

"What a tempting offer!" His voice rose with excitement. "I teach a course in ancient history, you know. The beginnings of civilization through the fall of the Roman Empire."

"Then, Vlad, you should experience our collection in more depth." Her blue eyes held his for a long minute. "You won't be disappointed."

"You convinced me, Elke. Where do we return this equipment?" He pulled the earbud out and turned off the device, slipping the cord over his head. Hers already hung loosely, microphone disconnected.

"Come with me to the front desk." She led him to an elevator marked *Staff Only* in English and German and punched the button marked One. Her perfume filled the elevator with the fragrance of sugar cookies freshly out of the oven. Unaware of how her closeness affected him, she kept chattering.

"Construction workers found another burial site as they were digging the foundation for a new office building. My colleagues in the field were able to excavate some jewelry and shards of glass. The real treasure was a small mosaic of a man and woman—only some of the tiles are missing."

He focused on the numbers over the door as they moved

downward. Three, two, one. Clearing his throat, he said, "Will it eventually be on display?"

"Come look. Judge for yourself if the quality is there." The door opened next to the desk in the lobby where the listening devices were handed out; Lutz was sitting in a chair next to the attendant, engrossed in his cellphone. Barely looking up, he gave them a perfunctory nod. As Elke handed over both sets of equipment, she said, "Professor Chomsky has decided to stay a bit longer at the museum. I told him about the artifacts recently discovered at an excavation. He's very eager to see them."

'We pick up the passengers down from the cathedral where we dropped you off at five o'clock. Do you remember where it is?" he said.

Vlad sadly shook his head, but Elke chimed in, "Is it at the Hohe Strasse?"

"Yes, right across from the Bier Garten," Lutz answered. 'You'll give him good directions?"

"Of course. I wouldn't let our distinguished guest miss his ride to the ship," she laughed. "You might ask for a different tour guide if I lost one of your passengers."

She led him through a side door marked *Restricted.*

"A professor of archaeology cannot tour Cologne without a visit to the Praetorium. And we have just excavated an ancient sewer tunnel that leads directly there from the museum."

"The Praetorium? What is that?" he asked as he followed her through a short hallway.

"The ruined foundation of the governor's palace from Roman times. Uncovered as a result of wartime bombing. I will show you. We walk on platforms above the main ruins. You can't imagine the size—though not as big as your Grand Canyon." She unlocked a massive steel door, then flicked on a light.

"You've been to the Grand Canyon?" Vlad arched his eyebrows with a sideways glance.

"I studied in the United States at the University of Nebraska for two years."

He nodded and said, "That explains why you are so proficient in English."

"In primary school we begin to learn English. I speak five

languages—French, Russian, Swedish, and English as well as my native German." She ushered him into a large room. "But first we'll look at the most recent artifacts."

Wall-to-wall tables covered in fragments of carved stone, pieces of statuary, and even some real bones filled the room. Vlad saw disembodied marble legs and torsos, the fragment of a delicately sculpted ear, Roman letters carved on a stone piece the size of a toaster. Shards of glass, green and yellow. She pointed out a small mosaic of a long-dead woman with her hair piled high and a somber-looking companion. "Here is the mosaic. What do you think?"

"I can barely tell that tiles are missing. The colors are still so rich. What a find!"

She indicated a pile of bones. "That is the skull of a dog."

Vlad recognized the long, bony snout, empty holes where there once were eyes. She leaned against him and gently touched his arm, pushing him closer to the table.

"Look at the top. See the large gash. This dog's head was split by a sword. I wonder what it did to annoy its human so much that he struck it hard enough to shatter the skull."

The warmth of her body so close to his made Vlad break out in a sweat so he moved away. Was this common body language among German people? Funny how they were stereotyped as cold and reserved. Elke was anything but. Her friendliness made him feel slightly uneasy, like she invaded his personal space. But then again, this was Europe. He remembered the topless sunbathers on his visit to Greece. They were mostly German or Swedish.

"Do you know what this is?' She pointed to a yellow terra cotta fragment that looked like half of a forehead over an empty eye socket.

"It's not a human that someone angered?" He swallowed hard at the thought of the sword coming down on a head.

She tittered, "Oh, no! It's part of a mask. You Americans weren't the only ones to celebrate in masquerades. The Romans liked to dress up, too."

She moved to a different table. "Here is another prize."

She pointed to a reddish-orange bowl with clear glass footing and only one nick on the rim, so translucent he could see the wood grain of the tabletop below it. It was perfectly balanced and symmetrical, yet delicate in appearance despite its large size.

"Beautiful, absolutely stunning," he sighed. Again, she stood companionably beside him, leaning ever so slightly against him.

"Yes, this will make it into the collection upstairs as soon as we can carbon date it. I just cleaned it up yesterday," she said. "But we should visit the Praetorium now, before more tourists start to arrive."

She led him to another locked door. This one opened onto a dark staircase.

"Have you ever seen the Roman sewer system? It's truly an engineering marvel, built to withstand centuries old disuse and decay."

She flicked on a light that barely illuminated the stairs leading down to an abyss of darkness. Vlad held onto the railing and stepped cautiously to find secure footing before venturing onto the next level. Ahead of him, Elke reached the bottom and turned on a light. Bare bulbs were strung out along a stone block tunnel and cast black shadows into the unknown expanse filled with the musty smell of damp earth.

"No, I've never seen any ancient Roman structures. I have three children and don't really get away very often. My ex-wife took the kids so I could do the cruise," he said as he stumbled on the last step. He reached his hand to the cold, dank wall to steady himself. Fighting the urge to turn around and head back to the welcoming light of the upstairs lab, he took a deep breath and took another step. She was already several feet ahead of him, striding confidently through the tunnel, whereas Vlad's eyes had not yet adjusted to the darkness.

"Elke, could you hold up a second until I catch up?" He floundered toward her, feeling like the walls were closing in.

"Of course. So sorry. I travel this site so often I scarcely need to turn the light. I forget others are not so familiar." She looked around at the sturdy tunnel walls that curved into the ceiling, massive blocks held in place overhead by the technical skills of ancient builders. "Truly amazing, don't you think?"

"Yeah, amazing," he said, hoping that the huge stones overhead wouldn't come loose as they were standing there. *This tunnel existed for a thousand years. There's nothing to worry about*, he told himself. He heard a rustling sound, and something scampered over his foot. He gave out a little yelp.

"I just felt something run over my foot," he said.

"It's nothing. Probably a rat or a lizard." she said reassuringly.

He closed his eyes and shuddered in spite of his determination to act calm. If he'd wanted to be around creepy, crawly things, he'd have studied biology, not archaeology. He remembered his father killing a rat in their basement with his baseball bat. He couldn't bear to play ball or even touch it for months, remembering the sound of the rat's squeal as its brains leaked out.

When he opened his eyes, she was there next to him. "Why, you are shivering!" she said. "It's so cold down here. Let me warm you up."

She put her arms around his neck. He felt the softness of her breasts as she pressed against his chest, the warmth of her breath in his ear as she whispered, "I can take you back to your ship. You don't have to meet the bus at five. We could have the whole day to get to know each other better." Then her lips found his in an insistent kiss, her tongue searching his mouth, grazing along his teeth.

"No!" he said, jerking away. "I'm afraid there's been a misunderstanding"

He put his hands on her waist and gently pushed her away. She disentangled herself from him and said, "What misunderstanding? You have an ex-wife, I have an ex-partner. You're an attractive, intelligent man. I don't meet many archaeologists from the cruise ships. I thought we had some chemistry."

"You are a very attractive woman, and I appreciate your offer to show me the artifacts. But it's purely professional. I have a fiancée on board the ship. This is our first vacation together."

"She doesn't need to know. I have a futon in my office. Sometimes I work late. No one will be around today, I promise you. No one need ever know." She reached for him again.

He caught her hands and held them as he spoke, "I love my fiancée and wouldn't cheat on her. I would know. I have to look at myself in the mirror and like what I see there. I hope you understand."

She pulled away and said, "You egotistical Americans. So self-righteous! You hold my hand when we meet like a come-on, stand close to me in the elevator. But when I respond to your advances, you turn me down. Such a pompous ass."

Pivoting away, she stomped off into the tunnel. "Hurry along. You can probably catch up with your group at the cathedral."

Without another word they traveled through the sewer tunnel, through another door, and into the brightly lit ruins of the Praetorium.

Vlad blinked rapidly at the brightness. They stood on a platform that looped around the remnants of once massive walls. He leaned against a rail and looked over the vast foundations of the ancient Roman edifice.

With a flip of her hand she pointed out a large door. "There's a small museum room with plenty of information about this, if you know German. Stay as long as you like. Now, please excuse me. I must get back to work. I've wasted enough time today."

She turned on her heel and went back into the dimly lit tunnel. He heard a click as she locked up behind her. A sign in bold black letters clearly stated *Authorized Personnel Only* in English and German. He stared at the closed door, wondering what just happened. He stood stunned as a steady stream of visitors passed by.

Chapter 21

SHIVERING STILL, DESPITE THE BRIGHT MAY sunshine, Vlad glanced around the large square in front of the entrance to the Praetorium as he found his way up the stairs and out of the exit. A line of tourists queuing up in front of the small unassuming entrance totally ignored him as he blinked and searched for something familiar in the bright light. He approached a young man with a New York Yankees tee shirt and a *Lonely Planet* guidebook in hand.

"Pardon me, sir," he politely said. "Can you direct me to the cathedral? I need to meet my group there."

The man flipped his guidebook open to a page with a small inset of a map of Cologne and pointed to the street upon which they were currently standing.

"We're right here," he said, pointing to a little symbol labeled Praetorium. "The Cathedral is this way." Tracing his finger along the map, he jabbed where a small cathedral was drawn on a large square. "Just turn left on the next block. Once you clear this area, you'll be able to see the spires. Can't miss them."

"Thank you," Vlad said.

He stumbled along the cobblestone street until he reached the designated corner and turned, looking skyward. Yes, there were twin spires rising in the distance. He traveled along, always keeping sight of the peaks. Soon he found himself at the edge of a large square. The cathedral lay in front of him; two enormous towers supported the tallest spires he'd ever seen, a paragon of Gothic design. A multitude of smaller spires atop the side buttresses directed his eyes heavenward. But, just as Elke warned, the sides were swathed in scaffolding. Mammoth stone steps led to a richly sculpted entrance of numerous saints hovering above. More people lined up, waiting to enter the famous church. None of them were from the ship, although he wasn't really expecting to see any familiar faces. This was to be the last stop before their free afternoon. Although time with Elke felt like hours had passed, it had been an hour at most.

Rather than join the throng, Vlad looked around for an outdoor café where he could indulge in a coffee and some *kuchen* or strudel. Kitty-corner to the cathedral entrance, he saw a small, unassuming cluster of tables and a harried-looking waiter buzzing about. He ambled over, feeling in his pocket and wondering how many euros he had left. He felt coins jangling, but he didn't know if he had two euro pieces or just coins of lower denominations. He'd hoped to find an ATM and draw out some more money, but the encounter with Elke had left him reeling.

How could she have so badly misinterpreted his intentions? He had been so pleased to meet a fellow archaeologist, maybe he had exhibited a little too much enthusiasm. But for her to think he'd plunge into a casual affair without a conscience, and betray Beatrice, was appalling. The thought never entered his mind. In his heart he had already forsaken all others, even though Beatrice held back on commitment. He hoped that on this trip she'd trust him enough to tell him why so he could allay her fears.

He sat down, and an acne-scarred busboy brought him a glass of water and a menu. "Your waiter will be here shortly," the gangly youth said and rushed to clear the next table.

Vlad surreptitiously examined the coins in his pocket—only small change, barely tip money—and pulled out his wallet. He found a twenty euro note nestled in among the American dollars. Only then did he pick up the menu and look over the offerings.

As he was perusing the photographs of the rich pastries, he noticed a family sitting down at the table next to him. A bored-looking preadolescent in a Nike shirt immediately pulled out a cellphone and began skimming his thumbs over the device. The man began drumming his fingers on the table, glancing around for the waiter, while the woman tried to corral a small girl with curly red hair escaping from a ponytail. The child loudly protested the interruption of whatever she'd been doing out on the street and kept tugging at the mother and sliding off the chair.

Suddenly, Vlad ached for his own children—Kaitlyn at that age, full of energy and a short attention span. How he and Maria worked to keep her from annoying other diners. Erin's cellphone seemed to be another appendage to her hands as he constantly asked her to put it away and converse with them. And Nicholas with his obsession for books. How many shouts did it take before he pulled himself out of the escape hatch of a book?

"May I take your order, sir?" the frazzled waiter suddenly appeared at his elbow, ignoring the waving hand of the man with the two children.

"Just a cappuccino, please," he said, slowly closing the menu with the tempting photos.

The waiter jerked it out of his hand and stopped at the table with the family. He handed the man the menu and yelled at the busboy who was bringing four glasses of water and a stack of menus over to them.

As soon as the boy set the glasses down, the woman pulled a sippy cup out of her voluminous purse, took off the lid, and poured some ice water into it for the child. The little girl gulped down the water, finally settling into her chair. Her mother opened the menu and pointed to the pictures of the various pastries. The child shook her head at each one, stubbornly repeating the same words, which Vlad hypothesized were "ice cream" in German. At least that's what Kaitlyn would have wanted.

The ache was so strong Vlad pulled out his cellphone and began composing an e-mail to Erin. Her troubling e-mail concerning Nicholas began to gnaw at him. How unlike his sweet-tempered boy to slam a door and refuse to come out of his room. He flagged down the German boy and asked, "Do you have Wi-Fi here?" gesturing to his phone. The boy shook his head. Vlad sighed. He'd have to wait until returning to the ship.

He was just finishing his coffee as Lutz led the throng of his shipmates into the square. Flagging down the waiter, he handed him the twenty euro note and blotted his mouth with the napkin. Then he watched as Lutz gestured toward the church, spreading his arms so wide apart he assumed the discussion was about the size of the spires. He'd been right about the little girl. The waiter brought him his change and the family their pastries, with a very prominent dish of vanilla ice cream set before the child. She contentedly spooned the treat into her mouth; no more squirming, the boy set down his phone, and the family made the ideal picture for a tourist brochure.

"Dr. Chomsky! Is your tour behind the scene of the museum already over? I didn't expect to meet up with you until five," Lutz exclaimed as Vlad joined the throng gathering in front of the cathedral.

"Uh, Elke had a pressing matter to take care of. Came up unexpectedly so here I am."

"Did you visit the Praetorium and the tunnels?" Lutz asked.

"Oh, yes. Quite interesting. Imagine the size of that building!"

"I wish there was time to include it on our tour, but I only have a morning. And you've missed most of my presentation about the cathedral, but perhaps some of your friends can fill you in."

Vlad drifted toward Beatrice, still wedged between Dougie and the Englishman. Narrowing her eyes with a slight shake of her head, she gave him the warning not to come near. Dougie was so engrossed in another one of his stories that he didn't notice Vlad. The English fellow nodded politely, but his eyes seemed focused on something far in the distance. That left Sandra as his only approachable friend.

The tall Englishman's head stuck out above the cluster of tourists, a vantage point much like the spires of the cathedral. Vlad waited as the group filed past him up the steps, leaving Sandra and her target bringing up the rear with Gaston trotting behind with nose to the ground in bloodhound fashion.

"So what did I miss?" Vlad asked.

"Lutz told us the cathedral contains the relics of the Three Wise Men. The spires are the tallest in Europe," Sandra said, urging Gaston to pick up the pace with a tug on the leash.

The Englishman picked up where she left off. "It was started around 1200, and they stopped working on it two hundred years later but never finished it. Legend has it the builder made a pact with the devil that when the cathedral was completed, his whole family would belong to Satan. His wife tricked the builders into stopping construction, thus saving her family."

"Looks pretty complete to me except for the scaffolding around the buttresses."

"Well, dearie, the city decided to finish it in the 1880s. For four years, it was the tallest building in the world until the Washington Monument was completed and broke the record."

"You Americans always find a way to beat out the Germans," the

Englishman said. "Name's Ollie Fleming, by the way." He extended his large hand and vigorously shook Vlad's. "You must be the professor friend."

"Yes, I'm Vlad Chomsky. First time on a cruise. How about you?"

"Actually, I've had a job offer to become a travel agent in Auckland. I plan on trying out some of the tours so I can describe these experiences to prospective clients. I spent about two weeks in Italy, and now I'm on this."

Suddenly, Gaston lay down on the cobblestones and refused to get up. Sandra pulled a bit harder, but the little dog dug in with his paws. She dragged him along for about a foot, but he refused to stand up.

"Oh, dear. My dog seems tuckered out. What's wrong, Gaston? Are you all tuckered out?"

"The pup looks knackered, for sure," Ollie said.

"Would you like me to carry him?" Vlad offered.

"Oh, no, dearie. He's much too heavy. I noticed a little outdoor café. I'll buy him a strudel, and perhaps they'll bring him a bowl of water. You two finish the tour. Perhaps we can all go out for lunch at one of those beer places. How about some strudel, boy?"

At the word strudel, Gaston slowly rose to his feet and seemed willing to follow her to the café. She gave a backhanded wave while the two men gave each other a sideways glance

"Well, mate, shall we take a look inside? Supposedly, it's just as bril on the inside," Ollie said.

As they climbed up the stairs, Vlad continued, "What made you decide to work in Auckland? You're not a Kiwi, are you?"

"No, mate. My daughter married a Kiwi, though, and my two grandkids are in New Zealand so I moved to be near them. Me, I'm just a bloke who likes to wander. Spent thirty years in the military. Started out when we took back the Falklands in '83. Got a taste for travel. Marriage went all to pot, though," he said.

"Lot of that going around. My marriage ended last year. My ex actually took the kids full time so I could go on this trip."

"Kids—how old?"

"My oldest, Erin, is fifteen. Nicholas just turned eleven, and my youngest, Kaitlyn, is four."

"Yours are a bit younger than my two grandkids."

"That's why it's been hard to get away. Especially with my ex working, too."

"Will you look at that?" Ollie pointed to a hideously ugly gargoyle hovering above them, looking like a demon ready to pounce. "That thing's wicked. Give you nightmares for a week."

As they followed the crowd into the cathedral, Vlad watched Beatrice pause in front of a stained glass window and take a photo with her cellphone. He gave a little wave, but she didn't look his way. The English fellow pointed to something in the next alcove, and they ambled forward with Dougie trailing behind.

The massive arches directed Vlad's eyes heavenward as he walked inside the largest sanctuary he'd ever seen. Numerous alcoves with the remains of kings and saints lined the sides, each adorned with stained glass windows and the ubiquitous kneeler for prayers.

"I'm not one for religion, but I'm gobsmacked by this one," Ollie said in a hushed voice. "Been inside of more churches on this trip than I can remember growing up. Me Mum wasn't much for kneeling and juggling between the Book of Common Prayer and hymnals. Dad spent Sundays at the pub."

"Lucky you. My father was a strict Lutheran so we spent every Sunday morning at church and sometimes even back again in the evening."

"Bloody hell! Christmas and Easter is about all I can take. All these dead saints give me the willies." He pointed to a sarcophagus with the life-size likeness of the long-dead holy man carved on the tomb. "Like that one. I wouldn't want to be around on Judgment Day when that ugly bloke rises from the dead."

"I agree. This place is depressing," Vlad said with a sweeping gesture. "Too much doom and gloom. The day's too nice to spend in this giant mausoleum. Planning on heading back to the boat?"

"I'd rather tour the Chocolate Museum," Ollie replied." Let's head for an exit."

They politely nudged past the clusters of tourists and hushed pilgrims, past the flickering votive candles and velvet kneelers, into the brilliant spring sunshine. Vlad blinked rapidly, then shaded his eyes, scanning the square for the café where Sandra had taken the stubborn dog.

"Shall we lunch with Sandra and head there after?"

"Good that. Chocolate it is."

Chapter 22

SANDRA AND GASTON WERE WAITING at a small table under a striped umbrella in the same outdoor café where Vlad had stopped earlier. The same harried waiter with the perpetual frown came up to them as soon as they sat down and plopped a menu before them. Sandra sipped what remained of her coffee and brushed some crumbs from her lap. Gaston had stretched out on a metal chair beside hers for a short snooze, obviously sated from strudel.

"Ready to head for a beer and some lunch?"

"Gaston just settled in. Mind ordering something from here?"

Ollie waved his arm, and the waiter took their order for Coke Lite and a sausage on a roll with sauerkraut. He directed the boy to bring them water.

"We're planning to visit the Chocolate Museum this afternoon," Vlad said. "Do you want to join us?"

"I would but Gaston may not cooperate. He's been a little bucky today. I may just catch the noon bus back to the boat. Besides, I feel like I could do with an afternoon nap myself."

"But I thought you were excited to see how your favorite chocolates were made. I hear they have free samples," he added enticingly.

"And the largest assortment of molded chocolate in Europe. Every animal in God's creation and vehicles, sports equipment, everything. They say it's pretty ace!" Ollie added.

"It's a tempting offer, especially from two of the most handsome men on the ship, but Gaston comes first." She coyly dabbed at her lips with her napkin, then fished out a tube of lipstick from her purse, smearing some on her bottom lip and then pressing them together.

"No worries, Princess. Vlad and I have been going great guns. We'll bring some chocolate back for you. Milk or dark?"

"Anything with sea salt and caramel. Make it dark, the darker the better. Healthier, they say. I do have my girlish figure to keep in shape."

The waiter brought the checks, and Vlad reached inside his special traveling vest with the inner zippered pocket, but Ollie held up his hand. "I'll get it. It's the least I can do for this charming lady and her pooch."

Sandra checked her watch and rose slowly to her feet, tugging gently on Gaston's leash. This time he cooperated and stood at a heel by her side. "We're heading to the pick-up spot. You boys go ahead and have a good time. We'll see you back at the ship."

Vlad watched as she slowly made her way across the crowded square. In the brilliant May sunshine she aged before his eyes as she hobbled across the cobblestones, Gaston obediently trotting at her side. He could see Lutz in his white shirt, gold buttons glinting in the sun, at the opposite corner of the square. A few other shipmates gathered near him waiting for the bus but most had scattered in all directions after the cathedral tour to enjoy Cologne and the beautiful day. Lutz noticed Sandra and waved a welcome.

"The old bird should be all right. She's found the steward; the bus should be on the way. Should we head to the Chocolate Museum?"

"Yes, let me dig out the map Lutz handed out on the bus. The museum appears to be along the river; we just need to head in that direction, I think." Vlad carefully unfolded the paper and tried to make sense of it. "Let's see. *Gasse* is street, I think. That street should be *Trankgasse*. We need to find something called *Am Leystapel*. That's the avenue that runs along the river. See here."

He held the map out to Ollie. The symbol for the cathedral stood out clearly on the map, but he couldn't tell if he was looking at the right orientation.

"No worries, mate. I've got Google maps on my cellphone. I'll get us to the museum in no time."

He drew his phone from his pocket and slid his thumb along the surface. "Actually, I think it's faster to walk past the Roman-German Museum and take that little side street down to the river." He showed him the small map on his phone. "I'll just click on directions, and my bird will tell us how to get there."

Vlad slouched down and held the paper map up to cover his face as they passed the museum. He hoped Elke was busy cataloging artifacts or writing or doing anything but walking to lunch. His face flamed as he recalled her kiss. How could she have so misread his body language? If he saw her, a brisk hello should right matters.

Luckily, no Elke appeared. As he and Ollie wandered past sleek clothing stores and unique home décor shops, he remembered he hadn't yet bought a souvenir for Maria. In two days they'd be in Amsterdam with more shopping opportunities and Beatrice to guide him in selecting something feminine.

As though he were a mind reader, Ollie said, "You said you've got kids. Say again, how many, and what are their ages?"

"I've got three—Erin's my oldest. She's fifteen. Then there's Nicholas—he just turned eleven, and Kaitlyn is four."

"Wow. That's quite a spread between the oldest and youngest. My girls are twenty-four and twenty-six—Nicole and Kara. Nicole's the one in New Zealand, the oldest, and she has my grandson, little Harry. Kara lives in Canada—just got married last year. Quite a bash. Married a techie."

"Neither live in England?"

"Nah—no good opportunities there for their college majors— journalism and teaching. Both ended up in sales."

"Seems like journalists are a dying breed. And teachers so poorly paid, at least in the United States."

"But aren't you in the teaching profession?"

"And, sadly, I speak from experience."

As they were wandered along the river, even the butterscotch May sunshine couldn't dispel Vlad's nagging worries of Nicholas and Norm and his inability to protect either of them. He squinted, wishing he had brought a hat or sunglasses to combat the bright reflection off the river. "Is that the Chocolate Museum?"

Vlad pointed to a building situated at the end of a short bridge, a semi-circle of windows overlooking the water with a larger sleek modern building attached. Even from this distance, he could smell the sweet scent of cocoa wafting through the air.

"I say, you're bloody well right! My mouth is starting to water already. Free chocolate, here we come!"

After the eleven euros charge, they were in. The ground floor ushered them into a museum presenting the history of chocolate, starting with the Aztecs in Mesoamerica.

"Look, the Aztecs believed that cacao seeds were a gift from the god of wisdom. They were even used for currency back then." Vlad gestured to a placard translated to English.

Ollie peered closely at the exhibit and said, "I'd like to taste that fermented drink. I bet it had a bloody good kick."

As they wandered through the exhibits, Vlad hoped that Beatrice was having more luck with her suspect. So far, Ollie seemed like a personable middle-aged man, clowning in front of a rainforest display, pretending to pluck a cacao bean from a tree, exclaiming. "Look. Aztec bit-coins!" He enjoyed his company more that Dougie's, that's for sure.

"Time to make a decision, mate," Ollie said as they came to a *You are here* sign. "This way leads into the glass greenhouse area or the elevators go up to the chocolate factory."

"We came here for chocolate samples so I say let's get on the elevator."

Glass cases displayed vintage chocolate molds of Easter bunnies, Santas, and Christmas trees, mostly for upper class consumption. At the end of a long line of visitors was a chocolate fountain, topped by what looked like a pine tree with gold cones instead of leaves. A candymaker dressed in immaculate white allowed them to choose a wafer or small cookie from a cart and dip it into the melted chocolate. In the next room Vlad could hear the faint sounds of machinery. As they were ushered along a glass wall they observed how a machine spit out bits of truffle filling, which then traveled along a conveyor belt to another machine that dipped the pieces into chocolate and sent them along to the final wrapping in bright blue foil. Another tray of freshly made samples stood at the end of the production line. The creamy milk chocolate goodness melted in his mouth.

"Too bad Sandra couldn't have seen this. She'd have loved this; even Gaston would be impressed."

"You do know chocolate is bad for dogs. Only a plonker would feed a dog chocolate."

Vlad flushed at the memory of taking care of Gaston when Sandra was recovering from her burns in the hospital, and the disastrous attempt at appeasing His Lordship Dog with a chocolate chip cookie. He said, "Yes, I learned the hard way."

"Down to the gift shop, mate?" Ollie said as the stood in front of yet another elevator.

"We still need to walk back to the bus pick-up so a quick stop to the gift store makes sense."

A glassed-in dark wooden counter along one wall was like a step back into the 1890s, complete with a clerk wearing a blouse with pork chop sleeves and a long skirt. However, the rest of the shop was a tribute to modern ingenuity with every conceivable sport or hobby immortalized in chocolate, even beefcake chocolate body builders and pin-up chocolate girls in bikinis.

"I've got to get my kids something from here," Vlad said. 'Little Kaitlyn would love the chocolate dog, and Nicholas likes to read about dragons. Here's one in chocolate."

"No worries, mate. Take your time. I'll just have a little wander. Meet you at the checkout in say a half hour?" Ollie looked at his cellphone, and Vlad checked his watch.

"Four o'clock sounds good. Gives us plenty of time to walk back to the square," Vlad said as he headed toward the stack of shopping baskets near the old-fashioned counter.

He picked up the beagle type dogs—unfortunately, there was no poodle like Gaston—and put it in the basket. He found a molded gargoyle that wasn't quite as expensive as the dragon. A bag of dark chocolate bon-bons with sea salt and caramel, as Sandra requested, and a large chocolate almond bar for Norm. When he saw the modern art paintings made of swirls of white chocolate and nuts on a "canvas" of dark chocolate, he had to get one for Beatrice and one for Maria, a thank you for taking the kids all week. Against his better judgment he settled on the beefcake man for Erin. Hopefully, it'd make her laugh.

The line at the checkout was just as long as the line at the chocolate fountain. No Ollie in sight, but he figured getting to the front of the line would take ten minutes at least. He was right.

When the bill added up to almost one hundred euros, Vlad dug out his credit card from his inner vest and reluctantly handed it over to the checkout girl. Good thing he signed on for teaching the summer session. Maybe he could pick up something else part time. The campus magazine was always looking for advisors, and he did have experience editing articles for the department newsletter.

Vlad stood near the exit with his bag of expensive chocolates and checked his watch. Nearly ten minutes after four and no Ollie. He thought he'd give him another five minutes but then he'd have to leave and walk at a fast clip to catch the bus back to the ship.

Suddenly, Ollie appeared out of a cluster of shoppers, walking as fast as his long legs would carry him.

"Sorry, mate. Had a hard time deciding and that threw a spanner in the works. I'm good to go now."

"What, no package?" Vlad said. "I thought maybe you'd pick something up for the daughter in New Zealand since you'll be seeing her soon."

"Nah, she's on a perpetual diet. Plus, after lunch, I'm a bit skint on funds. We'd better hustle. Don't want Lutz to get his knickers in a twist."

Just as they hurried out the exit and onto the bridge, Vlad heard a commotion from inside the shop.

"My wallet's been stolen!" An angry male voice at the back of the checkout rose above the chatter. "I just had it in my pants pocket. Now it's gone."

Turning to look at the group forming around the man, Vlad saw a grey-haired man step away from the cluster where Ollie had recently emerged. A woman carrying a shopping basket full of candy sat it down next to him and patted his arm as he wrung his hands. "I had two hundred euros in there and all my credit cards and my driver's license."

"Oh, dear. That was our souvenir money," the woman said in a teary voice.

"Seems to be some trouble back in the gift shop," Vlad said, glancing over his shoulder to watch the scene unfold. A store security man had joined the couple and spoke into a microphone attached to a headset. Another man dressed in a security uniform moved to the exit door. "Wonder what that's all about?"

The man started to point and wave his arms as a crowd gathered around him and the woman. "I felt someone bump up against me, but when I turned to say excuse me, whoever it was had disappeared."

The woman looked as if she was about to cry. She wrapped both arms around the fanny pack at her waist and rocked back and forth, the shopping basket filled with chocolate abandoned in the aisle as she followed her husband and the security man toward the back of the store. Vlad felt for his wallet safely tucked inside his travel vest and clutched his shopping bag a little tighter.

Ollie said, "Probably just a pickpocket. No big deal. People get nicked by thieves all the time. We'll be the ones in trouble if we don't get back to the ship. Let's move."

He didn't wait for a reply as he crossed the small bridge and rushed back onto the street. Vlad valiantly tried to keep up with his long-legged stride as he dodged pedestrians on the crowded sidewalks.

Chapter 23

WITH A WAVE OF HIS HAND, VLAD brushed off the ship attendant who was handing out some kind of green smoothie and said good-bye to Ollie in the lobby. Little groups of travelers swapped stories of their Cologne adventures but he went to an isolated corner and tapped out an e-mail to Erin: *How are things going with Mom? Did you have a chance to talk to her? Is Kaitlyn behaving? What about Nicholas: still acting weird? Went to the Chocolate Museum. Hope you aren't on a diet. lol. Dad*

Sighing, he sent a greeting to Maria as well—a simple update and kid status inquiry. Would she reply? They had done most of their e-mail correspondence through Erin on this trip so he didn't hold out much hope for a prompt answer. But if something was bothering Nicholas, maybe she noticed the changes.

Then on to Sandra's suite.

Beatrice answered when Vlad knocked on the door. The elderly lady was lying on the sofa, her feet elevated on a pillow, ice pack on one ankle. Gaston was stretched out on the couch beside her, eyes half open. When he saw it was just Vlad, he closed his eyes, falling asleep. Soon a gentle doggy snore filled the air of the suite.

"Oh, no! What happened to you?" Vlad said as he strode over to where she lay.

"Nothing much. Just a foolish old lady missed a step coming off the bus. Twisted my ankle a bit. Nothing's broken. Just hurts like hell. Getting old is the pits," she groused.

"There's a nurse on board who examined her. She was able to move it around, and she could put a little weight on it but she needs to keep it iced and elevated. Not much swelling but if she's still experiencing pain, they have a doctor in Amsterdam that can look at it more closely," Beatrice said.

"I should have come back with you," Vlad said.

"Don't talk so foolishly." She rose to a sitting posture, careful to keep her leg still. "What could you have done? Catch me at the bottom of the step? Carry me to the ship? Nonsense. You were needed to investigate the suspect." She sank back onto the pillow. "How did it go with Ollie?"

"He seems like a nice guy. Divorced, two grown daughters, one in Canada and one in New Zealand. In fact, he's moving there next month, got a job as a travel agent. That's why he's on this ship, scoping out the tour."

"You didn't notice anything suspicious about him?' Beatrice said.

"Not really. He did seem to use some British colloquialisms at times, but no worse than some of the slang I hear from my students. When they say something's dope, it's a good thing. Ollie's not much different. I found it somewhat amusing."

"I told you my Super Hunk was a charmer!" Sandra said to Beatrice. "He even asked for a bowl of water for Gaston, right, Luvy Puppy?"

Gaston opened his eyes and answered with a happy bark.

"I did witness a pickpocket incident on the way out of the Chocolate Museum, right in the checkout line of the gift store where we'd just been standing. So glad you lent this traveler's vest to me. I had no idea even in a fancy candy store you could get robbed." He straightened the vest and again felt for his wallet in the concealed pocket.

"Did they call the cops?" Sandra asked.

"I have no idea. Ollie rushed me to the street so we made it to the bus stop in time. Rather hard keeping up with Paul Bunyan. No time to investigate pickpockets."

He turned to Beatrice. "How did it go with big Lord Fauntleroy?"

"At first, he was very close-mouthed about his background. I tried to draw him out at the Roman Museum, but he didn't volunteer much. He seemed to have a lot of knowledge about antiquities as we looked at the exhibits. Turns out he's a dealer in art and antiques. From Brighton, he said."

"So what's he doing on a cruise by himself?" Sandra asked, holding the notepad and pen up. "Who wants to write today?"

"I'll do it. Beatrice wrote last time." Vlad snatched the pen and pad, then sat down to write.

"It wasn't until the incident at the museum that he opened up."

"What incident at the museum?" Vlad said with a puzzled expression.

Sandra shook her finger at him and said, "We saw you leave with that blonde, you naughty boy. I was surprised to see you so soon at the café."

"That was purely a professional courtesy," he stammered.

"Hmmpf! The way she draped herself around you was anything but professional, unless she was a lap dancer," Beatrice said bitterly. "When you disappeared through that doorway with her, I guess I lost it a little. And Nigel was very comforting."

"Comforting?" Vlad's tone grew sharp. "Exactly how was he comforting?"

"We'll discuss that later when we're alone. Right now let's compare notes on what we found out. Like I said, Nigel is some sort of antique dealer. He said his shop specializes in Victorian furnishings, although he does scout around for Art Noveau pieces for clients who are collectors. He's hoping to spend some time in Amsterdam talking to other dealers."

"And casing the Gasson for a diamond heist." Vlad scribbled a row of question marks after Nigel's name.

"Really, Vlad. He doesn't appear to be short of funds. We visited a cute antique store outside the art museum, and he bought an original Mucha poster for two thousand euros. He's having it shipped to his shop for a customer. Says she's willing to pay double what he did. It's rare to find them outside of Prague, supposedly."

"Did you bring up the subject of jewelry? It seems like a dealer in antiques would have some knowledge of what jewelry is worth, especially vintage jewelry."

"Actually, he was wearing a pinkie ring with a small diamond. When I asked about it, he said it wasn't that valuable—just a fifty-point diamond."

"What does that mean?" Vlad asked.

"My question exactly. He said that meant it was half a carat. He showed me its faint yellow color, which also made it less valuable. The more colorless, the sparklier, the better. It was also slightly included, which made it less valuable."

"Included? What's that?"

"Included means a lack of clarity. A flawless diamond means no inclusions or blemishes. Inclusions are internal variations that can't be seen without magnification whereas blemishes are visible to the human eye."

"For an antique dealer, he seems to know a lot about diamonds," Vlad said suspiciously.

"Honestly, Vlad, the Four C's of Diamonds are common knowledge. Even I've heard of carats, clarity, cut, and color. Haven't you, Sandra?"

"I only know about the Seven Seas, and even then, I doubt if I can name them. Sorry, dearie, can't help you there."

"Well, I'm keeping a big question mark by his name," said Vlad.

"Put a question mark by Ollie's, too. Your idea of colloquialisms might be Norm's idea of gibberish."

"We can't rule either of them out," Sandra said. "You're just going to have to dig a little deeper."

"How do you propose we do that?"

"You're going to start by dining with one of them tonight. BOTH of you so you both hear the same thing."

"And what will you be doing?"

"The captain said I could have my dinner brought to my room because of my injury. And Clarence's, too. We're going to have a romantic dinner, just the two of us. I've even ordered a bottle of champagne."

"Just the two of you? What about Gaston?"

"Why you're going to lock him in your room. Don't worry. I'll give him a doggie downer before you take him for the night."

"What if Norm comes home?"

"I think he still has your extra key if I'm not mistaken."

Vlad looked with dismay at Beatrice, who pointedly ignored him. No mistaking the venom in her voice when she brought up Elke. The way she twisted her hands together betrayed how upset she was. The cruise was half over, and she was drifting out of his reach. Soon he'd be back in Crawford with teaching schedules and faculty meetings and driving kids to swim lessons while Beatrice buried herself in the library. All his hopes were sinking faster than the Titanic.

Chapter 24

AN ANGRY SILENCE FILLED THE WALK BACK to their staterooms. Vlad tread cautiously, feeling like he was stepping into a wasp's nest. He recalled when, as a child, he had been playing in the woods, blissfully ignorant that a mound of weeds hid a nest of mud wasps until he stomped on it. They attacked, even flying under his shirt, covering his legs, arms, and stomach with painful welts. He ran crying to his house. When he stripped off his shirt, several escaped, and his mother hunted them down with a fly swatter after she iced his stings. He'd rather face a thousand wasps than endure the glare in Beatrice's eyes.

"I saw you disappear with that blonde, that so-called archaeologist. What the hell happened to our plan to interview the suspects?" she hissed as they neared his room.

"Please come inside. I'll explain everything," He shot her a hopeful glance and slid the card into his lock. She stared coldly at him as he closed the door and gave her a timid smile. He took a step toward her, but she stepped back, keeping her distance.

"Where did the braless wonder take you?" she snarled. "She was hanging all over you like flies on garbage. Everyone noticed. I heard them whispering."

Vlad tried to widen his eyes in an innocent look. "Some sanitation workers uncovered a tunnel that held new artifacts. Elke mentioned some exciting new discoveries."

"Elke! Now you're on a first name basis with her?" Beatrice broke in.

"Merely a professional courtesy. She just wanted to show me what they unearthed—more statue fragments, a small mosaic, a glass bowl—objects like that. Even a dog's skeletal remains. Reminded me of the discoveries at Pompeii."

"I'll bet she wanted to show you stuff, like her boobies. Do you really expect me to believe she was just another scientist?" Beatrice spat the next words out. "She kept looking at you like a cat eyeing a plate of salmon. Maybe you were oblivious but the rest of us saw plenty."

"I swear. I only wanted to see the artifacts." He held his hands up in protest. "I never had the opportunity to go behind the scenes at a major museum before. I wasn't thinking clearly."

"Not thinking clearly! I'd expect that kind of excuse from Norm who, by the way, still hasn't appeared from Koblenz. Have you forgotten about him?"

"No, of course not. I tried to surreptitiously question that tall fellow Ollie. I didn't get very far." He shrugged his shoulders.

"Your mind was still probably on that blonde bimbo," she said. She took a deep breath and wrapped her arms protectively around herself. "Tell me the truth. Did something happen between you? I can't be involved with a man who lies to me. I won't go through that kind of pain again."

Vlad looked at her eyes welling with tears, and a pang of remorse stabbed him. Beatrice's beautiful spirit shone brighter every day they were together. Lying about Elke would leave a cloud over their happy beginning.

After a moment of tense silence, with her blinking away the tears, he sighed. "She came on to me. I swear I wasn't expecting her to do that. I sincerely thought she just was proud of her discovery and wanted me, as a colleague and fellow archaeologist, to appreciate the find."

"I knew it. I knew she was trying to seduce you." She clenched her hands into fists, then slowly opened them as she spoke "You have that puppy dog look that some women find appealing. Fairly panting with enthusiasm. Easy prey to cougars and sharks."

"I wouldn't exactly call her a shark. She's a well-regarded archaeologist. Just a case of misreading signals."

"Misreading signals?" Beatrice exploded. "She was flashing hers like the Jumbotron in Times Square! Only you—you, Mr. Magoo—would fail to notice!"

"I'm sorry. I guess I just didn't think." Vlad looked down at the floor, hoping it would swallow him.

A tone of bitterness crept into her voice. "I'm sorry, too. I'm beginning to think this whole relationship is a big mistake. I never should have left Crawford."

"I made a mistake. I was a fool. Privileged access at a major museum. Something to brag about back at department meetings. I wasn't thinking how it looked to you. You know you're the best thing to ever happen to me." He looked at her pleadingly.

"You don't understand. I was engaged before to a man named Tom." She took a deep breath and continued. "Met him right after grad school. My first real job and my first real boyfriend. We met at Summerfest. Listening to my favorite band, The Foragers. He asked me if I wanted a beer. Said it was his favorite band, too. Pulled me up to dance with him on a picnic table."

She walked slowly to the small porthole and looked into the distance, not meeting his eyes. "I couldn't believe this cool guy was attracted to me. Tall, tan, hair a little long, dressed like he got off a yacht, designer shirt, deck shoes. He said he liked how I was different, sweet, the real deal. Not just out for a good time like other girls."

Vlad tried to mentally wipe away the image of a younger, handsome man dancing with Beatrice. Ignoring the stab of jealousy, he asked, "So what happened?"

"We dated for almost a year, set a wedding date, invitations sent out, deposit on the venue, everything ready for our perfect life together. We started looking for a house. I pictured myself with a baby in the nursery, a big backyard for the baby to play in when he got a little older. Typical stupid dreams. I was so naïve."

"You didn't get married? Why not?" Vlad held his breath waiting for the answer.

Her voice broke. "I called the wedding off when I found out what a liar and a cheat he was!"

"But I'm not like that. I would never lie to you. Didn't I just tell you the truth about Elke?"

"I trusted Tom, too. He told me the same thing, 'I'll never lie to you. I'll always be true. You're the only woman for me.' Yeah, I was the only woman for him—in Germantown. He neglected to mention the other women he was corking when he went on supposed business trips. Yeah—monkey business."

"I'm so sorry. I'd never do that to you. Maria cheated on me. I know how it feels to be hurt like that."

She paced the small room like a caged wolf. Two steps from the bed to the counter. Shoving the chair aside, she pivoted back and forth in front of the porthole as Vlad watched anxiously, hoping she wouldn't flee.

"You want to know how I found out? Thought I had a yeast infection or a urinary tract infection. It burned like fire every time I peed. And hurt when we had sex, even though I pretended it didn't. Thought there was something wrong with me. I didn't want to lose him so I faked it even though it hurt like hell. Finally, I went to the doctor. Turns out it was an STD. And Tom was my only partner, EVER. I was a virgin when I met him. Hard to believe, a twenty-three-year-old virgin. I was such a fool."

He moved closer, reaching for her, saying, "My poor darling. You weren't a fool. He was a bastard."

She pushed him away and gritted her teeth. "I vowed I would never be deceived again. I moved away from Germantown, started a new life in Crawford. Gave myself time to heal. It took years. But then you came along. You and your stupid poem."

"I'm so sorry for the mix-up. I tried to make it right. You know I would never intentionally hurt anyone. I was an idiot on the rebound when I gave you the so-called love poem by mistake." He slapped himself on the forehead.

"I knew you were going through hard times with Maria. I heard the rumors. It's a small campus after all. And the gossip about you being seen with a co-ed." Her voice grew tender. "But I'd seen you in the library with that earnest look on your face, so eager to find new materials for your students. Always so kind to me, treating me with respect. Like I was a person who mattered, not some automation whose sole purpose was to search the stacks for books."

Vlad's face softened at the memory. "Because even back then I could tell you were a good person, always ready with a smile, so genuine. Never judging me. Sometimes talking to you was the high point of my day."

She nodded in agreement. "Me, too. So when I saw you dodging me at the bookstore, I just had to do something. You looked so lonely and lost. So vulnerable. I confronted you about the mistaken note just to put your mind at ease. I thought you were trying to cover up a serious illness, but then I realized it was really a broken heart."

"I had lost my way, taken a wrong turn in life. I was struggling to adjust to the separation, missing my kids every day," he said. Just talking about that confusing time reawakened the despair.

"Then I saw how kind you were to my parents when you came to dinner and brought Norm with you. How tolerant you were of their quirks. Ignored my dad's confusion and treated him with respect," she said.

"Hey, you let me bring Norm. Not many women would want a character like him at their dinner party."

"Because you didn't want him to spend Thanksgiving alone after Sandra had her accident. You supported her all through her recovery. Became her guardian. Cared for her beastly dog." Her grey eyes shone as she held his gaze.

"She had no one else. I had to do it or she'd still be in the nursing home where she obviously didn't belong."

Suddenly, her eyes glinted like a hammer hitting steel. "Only Tom pretended to be caring, too. Took me to visit his grandfather in assisted living. Broke dates with the excuse that Grandpa's Parkinson's got worse. Made it seem like the old man was on death's doorway. All the while he was screwing some other woman."

"He was an asshole, a total asshole." Vlad said. "I'm not like him. Can't you tell how I feel about you? My love for you is as eternal as the North Star."

"Yeah, eternally in the darkness. Sometimes you haven't a clue. You couldn't tell what that blonde slut wanted. I had to fake it again. Keep on talking to Nigel, pretend like I didn't care that the man I just gave my heart to had flitted off with the first available blonde. Again. And I had to play detective while you were missing in action. I'm a loser again."

He swallowed hard, searching desperately for the right words to repair this break and restore her to him. He'd paraded all the reasons why she should forgive him like floats at a homecoming parade, and she'd blown them away like the tissue flowers in a blast of wind. Useless words. Perhaps the ring was useless, too. He'd never propose, never even show it to her. Return to his sad little life in Crawford so full of missed opportunities. If only she could see into his heart as he opened it up to her. If eyes were windows to the soul, then why couldn't she see how much he loved her? If only she loved him, too.

She looked out the porthole at the darkening sky. Pink shreds of clouds gradually made way for purple, inky splashes. Shadows from the encroaching twilight engulfed the room but neither made a move toward the light switch. He took a step closer, close enough to smell her unique scent, a sweet muskiness, a hint of verbena. This time she didn't move away, sadness etched on her face in the fading light. If he slightly shifted his body, they would be touching. Maybe his touch would persuade more than his words.

The shrill ring of the bedside phone shattered the quiet, the moment lost in the persistent noise. Vlad reluctantly turned and strode over to the counter. When he picked up, he heard Sandra's voice filled with urgency.

"I got a message from Norm. You need to come to my room as fast as you can. There's a new wrinkle in the case."

He turned to Beatrice. "Sandra just heard from Norm. She wants to see us right now."

"Let's hope it's good news. We could use a break in the case." With that, she swept out the door.

Chapter 25

SANDRA STOOD FIRMLY ON BOTH LEGS, wildly waving a sheet of paper as she opened the door. She stepped aside to let them both in as Gaston barked a happy greeting, then dashed over to Beatrice, wagging his tail so rambunctiously his whole behind shook with pleasure. Jumping up, he yipped until she petted him.

"You're certainly in a good mood today," she said. "Glad one of us is."

"Look at this! What do you make of it?" Sandra said, thrusting the note in Vlad's face.

"What do we make of you? I thought you injured your ankle in a fall from the bus?" he said, frowning as he stared at her ambulatory leg.

"It seemed like the only way to get room service around this joint. How else can I get a romantic dinner alone with Clarence? I needed to use a little subterfuge," she said with a sheepish look on her face. "All part of being a detective. You two should take note."

"Yes. Appearances can be deceiving. You think someone is a straight arrow, and they turn out to be crooked as hell," said Beatrice. She bent down to scratch the dog under his jaw, as he licked her face. "Everybody but you and me, boy. With us what you see is what you get. A bipolar poodle and a mousy librarian. So glad you're a little manic today. Wish some of your mania would rub off on me."

As though to prove her point, Gaston began to run wildly around the room as though he was chasing an invisible cat, yipping excitedly. He nearly toppled Vlad on a swing through, and Beatrice half-smiled as he awkwardly grabbed at the cabinet to right himself.

"Good boy, Gaston. You show them. You're ready for whatever comes our way, aren't you, boy?"

The little dog yipped even louder.

"Gaston! That's enough!" Sandra said. "Do you want to get us in trouble? I don't need any complaints from next door to spoil my evening. Settle down."

The little dog growled and slunk behind the couch. Sandra handed the note to Vlad. "Read this. What do you think?"

He read aloud: *Meet you in Amsterdam. Still with police in Koblenz. Call to INTERPOL. Don't worry.* What the hell?" He stared at the terse message with a puzzled expression. "INTERPOL only handles the big stuff, like terrorism or organized crime. They wouldn't respond to the petty theft of some rich lady's missing diamonds."

"Maybe there's another terrorist on board," Sandra cackled, rubbing her hands together. "Another case for the Wonderdog. I knew you and Gaston were on to something big. Didn't I tell those police he was a crime-solving miracle?"

"I'm not sure that's what Norm means," said Beatrice. "You know how he gets confused sometimes."

Sandra sank back on the couch and hoisted her leg onto the coffee table. "Could you be a love, dearie, and put the ice pack back on my ankle?" she said to Beatrice. "Just in case the attendant comes in to clean."

Picking up the towel, she wrapped it around the ice pack and placed it on Sandra's ankle, shaking her head. 'I can't believe I'm a part of this."

"Tonight's the big night. You need to zero in on the suspects at dinner. One of you does the talking and the other observes. Maybe you should do Good Cop, Bad Cop."

"I think that only works if you have a suspect in lock-up," Vlad said. "I'm not sure how effective that is at the dinner table."

"Maybe we should just let the police do their job," Beatrice muttered.

"Dearie, just give it one more chance. If you don't get anywhere tonight, we'll give it up."

"Let's focus on Nigel first. If we don't get anywhere, I'll offer to buy Ollie a drink in the lounge," said Vlad. "Nigel looks like he knows his way around an exclusive jewelry store. I imagine he could sweet-talk some female clerk."

"He does have the looks, sort of Cary Grant like," said Sandra.

"Really, you think so? I think he looks more like George Clooney," Beatrice said, tapping her cheek.

"And Ollie looks like Clark Gable. So rugged and manly. Wish I were thirty years younger." Sandra sighed. "I'd give him a run for his money."

"I disagree. He resembles Liam Neeson with his height and broad shoulders. More of the rough and tumble type." She swatted the air with a playful punch.

"If you two are done drooling over the suspects, perhaps we should dress for dinner," said Vlad. "We need to be prepared to nail this down. We're running out of time, and Norm's still in police custody."

"You're right, dearie. You need to be on top of your game. A lot's riding on this. Just don't forget to pick up Gaston before dinner. You can lock him up in your room. I'll pack lots of treats.'

"I nearly forgot about him," Vlad groaned. "Let's make it after dinner."

"Just so Clarence and I have this last evening alone." Sandra clasped her hands over her heart. "A last chance for romance."

Vlad walked to the door and paused with his hand on the knob. "Beatrice, aren't you coming?"

She thrust out her chin, making no effort to follow him, and waved him away as she said. "You go on ahead. I need to talk to Sandra—alone."

Chapter 26

THE WAITERS HURRIEDLY PLACED FROWSY PINK peonies in crystal vases on the crisp white tablecloths for the evening dining service. The wine servers uncorked bottles of reds and whites at their stations in anticipation of the usual demands. Vlad observed the bustle inside from the translucent closed doors. When they opened, he planned to station himself near the center where he could survey the room unimpeded until their quarry came into view. Hopefully, Nigel wouldn't dawdle.

The doors opened, and Vlad moved into the strategic position. Hungry diners flowed on both sides, exchanging greetings with friends, sliding into empty chairs. A waitress carrying a tray of what looked like bruschetta approached. "May I help you, sir?" she said.

"No, thank you," he said. "I'm just waiting for my friends. One of them is an English fellow, a sharp dresser, neatly trimmed mustache. You haven't seen him, have you?"

"I know who you mean. He usually sits nearest the window on the last table on the left. I can tell him you're looking for him if you wish to sit down and wait."

"I'd rather stand here, if you don't mind."

She shrugged and started handing out small plates to the diners who were settling in her area. Sam came from the kitchen, carrying a stack of menus. Vlad raised his fist to his face and pretended to cough. He slouched to the left, hoping Sam didn't see him. Apologies weren't enough for all the hassle. When the envelope came at the end of the voyage for gratuities, Vlad planned to give Sam a huge bonus to make up for all the trouble Norm had caused him.

In a swift movement Vlad stepped aside to let a gaggle of chatting ladies pass. The place was filling up. He checked his watch—the time to serve the appetizers had almost passed. No Nigel and no Beatrice. Had she made a secret assignation with the man?

Finally, the Englishman sauntered in the room, wearing his usual fitted jacket and tie for dinner. Just as the waitress noted, he headed for the left at the back of the room. He chose the empty chair that commanded an excellent view of the river vistas. Vlad sighed in relief, then hurried to join him, still checking the entrance for Beatrice. Sitting across from him, he tipped an empty wine glass over at the adjacent place setting for her. A small plate with the appetizer appeared almost like magic in front of him, along with the menu of the night's offerings.

"Hope you don't mind if we join you for dinner? My friend Beatrice should be along any second." He bit into the bruschetta, chewed slowly, trying to think of what to say next.

Nigel stared coldly at him and hesitated for a fraction of a second before he replied, "Yes, your friend and I became rather well-acquainted at the art museum. It seems we have common fondness for vintage jewelry and Art Nouveau pieces."

"Really. Is that ring you're wearing an example of vintage jewelry? Or are you more interested in current styles featuring diamonds?"

"Well, what have we here? A discussion of the old and the new? Are we talking jewelry or art?" Beatrice's lilting voice came from behind. Vlad turned at the sound. It was definitely her voice but the woman standing before him was not the sweet, demure Beatrice, so pretty in pastels. She wore a black silk camisole trimmed in lace, one of the spaghetti straps slipped down to expose her bare shoulder. Red high heels with dagger-like toes combined with a red mini-skirt showcased her legs, looking long and lean.

She settled into the chair beside him and waved her arm to attract their waiter's attention.

"Could you please send the wine steward over? I'm parched." Turning her glass upright, she picked it up, jiggling it back and forth until the girl with the wine came over.

"White or red, madam?" she said.

"I'll have red, and you may as well just leave the bottle. These two gentlemen and I are celebrating tonight." She smiled broadly, gesturing to Nigel and Vlad.

"Is it your birthday?" the girl asked as she filled her glass and Vlad's.

"In a way. We're celebrating the birth of a new me. Out with the old mousy librarian and in with the glam," she said with a toss of her head.

"Madam, I would never call you mousy. You are so chic, like Adriana Lima, the Victoria's Secret girl," she said.

"Neither would I," said Nigel with an admiring glance.

"Thank you. I may have borrowed her lips for tonight," Beatrice said, pursing hers into a sexy pout. "It's a wonder what good cosmetics can do."

She tittered, her laugh ringing like a tiny bell, and batted her eyelashes, thick and dark. Her hair, lifted to a new height by teasing, added to the supermodel look. She twirled her finger around a loose strand and smiled bewitchingly. Vlad stared, openmouthed. Gone was his beloved lady, replaced by this wild woman so unexpected in her behavior. He didn't know whether to cover her shoulders with his sports jacket or throw her over his shoulder and drag her off to his room.

Gulping a swig of wine, he stammered, "I was just, ah-h-h, just admiring Nigel's diamond ring. He was about to tell me more about vintage diamonds, I mean, vintage jewelry."

"Yes, please tell us what you know about diamonds. I find it fascinating. After all, diamonds supposedly are a girl's best friend. But Vlad probably needs a little background in diamond shopping, right, sweetie?" she said as she slowly slid the errant spaghetti strap back into place. "Bugs Bunny knows more about carets than he does. But if you want to know about ancient Roman artifacts, then he's your man. He had a special private presentation at the museum today. Most enlightening, I'm sure."

Vlad nearly choked on the mouthful of wine and hastily blotted his mouth with his napkin. "Nothing more interesting than a few shards of pottery and a pile of bones, the remains of a dog. Diamonds are much more interesting than an excavation."

Nigel held up his hand with the pinkie ring and said, "This ring is just something I picked up in Paris for fun. It's not very valuable. I liked the look of the setting."

"So what makes a diamond valuable?" Vlad asked.

"The key to a diamond's value is its rarity, and the most important factor is its color. The perfect diamond is colorless, and any hint of color makes an enormous difference in quality," he answered matter-of-factly.

"But I heard somewhere that blue diamonds are valuable?" Vlad continued, remembering the conversation with Katherine Beaumont.

"There is a category called fancy diamonds, which are valued for their striking color. Once again, it depends where the gem falls on the gradient. Really, cut is more important than color. It's the biggest factor in creating brilliance, sparkle, and fire. Even though it can be high quality, a poorly cut diamond can appear dull and lifeless."

"Wow, diamonds are like people. On the surface someone can seem dull and boring, just because of the cut of their clothing. Like a drab librarian," Beatrice said. "Change the cut, show a little cleavage, and watch out for the flash."

She poured them each another glass of wine. "All this talk about diamonds and bones creates a colossal thirst." She drained her glass and waved the empty bottle of wine to catch the server's attention. "More red, please."

"None for me," said Vlad, covering the glass with his hand. "But I'd like to order dinner. I'll have the shrimp scampi and the tiramisu for dessert."

"I say, that sounds like just the ticket. Me, too," said Nigel, handing her the menu.

'I'll have the lamb with risotto. No dessert for me. I'm going to have an after-dinner drink in the lounge. More wine, Nigel?" She raised her glass, ignoring the server who placed her risotto before her.

"I'm still working on this one," Nigel said with a smile. "I do like the analogy between diamonds and people. When you find the perfect one, you never want to part with it." He arched an eyebrow at Vlad, then picked up his fork to attack the scampi.

Ignoring the look, he asked, "What about carats? I thought the bigger the carats, the more valuable the diamond."

He thought of the ring, forlorn and forsaken in the wall safe. Probably didn't matter if it was ten carats, Beatrice would scorn it.

"Carat is the way to describe the weight of a diamond, not necessarily its size. Think of art. You wouldn't determine the value of a painting by the size of its frame. There is an aesthetic quality, the same with diamonds. A small carat diamond with a good cut can look larger than a high carat diamond with a poor cut." Nigel smiled at him like he was a struggling elementary student slow to catch on to the lecture. 'Don't forget clarity, the last of the Four C's and probably the least important."

"Why is that?" Vlad said out of politeness. He wished the pompous gasbag would choke on his shrimp scampi.

"The small imperfections are very hard to see. These tiny inclusions are microscopic and don't affect a diamond's beauty in any way. Very hard for the untrained eye to assess."

"Now I want to look at some diamonds to see if I can tell the difference in quality," Beatrice said. "Can you recommend a place in Amsterdam? I heard it's the diamond capital next to Antwerp."

Vlad gave her an amazed look. Clever girl, checking his familiarity with the Gasson. Now they were getting somewhere with the interview. How much did Nigel know?

"I'm more familiar with antique dealers than diamond establishments. I'm sure the concierge can make some suggestions." With that he picked up his fork for another bite, signaling an end to the diamond discussion.

Chapter 27

"I'LL HAVE A B AND B," Beatrice said to the bartender. "Please start a tab for me, Room 324." She perched on a stool and set her sequined purse on the bar. There were still some empty tables in the dimly lit lounge but they were filling fast.

"Should we grab a table?" Vlad said, surveying the room.

"No, I think I'd rather sit at the bar. Closer to the music," she said, waving her hand at the nearby piano. The musician was warming up with a few soft chords. "Won't you join us, Nigel?" She patted an empty bar stool on her left as Vlad sat down on her right.

"I'd be delighted," he said, straightening his tie." But I'm sticking with wine. Your best cabernet, please."

"Yes, sir. What can I get for you?" the bartender asked Vlad.

"Just seltzer water with a twist of lime."

"What? You're not joining the celebration? You of all people should cut loose where nobody knows you. No worries about pink slips in your file or gossiping secretaries."

Vlad nodded across the room where Katherine and Warren Beaumont sat glaring at them. "I'm not sure we really want to draw attention to ourselves."

'Oh, those stuffed shirts. I'm not sure they didn't make up a story about stolen diamonds just for the insurance claim. I'm not going to let them spoil my evening." She tipped the bartender with a five euro bill as he set down their drinks. "Just keep them coming."

"A false insurance claim. How clever!' Nigel said. "Do you think they're smart enough to get away with insurance fraud?"

"Don't know and don't care. Tonight I'm all about having fun. Long winters in Wisconsin. All bundled up with sweaters and coats and layers of clothes. You get so buttoned up you forget what it's like to be free." She gave a little shake of her shoulders, and both spaghetti straps came cascading down. She laughed as she moved them into place.

Soon a singer dressed in a shimmery pink evening gown brought out the microphone stand. The piano player began to play an old Beatles tune, *Michelle*, as the woman softly crooned the familiar lyrics. Beatrice quietly hummed along. A few couples moved to the dance floor and swayed in front of them.

"Would you care to dance?" Nigel asked.

Beatrice slid off the stool and gave him her hand. He tucked her hand close to his chest and put his other arm around her waist.

Vlad watched sullenly as they glided past him on the dance floor, Nigel expertly directing their movements like an Arthur Murray instructor. He whispered something in her ear, and she threw her head back with laughter, never missing a step.

"Your lady friend seems taken with that English fellow," said a voice behind him.

Vlad turned to see Dougie and lowered his head to hide his dismay.

"You two on the outs?"

"Just a little misunderstanding. Nothing we can't work out, if that's any of your concern," he answered coldly.

'It wouldn't have anything to do with that sexy tour guide that had the hots for you today?" Dougie gave him a big wink.

"None of your business." Vlad glanced around the room and said, "I think I see two women at a table by themselves. I met them this morning, Sally and Jo-Lynn. Very nice ladies. I'm sure they'd enjoy your company."

"Thanks for the suggestion but I want to buy a drink for Beatrice first. She looks pretty hot tonight herself. You're a lucky guy," he said, elbowing him in the ribs. He waved to the bartender. "I'll have a bourbon Manhattan with olives and another one of whatever the lady is drinking." He gestured toward Beatrice's half-empty glass.

The music ended, and Beatrice and Nigel ambled back to the bar.

Dougie whistled as she sat down. "You look gorgeous tonight. What's with the new look?"

"It's my birthday, sort of, so I wanted to look more festive. Please join in the celebration. This only happens once in a lifetime," she said.

"Is it one of those landmark birthdays? Dad had one of those a few years back. Sis rented a big hall and invited half of Pittsburgh, it seemed."

"You might call it a landmark day. I realized life's too short for what we put ourselves through. So tonight I'm starting a new chapter. No more buttoned-up Beatrice. Just call me Boisterous Bea." She made a ta-da gesture with her hands.

"I think you look like more like a Beezy," Dougie said. "How about Beautiful Beezy?"

"Brilliant!" Nigel chimed in. "Beezy it is."

"Beezy? I kind of like that. What do you think, Vlad? Or maybe we should start calling you Vladdie?" she laughed and reached up to mess up his hair and unbutton the top button of his shirt. Leaning back, she gave him an appraising look. "There, now you look more carefree, too."

The piano player switched to a lively song, and Vlad grabbed her hand and said, "Then it's my turn to dance with you since the music's livened up, too."

She drained the rest of her drink and stood up. "Vladdie, I thought you'd never ask. Let's rock."

She shook her hips in a shimmy and clapped her hands overhead as she led him out on the dance floor. "Not only did I borrow this outfit from Sandra, I learned a few of her dance moves. You'd be surprised at what make-up tricks she showed me, too, to help celebrate. That woman knows how to live!"

"I'm never surprised by what Sandra does. I've learned to expect the unexpected from her and Gaston."

"Speaking of Gaston, aren't you supposed to dog-sit tonight?"

"He'll have to wait. I'm not leaving you here to celebrate without me." He made quotation marks with his fingers when he said "celebrate."

"Great. The more the merrier. I'm not going to be the good girl who's home with a broken heart anymore. 'Cuz I'm free." She broke into song, an off-key imitation of Tom Petty as she waved her arms into the air. "Yeah, I'm free-ee. Free falling. Da-da. Da-da-dadut."

With the last syllable, she struck the man dancing next to her, a light glance to the shoulder. "Oh, I'm so sorry. I got a little carried away," she apologized as the man's partner gave her an annoyed look and pulled him away.

"She must be related to Katherine Beaumont. They have the same tight-ass glare," she giggled, waving to Katherine across the dance floor. Vlad could almost hear Katherine go hmpf in reply.

"Maybe we should dance more at the edge where it's not so crowded," Vlad said, inching toward the back of the dance floor where the shadows revealed an empty space.

"Whatever you say, Vladdie. I can dance anywhere. When I get this feeling, I can dance, dance, dance." To prove her point, she did a little pivot left, then twirled around to the right.

Vlad grabbed her arm as she careened near a cluster of couples and muttered, "Excuse us. Sorry," deftly steering her toward the open space.

"Oh, you want to do some old-fashioned rock and roll?" She jerked back on the arm he was supporting her with and stepped forward, then back. Raised his hand high, then twirled under it. They broke contact, and she gave a Flashdance flourish. By this time they were in the shadows. The shimmy loosened her straps again, and he caught a glimpse of flesh.

"Darn strapless bra," she said, yanking up the black padding. "I told Sandra I didn't need it but she said the top looked better with a little push-up. Maybe I should just go to the ladies room and take it off. Then the girls could be free. They've never been loose in public."

"I think Sandra's right. You look good just the way you are."

"The night's young. I can still change my mind," she said with a flip of her hands.

Thankfully, the music stopped, and she rested against him for a second, wobbling in her high heels, her stiff, teased hair tickling his nose yet the scent of verbena lingered beneath the hairspray. His arm crept around her waist, and she didn't push him away. Her eyelids lowered a bit, and she took a few deep breaths. The river flowed past the darkened window where they stood. Just as he turned her to face him and plead his case once more, Dougie shouted from across the floor.

"Hey, Birthday Girl. I bought you another drink."

She pulled away. "Another drink. Jusht what I need." Her speech slurred. "Can't let him get ahead of me."

Falling out of her shoes as she started to walk, she said, "Ouch! Damn sh-shoes. Beauty seems to involve a lot of pain." Kicking them off, she stooped down and scooped them up, then padded back to the bar, Vlad in her wake. She tossed the shoes next to her purse and picked up the full snifter. "Cheers!" she said with a huge gulp.

"You might want to go easy on that. It's pure alcohol," Vlad said with a worried expression.

"Don't get your undies in a bundy. What is it you English say?" She turned toward Nigel. "Knickers. You call then knickers. Your knickers in a knot."

"Close. We say *Don't get your knickers in a twist.* Perhaps Vlad is right. Perhaps you should slow down a bit. The evening's just begun."

"No way. I lived my whole life in the slow lane. I'm fast and furious tonight."

"In that case, let's dance," Dougie said. "The piano player is playing our song."

Another Beatles tune, but this time with a jazzy beat. Dougie struck his best Disco pose and held out his hand. She hopped off the stool and cavorted out on the floor. "Who knows? Tonight may be the night I dance on the table. Maybe on the Beaumonts' table"

They disappeared into the throng.

"I hope that museum guide was worth it," Nigel commented. "Your lady has been building up to this all day."

Vlad exploded. "Nothing happened! For God's sake! She just showed me some damn artifacts. I was back on the tour by the time you entered the cathedral."

Vlad took a sip of Beatrice's drink. It burned all the way down his throat.

"This is pretty potent. I'm going to order her a glass of club soda to dilute it." He caught the bartender's eye and gave him his request.

Dougie and Beatrice were shaking and gyrating to the music. In her stocking feet she was able to spin without colliding into anyone. By this time the other dancers cleared a section for them. In fact, some had paused and were clapping to the beat as the couple swooped and twirled.

The song ended just as the bartender brought the water.

Beatrice stared at the glass and said, "What's this for?"

"I thought you might like some water for a chaser," Vlad said.

In a bad imitation of W.C. Fields, Dougie said, "Never drink water, my dear. Fish fornicate in it." He flicked the ash off an imaginary cigar.

Beatrice giggled as she downed her drink. "I didn't know you were so talented." Suddenly, she swayed in a figure eight motion, her head tilting right, then left. Her eyes widened in surprise.

"Wow! This strobe light is making me dizzy." She slightly collapsed against Vlad. "When did they turn that on?"

"There is no strobe light," he said. "Maybe you're a little tipsy. I better take you back to your room." He held onto her and helped her stand.

'No. No. The party is just getting started," she protested. "The room is a little swirly. I just need a breath of fresh air."

"Let's go out on the deck for a bit. I'll grab your things." He picked up her purse and shoes as he steadied her with one arm.

"Keep my seat warm, fellas. I'll be back in a jif," she said with a dramatic wave of her arms.

Vlad steered her out of the lounge and onto the promenade. The lights from the ship flickered on the tranquil water. They could hear a murmur of voices from the deck above. Slowly, they walked over to the railing. She inhaled deeply, letting out an audible breath. Still she swayed a bit, grasping tightly to the railing.

"This ship sure is moving a lot. Did-did we hit some rough water?" The quiver in her voice matched the trembling of her body.

"We're still tied to the dock."

"I think I need to sit down. I'm getting a little light-headed." As she pushed away from the railing, she surveyed the deck.

"There's no benches out here. We'll have to head into the lobby if you need to sit," Vlad said as he gripped her arm firmly with his free hand, steering toward the door.

"When did they put a strobe light out here?" she wondered. "It's still swirling."

Before they could take another step, she crumpled into his chest.

"All of a sudden. I don't feel so well," she moaned. She clung to his arms, tottering back and forth.

With a loud URP, the evening's libations exploded down his shirt. He watched in dismay as she swallowed hard, threatening a second round. However, this time she staggered over to the railing. Hanging tightly onto her, he watched as she hurled over the side of the ship. The peaceful river swallowed all traces of the projectile vomit.

Chapter 28

VLAD HALF-LED, HALF-CARRIED BEATRICE back to her room, down through the empty staircase, struggling to hold shoes and purse in one hand and the ailing woman in the other. She floundered on the steps, placing one stocking foot down, slipping a bit. Then misjudging the height of the next step, she missed it and tumbled forward, nearly toppling them both. He tossed the shoes and purse to the bottom, grabbing with both hands to steady her. Slowly, they inched down the remaining narrow steps of the metal staircase.

"I'm so sorry. I feel horrible," she moaned as she grabbed the railing to right herself.

Vlad stooped down to pick up her scattered possessions.

"It's all right. I'll send my clothes to the laundry in the morning," he said. "Don't worry about my shirt." He slid his arm firmly around her waist.

"No, I feel really terrible. I'm so dizzy. I could upchuck again at any second."

They tottered along the corridor to her room. He stepped up the pace, hoping to prevent another smelly mess.

"The card is in my purse. I can find it." She grabbed the glittery bag from him and opened it upside down, spilling the contents onto the carpet. "There it is." Dropping to her knees to grab the card, she shakily stood, weaving back and forth as she attempted to slide the card in the lock.

"The damn thing keeps moving. I can't get it." She jammed the card in upside down. "Still red. Maybe they rekeyed my room."

"Here, let me do it," he said, tucking her shoes under his arm and taking the card from her. A green flash. "Voila! We're inside."

She pushed past him in the doorway and dashed to the

bathroom where he heard her upchucking again. He picked up the lipstick, comb, and breath mints scattered on the floor, shoving them back into the bag.

Next, he followed her into the bathroom. She huddled over the toilet and vomited again, making a horrid gurgling sound like a sewer malfunction. Finally, the dry heaves. Then she sprawled back on the bathroom floor, arms outstretched and eyes closed.

"I wish the room would stop swirling," she moaned. "It's making me so sick. I don't think I can leave the bathroom. I could throw up again any second."

He ran cool water over a washcloth and gently wiped her face.

"Rest a minute. I think you've emptied your stomach. It just feels like you could throw up again."

She opened her eyes and said, "Look what I've done to you. You're a mess. So gross. I'm so sorry."

"I'm going across the hall to my room for some clean clothes. I'll be right back," he said.

"'S okay. I'm not going anywhere." She raised herself up and slumped between the toilet and the shower, leaning her head against water tank. "That cold porcelain feels good. My head is throbbing."

Digging his keycard out of his back pocket—luckily, it wasn't in the front—he quietly slipped out of her room and went to change clothes. He rinsed off his shirt as best he could, found the plastic laundry bag in his closet, and bundled up the stinking shirt. He took a brief shower, lathering up every inch of his body and turning the water as hot as he could stand it. Not even bothering with socks, he dressed quickly and hurried back to her room. Beatrice hadn't budged from the corner where she wedged herself.

"Let's clean you up," he said.

"I think I'm dying," she groaned. "Just let me die in peace. Throw me over the side of the ship in the morning."

"You'll feel better after a shower. Let's try rinsing your mouth out first, get rid of the taste of vomit."

Vlad gently lifted her to her feet and brought her over to the sink where a plastic glass sat on the counter. He filled it with cold water and handed it off.

"Here, rinse."

Propping herself against the sink, Beatrice took a sip, swirled it around her mouth, and spit. Drops slid out of the corner of her mouth. She wiped them away with the back of her hand.

"That's good. Do you think you can handle a few sips of water? You're probably pretty dehydrated right now."

"I don't know. I still feel kind of gaggy." Reinforced her statement with a loud *urp*. Lipstick smeared and mascara ran in rivulets down her cheeks. A fleck of vomit decorated her teased hair. Glancing in the mirror, she whimpered, "Oh, god, I look ghastly."

"We'll try some water after your shower."

He peeled the nasty clothes off her and tossed them into the vacated corner. She collapsed against him, clad only in her bra and panties.

"Don't make me move. My head hurts too much," she moaned. "I don't think I can stand by myself yet."

Propped up on two feet, she wobbled back and forth like a toddler's toy, always returning to an upright position. Vlad perceived this as a good sign and said reassuringly, "I'll be right here. It'll be quick."

He one-armed her to the shower door, turned the water temperature to lukewarm, and shoved her in, despite her howls. She didn't try to remove her underwear, just stood in the flowing water, letting it course over her. Her face lifted up to the shower head; she braced herself with an arm against the wall. The stream of water washed away the make-up and hairspray and disgusting spittle.

He bundled her in one of the fluffy towels, helped her towel-dry her soaking hair, used a hand towel to wipe off the shreds of make-up. Without make-up and her glasses, she looked younger and vulnerable, like a novitiate in a convent unsure of going through with orders. She shakily accepted the glass of water and took a few small sips as he watched her warily.

"Better?"

"Yes, thanks. I'm past dying, moved up to just feeling awful. My nightie is under my pillow. I think I can make it that far on my own."

"I recommend some aspirin if you can tolerate it. Voice of experience. Remember our first night?" He arched an eyebrow.

"Yeah. You looked like death warmed over. I hope I look that good tomorrow morning." She handed him back the glass and said,

"There's aspirin in the small travel bag on the bathroom counter."

While Vlad ferreted out the aspirin and refilled the glass of water, Beatrice stripped off the wet undies and slipped into the cotton nightgown. She was already under the covers by the time he returned. Her hand lingered against his as he handed off the aspirin; she gave his fingers a gentle squeeze. She gulped down the medicine with the water and sank her head back into the pillow.

With a muffled voice, she said, "Please move the wastebasket next to my bed, just in case."

Searching the room for the larger receptacle, he moved it closer to her bedside. Surprised by her hand grasping his arm as he turned out the lamp on her nightstand, he heard her whisper.

"I was wrong about you. You aren't like Tom or any of the other players. None of them would have done what you did tonight. You're the real deal. I hope you can forgive me."

"Of course I forgive you. We'll talk tomorrow."

Vlad kissed her cheek and quietly left the room.

Chapter 29

WITH BEATRICE SAFELY ENSCONCED in her bed, Vlad considered his options. He could go to bed, chalk the whole escapade up to a fool's errand. The thought of a jewel heist at the Gasson seemed totally unlikely. Probably the place was surrounded by armed guards. Yet Katherine's diamonds had been stolen on board the ship. Or he could return to the lounge, try to find Ollie or Nigel, and continue sleuthing. Which undercover appealed more? His bed beckoned fiercely. Yet this was the last night on board, his last chance to discover the thief before everyone vanished into the crowded streets of Amsterdam. Duty overruled common sense so he headed back to the lounge.

Then he remembered Gaston and his promise to dog-sit. He sighed heavily and slowly made his way to Sandra's suite. Maybe the dog had settled down and was sleeping peacefully on the sofa. Hesitant, he manned up and softly knocked on the door. He heard a flurry of footsteps and a loud yipping. Sandra flung open the door and thrust the pooch into his arms as he struggled to break free.

"About time! He's been a bad boy all evening. Don't know what's gotten into him. Wouldn't let Clarence get near me with all his growling."

"What about the rest of his things?"

"Just a minute, dearie." She soon reappeared with an armload of dog paraphernalia. Hanging the leash around his neck, she stacked the sock monkey, doggie treats, water bowl, and a can of dog food with a pop-top lid into a hot pink sequined tote bag and balanced it over his shoulder. He hunched his shoulder to his ear to keep it from slipping off as she slammed the door behind them. Like Quasimodo on his way to the belfry, he trudged down the hallway with the snarling dog firmly in his grip.

"Knock it off, Gaston," he said in his best Leroy Jethro Gibbs imitation.

The poodle nipped his wrist in reply.

"Yowch!" he yelped as he jerked his hand away from the sharp canine teeth. Gaston planted his back paws firmly in Vlad's privates and lunged out of his grasp. Buckling under in pain, he dropped the bag and the pooch. Sensing freedom, Gaston sped away.

"Come back here, you mangy mutt!" he shouted, but the dog bolted like someone had lit a firecracker under his tail, his four little legs moving at breakneck speed. In a blur of pain, Vlad managed to scoop up the bag and follow, amazed that the fat little poodle moved faster than a group of dieters at the discount all-you-can-eat buffet.

Down the hallway. Across the lobby. Into the inviting lights of the lounge.

Vlad limped after him but lost sight of his puffy tail as he ducked into the open doorway.

"Damn you, Gaston. You better not get us in more trouble."

He paused in the archway, surveyed the crowded room. Beatrice's two male companions still drank at the bar, light glinting off Dougie's bling and smarmy turquoise sateen shirt while Nigel tugged thoughtfully at his ascot. The Beaumonts, seated in a dark corner on the left, frowned at all the gaiety surrounding them, the harbingers of doom. However, on the right side he noted a flurry of movement like the dorsal fin of a shark stalking innocent swimmers on a crowded beach.

"What the hell?" Patrons shifted in their seats to avoid the furry missile.

"It's that old lady's service dog!"

"Nasty mutt, more like it."

"Watch out. I heard he bites."

Vlad followed the waves of commotion, then dashed to intercept Gaston mid-room, his ears burning at the sound of excited yipping and loud grumbling.

"Excuse me. I'm after the dog. Something startled him." He brushed by the amused onlookers, careful not to tread on anyone's feet.

"The little fellow's gone that way." A grey-haired lady pointed to the back of the room.

At the next table, a man complained. "That dog should be kept on a leash at all times. He's a nuisance."

Suddenly the yipping changed to an ominous growl.

Another man declared, "More like a lawsuit waiting to happen."

The growling grew louder.

"This is not good," Vlad muttered, hastening his steps.

He bumped into a table, jostling the drinks. "Pardon me."

"Gaston, come here," he ordered.

No response but growling. What did the dog trainers say?

"Gaston, heel!" He tried again in a gruff, no-nonsense voice.

"Ow! This damn dog tried to bite me!"

To Vlad's surprise, it was Ollie who leapt to his feet and yelled. "The little beast attacked me." He kicked at the poodle but Gaston deftly dodged his foot. He lunged again, sinking his sharp little teeth into Ollie's pant leg. R-r-i-i-p!

"He tore my trousers!" He stared in dismay at the two jagged edges, exposing his bare ankle and black dress socks. "Look what he's done to my new khakis."

This last comment was addressed to Vlad as he finally reached the table where Gaston had taken refuge after the attack, still growling softly, haunches poised to lunge again. He shifted back and forth threateningly. Vlad stepped between the dog and Ollie, blocking any further attack.

"I'm so sorry. He's never acted like this before." He tried to look apologetic as he lied. "It's totally out of character. Don't know what's gotten into him."

"I thought he liked me. I even bought him a pastry with the old lady at the café."

Vlad scooped the growling, snarling dervish into his arms and held him tightly. "Hush, Gaston. This is Ollie. You know Ollie from the excursion in Cologne. He won't hurt you. He's our friend, for goodness sake."

He grabbed his paw and waved it at the glowering man. "Say hi to our friend Ollie."

"Some friend. Ruins my good trousers."

Vlad noticed he'd been sitting with the two ladies he'd met that morning, Sally and Jo-Lynn.

"Hi, ladies. Did you find that Kölsch beer you were in search of?"

"Yes, we did. In fact, we're enjoying the same with Ollie," Sally said, lifting a pint glass of beer. She took a sip. "Almost as good as the beer garden's."

"I apologize for Gaston's bad behavior. I'll be locking him up for the evening."

"I'll change my pants," Ollie said. "Be back in a flash, ladies."

Gaston stopped growling and gave Vlad a big lick on the cheek, then a wide-eyed look at the ladies and a doggy grin.

"Aw, he's giving you a doggy kiss," Jo-Lynn giggled. "Isn't he cute?"

"Just keep that schizoid beast away from me," Ollie said as he walked past the cluster of tables.

"Maybe the music spooked him," Vlad said. "Usually he's friendly as can be. He's a service dog, a working professional."

"Rubbish. He's a blighter—a four-legged blighter."

"No, really. He's highly trained. Used to be in show business."

"What a load of bullocks!" Ollie hissed as he stalked away, Vlad trailing him through the crowded bar all the way to Ollie's room on the top tier.

"I'm so sorry. Sandra will feel terrible when she hears about this."

Ollie snorted, "No worse than me. Just keep him on a tight leash from now on."

As he hastily pulled his keycard out of his pocket, a second card slid out, dropping unnoticed to the floor. Thrusting the card into the slot, first the red light appeared. "Damn it," he said as he turned the card around and thrust again. The green light signaled the door was open, and he pushed through, leaving Vlad still mumbling his apologies. Vlad saw the second card in the hallway.

"Ollie, I think something fell…" he began, but the irate man slammed the door in his face.

Vlad bent down, still firmly grasping Gaston by the collar. He picked up the card.

"What's this?"

He slowly turned the American Express card over to the front side and squinted at the name on the card

It read: Henry MacLaughlan.

Chapter 30

VLAD STARED AT THE CARD IN HIS LEFT HAND while Gaston tugged on the collar, still attempting to abscond once more.

"What the hell? What's Ollie doing with a credit card made out to somebody named Henry MacLaughlin?" he whispered to the squirming dog. He set the glitzy bag down and fished out the dog's leash, clipping it to his collar. He thought about tossing the card back on the floor and walking away. There had to be a simple explanation. Maybe he should just knock on the door and ask. He raised his fist to knock but Gaston refused to cooperate.

The rambunctious dog yanked on the leash, wrenching Vlad's shoulder so suddenly it gave a little pop.

"Ouch!"

He tried to rein him in, grasping the leash as taut as a lasso around a stampeding steer. Gaston proved unmanageable, jerking and weaving his way down the hallway. Vlad followed in his wake. When he reached the door to the stairs, he raised up on his two hind legs and clawed it with his front paws, like he was trying to dig his way through the steel.

"Cut it out, you crazy mutt."

Vlad snatched him up and gave him a little shake.

"What's gotten into you?"

Gaston strained against his grip and gave a little whine, then a few short barks.

"Ok, Lassie. Did Timmy fall into the well? Is that what you're trying to tell me?"

Vlad slipped the credit card into his pants pocket and opened the door, still firmly grasping Gaston. Stumbling down the stairs, he juggled the sequined tote and frenzied dog, nudging the door to his tier with his sore shoulder. He paused outside Beatrice's door.

"Should we wake her up?" he whispered. "Maybe she'll know what to do about this bogus card?"

Gaston yipped.

"Yeah, you're right. She probably wouldn't be much help in her present condition. It's just you and me, kid." He brushed the top of the dog's head with his chin. The gesture calmed Gaston down, and he stopped wriggling.

Vlad sidled down the hallway on the lookout for fellow passengers. He didn't want to explain what he was doing with an unruly canine that all two hundred on board knew was Sandra Tooksbury's service dog.

When he finally got to his room, he fished his keycard out and wrestled the dog safely inside, then slammed the door shut with his foot. Unceremoniously dropping the tote bag on the floor, he massaged his aching shoulder as the little dog tore around the room in circles, yipping excitedly, until Vlad reached into the tote and pulled out a bag of treats. Scritch! The noise of the recloseable bag opening stopped Gaston dead in his tracks, and he plopped down, drooling expectantly. Flipping him a nugget, Vlad listened as Gaston crunched and gulped it down. Then he put his front paws against Vlad's pant legs, begging for more. Chewing and swallowing calmed him down so much he hopped on the bed and closed his eyes.

Vlad sank down beside him and once again studied the card. American Express. "Why would Ollie be carrying an American Express card in someone else's name? Maybe he picked it up at the bar by mistake and hadn't realized it wasn't his? Maybe I should march up to his room and point it out?" he said aloud.

The poodle gave a little snore in reply.

"You're no help," Vlad complained. "Next to worthless."

Too restless to sleep, Vlad decided to take a walk to the top deck, a perfect place to deposit the vomit-encrusted shirt—an anonymous drop in the trash receptacle. Holding his nose, he gathered up the plastic bag and stole up the stairs.

The ship was heading through the last set of locks before sailing into Amsterdam. Because of a scheduling snafu with the locks, their stop at Kinderdijk to see the windmills was canceled.

A slight breeze rustled through the taller potted plants. The deck was deserted except for him and the murmur of voices coming from the wheelhouse. A loose awning flapped in the wind, snapping the night air like a wet towel in a locker room free-for-all. The ship passed by a small village nestled on the banks, its scattered lights wavering on the water. The half-moon scuttled behind a cloud as a dreary darkness settled over the ship, broken only by the occasional overhead lamp. More clouds gathered, blotting out the night sky. Vlad thrust the telltale bag under some trash in the large receptacle.

The ship slowed, and he observed the lights of another riverboat stalled before an enormous steel gate, at least three stories tall. Slowly, the gate lifted, the boat eased forward, and the maw of the giant lock swallowed it. Their ship moved into the spot vacated by the smaller boat and drifted to a standstill. Engine off. Thump. Thump. Thump. Only the sound of the pump broke the stillness. Thump. Thump. Thump.

Someone from above the lock shouted in a language unfamiliar to Vlad, and the gate opened once again. The boat slowly slid into the lock, and then the gate closed. Concrete walls towered over the ship. Thick, dark clouds hung like a black-out curtain overhead.

This is like being inside an immense coffin with the lid upraised. Fighting a bout of claustrophobia, Vlad noticed a long yellow ladder extending from the top of the lock into the water. He could barely make out the rungs in the dim light. All movement was imperceptible; only the disappearing rungs let him know the ship was rising. They had spent so much time waiting for the lock that the grey light of dawn seeped into the patch of sky signaling night's end.

More and more light, shadowy white pumping station, swatches of green land. More grey water poured into the walls. The ship gradually rose to the level of the next section of river, a rim of steel still separating the lock from the canal. Vlad breathed a sigh of relief as the gate disappeared and they were once more sailing on the river. However, a patch of fog loomed ahead, threatening to engulf them.

By this time he felt beyond tired. All the events of the evening swirled around in his head: Nigel's lecture on diamonds, Beatrice's transformation into a Victoria's Secret clone, the disastrous conclusion of her walk on the wild side, the tender moment in her stateroom.

Then he touched the credit card still in his pocket, running a finger over the raised numbers, the unknown name on the front. Fidgeting with edges of the card, he contemplated his next move. *What should I do with this?* he thought. Tempted to fling it into the river and go to bed, he stood on the deck, still surrounded by the potted plants, frozen with indecision.

A movement at the back of the deck caught his eye. Another insomniac exited the stairway and moved to the end of the top deck, past the deck chairs and chaise lounges. Vlad crept to the opposite stairwell, drifting from tall potted fir to tall potted fir.

In the dim light he observed the glint of gold and the shimmer of a turquoise shirt. Dougie—deeply engrossed in a conversation on his cellphone, waving his arms and veering erratically between tables and railing. Back and forth, back and forth. He hissed into the phone so Vlad couldn't distinguish his words, his face obscured in the dim light of dawn. As Vlad ducked into the open stairwell, Dougie's thick lips pulled back into a snarl as he swore into the phone and kicked over a chair. Then he slammed the phone onto a table, glaring out over the river. Hands balled into fists, he stamped his feet and snorted like an angry bull, then punched the railing.

As the ship entered a foggy patch, the helmsman slowed their speed to a crawl. The thick fog engulfed the ship with an almost supernatural swiftness, blurring the outlines of the deck chairs and plant containers, erasing the opposite railing. It obliterated the figure still standing near the railing like dirty cotton batting dropping from the sky.

Shrinking into the shadows, Vlad shook his head in disbelief. He stood silently, waiting to see what Dougie would do next. But the shroud of fog inched its way toward him. Vapors like the tendrils of icy bracken surrounded the deck, surrounded him. The fog seemed to reach inside him as he inhaled the cold mist. It muffled the sound of the ship's movement, blotted out the visible world. He felt chilled to the bone as he retreated and stumbled down the three flights of stairs, his footsteps clanging on metal the only sound.

He paused to catch his breath at the bottom before he plunged into the brightly lit hallway. The cold permeated his clothing and made his fingers stiff and clumsy as he fumbled with the keycard.

Vlad didn't stop shivering until he tumbled into bed next to Gaston and huddled under the duvet.

From: erinflamethrower@gmail.com
To: Chomskyv@crawford.edu
Finally got Nick to spill what's bothering him. Some kid's bullying him at school. Threw his gym shoes in the toilet. Teacher yelled at Nick for not having the right shoes. Next day the kid ripped up his math homework. Nick had to redo it.
I told him to tell the teacher but he says that'll make it worse.
Mom says Nick has to learn to fight his own battles.
When are you coming home?

From: Chomskyv@crawford.edu
To: erinflamethrower@gmail.com
Three more days of cruising. Two are over the weekend in Amsterdam. Tell Nick to stay out of the kid's way as much as possible. We'll figure something out.

Chapter 31

THE FAMILIAR CHIME SIGNALING THE SHIP'S announcements woke Vlad. Lutz's voice boomed over the intercom. "We are sorry, dear guests, but our plan to arrive this morning at Amsterdam has been delayed due to the thick fog. Visibility is reduced to unsafe conditions. The captain invites you to enjoy a complimentary mimosa or Bloody Mary with your breakfast today. A special screening of *The Sound of Music* will be shown in the Sky Bar for your viewing pleasure. Once the fog clears, we will be on our way. The walking tour of Amsterdam and buses for those of you still wishing to visit Kinderdjik will be available once we disembark."

Like a twenty-pound cannon ball, Gaston dropped on his chest and planted a sloppy lick on his cheek.

Yip! Yip! Yip!

"Okay, okay. I get it. You're hungry. Let's find you some kibble in the overnight bag."

Gaston launched himself off the bed and pounced on the glittery bag, sinking his sharp little teeth in it and giving it a shake. A Tupperware container bounced out, and he pushed it across the floor with his nose.

"Hold on. Hold on. I'll open it for you." Vlad flung back the duvet and trudged over to the yapping dog. He popped open the lid and watched as the dog gobbled up the kibble, scattering chunks of partially eaten crumbles on the carpet.

He emitted an unhappy *snurf,* sniffed disappointedly at the empty bowl, then plodded over to the bathroom and hopped up to the toilet. Placing his front paws on the edge of the water in the bowl, he slurped away, balanced on his hind legs, tail happily wagging as he drank deeply. Then he hopped down, soggy maw, and dripped on the floor all the way to the door.

"I'll skip a good morning kiss today," Vlad said to the poodle scratching at the door. "I suppose you want your morning walk. Be prepared for the fog. We'll have to use the upper deck facilities."

Vlad found the *Service Dog* jacket in the tote and fitted it on the dog before he snapped on his leash. Then he grabbed his own jacket from the closet.

"It was really chilly at five o'clock. Hopefully, it's warmed up a bit," he said, then shook his finger at the poodle. "I need you to behave. None of last night's shenanigans."

Gaston gave a quiet yip and stood patiently while Vlad opened the door, then trotted obediently at his side as they made their way down the hall to the staircase.

"Last night was so strange. I swear I saw Dougie on the upper deck in the fog, and he lost his temper at someone on his cellphone. Looked scary in the eerie fog. Perhaps the lack of sleep altered my perception. What do you think, boy?"

Gaston made a little whining sound as he trotted up the stairs.

"Me, too," Vlad said. "The phone call clearly delivered bad news. I wonder what could possibly be so upsetting to make the Playboy of Western Pennsylvania lose his cool?"

A wisp of fog filtered in under the door to the top deck. As he pushed open the door, Vlad ushered the dog into the surreal setting. No longer so dense as to obliterate the familiar patio furniture, the fog still clung in thick patches to the deserted deck. Vlad made out the dim light shining from the wheelhouse. The flower planters nearest them were visible, but the distant Norfolk pines were hidden behind the damp veil.

Gaston scurried to the nearest large pot of geraniums and lifted his leg. After less than a minute, he scooted back toward the stairway, tugging on the leash as if to say *hurry it up*.

"I don't blame you, pal. I felt the same way earlier. Wanted to get back to light and warmth."

The compliant behavior only lasted down one flight of stairs. When they reached the doorway to the top tier of rooms, the pooch hurtled through the opening toward Sandra's suite, dragging Vlad behind him. He stopped at her door, scratched furiously at it. *Ruff. Ruff.* Immediately, Sandra opened the door. Gaston gave a happy yip as she slowly bent down to caress him, wagging his tail so hard his behind was shaking as he pelted her with doggy kisses.

"I'm happy to see you, too, little Luvy Puppy," she said.

Vlad stepped inside and quietly closed the door behind him. He whispered, "Is Clarence still asleep?"

"No, his phone dinged in the middle of the night. Some text message. He left. Not a good-bye or a word of thanks for the lovely evening. He just threw on his clothes and took off." She opened a drawer on the end table and pulled out a bag of doggy treats. "Come to Mama, Luvy Puppy. That's a good boy. Here's your reward."

The dog gently mouthed the kibble and crawled under the table to chow it down.

"That's weird because I saw our friend Dougie up on the deck at the crack of dawn, and he was in a rage about something." He gave her an appraising glance. "You look like you've recovered completely from your fall."

She sheepishly laughed. "Oh, that was just a ploy to get out of the way so you and Beatrice could get on with your sleuthing."

"I thought you did it to be alone with Clarence?" Vlad raised an eyebrow.

"Our shipboard romance is nearing the end, I'm afraid. Last night was our final fling. Today we arrive in Amsterdam, and then we go our separate ways. I always knew we were just temporary. I'm grateful Clarence survived our romantic endeavors."

"Better living through chemistry?" Vlad suggested with a chuckle.

"Speaking of chemistry, Beatrice turned on the sex appeal last night. Borrowed my best outfit. What did you think of her new look?" Her eyes twinkled as she waited for his reply.

"It was certainly a side of her that I'd never seen before. Unfortunately, we may never see it again. She overindulged—a lot. She was really hurting. I had to help her to her room."

"Oh, dear. I was afraid something like that might happen. She was very pissed at you, you naughty boy."

"I understand her feelings. I was a fool. I don't know how to make it right," he said as he slumped down in the chair. "Last night she said she appreciated my help. I'm not certain it was enough."

"Every relationship hits a rocky patch now and then. Alfred

and I certainly had our share of spats. Making up after a tiff was the best—if you catch my drift," she chuckled as she gave him an exaggerated wink. "You and Beatrice are meant to be together. You complete each other."

Vlad sighed. "Once I thought so, too, but now I'm not so sure. It's complicated. We both have baggage—heavy baggage."

"Then do some heavy lifting and throw it to the curb. Start fresh. It's a new day. Be grateful for every morning you wake up above ground and make the most of it. That's what I do."

"But she's been hurt, badly hurt, by another man, and she doesn't want her heart broken again."

"Dearie, if our hearts really broke every time love went wrong, you'd have a bag of wood chips beating in your chest. Hearts don't break, they bruise, and bruises can heal. Why are you sitting here talking to me? Take your curative powers to Beatrice and help her mend."

"You're right. I need to go to her this minute." He swiftly rose and strode to the door But before he reached for the handle, he heard someone softly cursing.

"Damn. Red again. Why ain't this damn thing workin?"

He took a step back as he heard the voice say, "'Bout time ya turned green."

The door swung open, and there stood Norm.

Chapter 32

S‌ANDRA CRIED OUT, "N‌ORM. I CAN'T BELIEVE it's you. We're so relieved!" She hobbled over to him, elbowed Vlad to one side, and flung her arms around him.

"Dearie, you had us very worried. And then you sent that rather cryptic e-mail, you naughty boy!" She clung tightly to him as Gaston leapt down from the couch and started running around him in frenzied circles, yipping excitedly.

Norm stepped into the room, kicking the door shut behind him.

"Look how happy Luvy Puppy is to see you," said Sandra. "Come and give Uncle Norm a big kiss."

The dog dashed over and jumped up, planting his front paws firmly on Norm's thighs, still barking a happy greeting. When he bent down, Gaston licked his face several times.

"That's my boy," Norm said, embracing the dog. He offered up both sides of his face for the slobbery kiss. The poodle attempted to crawl into his lap, knocking him off balance, but Vlad reached down and steadied him with a firm hand on his shoulder. Norm hugged the dog one last time, then tried to stand up with Gaston wagging his whole body.

As he clambered to his feet, Vlad grabbed his hand and shook it vigorously as he said, "Man, I'm happy to see you."

Norm punched him affectionately in the shoulder. "Me, too, dude."

"Where the hell have you been?" Vlad said, brow furrowed.

"In Koblenz. Been real busy."

Sandra eyed him. "Those aren't the clothes you left with."

Norm was still wearing his Green Bay Packers cap and motorcycle boots, but the crumpled jeans and flannel shirt had been replaced with a classic-looking chambray shirt and black dress pants that still held a pleat.

"Oh, these," he said off-handedly. "Helga picked these up for me. I couldn't keep wearing the same clothes 'specially since I'd worn them in the tavern all night."

"Helga!" Both Sandra and Vlad exclaimed, locking eyes with each other.

"Who's Helga?" Sandra shifted her eyes to Norm.

"Polizeimeiser Ashenbrenner. Her name is Helga." He shrugged.

"So you're on a first name basis. That must have been some interview!" Vlad said. "She got to know you pretty well if she's buying you clothes."

"I'm going to pay her back as soon as I get to an ATM in Amsterdam. She wanted me to look my best when I met with Interpol. I had to appear credible." He gestured with an open hand.

"You met with Interpol? Since when do they get involved with a petty theft?" said Vlad, eyes wide with disbelief.

"I think I need to sit down. It's been a helluva two days. And I thought this kinda stuff only happened in the movies." Norm strolled over to the couch and plopped down. "Ya got anything to drink? I could use a beer."

Gaston jumped up beside him and laid his head in his lap. He absent-mindedly stroked the dog's ears.

"I got half a bottle of Prosecco over here." Sandra toddled over to the small refrigerator, pulled out a bottle, and handed it to him.

"That's great. Don't bother with a glass," he said as he took a big swig and continued. "At the station they shuffled me into a small interrogation room. When I told them what I overheard on the top deck, they didn't believe me. Helga kept asking the same questions over and over, but my story stayed the same. She sent PM Griesbach for some coffee and a roll. When he came back, he brought the head honcho with him."

"Were you worried when they brought in the big guns?" Vlad asked.

"Nah, cuz I was telling the truth. Long as I kept telling exactly what I remembered, I knew they'd come round."

"Dearie, I hate to tell you this, but sometimes your memory is a little spotty," Sandra said as she gently patted his hand.

"Not this time. I had told the story to Vlad and you. I had all my ducks in a row."

"So what happened when the chief detective started in?" Vlad asked.

"By this time Helga was taking the notes. She kept getting more excited as the questioning continued."

"I have a hard time picturing her getting excited about anything! Seemed like an earthquake couldn't roil her," Vlad chortled.

"Well, it seems an informant had heard some chatter about a big jewel heist in the planning. In Amsterdam at the Gasson. And my testimony fit the rumor," Norm said brightening. "Interpol has been looking for these guys for years. They think it's the same gang that hit a jewelry store in Paris in '04. They were dressed up as women and got away with $107 million dollars worth of gems."

Vlad whistled and said, "Wow! 107 million! Think I read about that. Four guys dressed up like women pulled off the big heist?"

"Yeah, and they even called the staff by their names and knew the location of all the secret safes. Disappeared without a trace. Cops found out all the warning shots they fired were blanks. Almost seemed like an inside job, but no one ever was caught," Norm said as he drained the bottle and set it on the low table.

"You'd think the jewels would show up somewhere." Vlad shook his head.

"Not if they removed them from their settings. Even I know that much, dearie." Sandra poked him good-naturedly in the bicep. "Once diamonds are loose stones, they can fence them a lot easier."

"Interpol thinks it's also the gang that did the Antwerp Diamond Center in 2006. Another inside job. The mastermind acted as a diamond merchant for years. Bought a few less valuable stones and stored them in the vault. Somehow passed the background check with a stolen passport."

"Stolen passport?" Vlad hopped to his feet. "Ollie dropped a credit card last night with a different name on it. Maybe he's the one!" He snapped his fingers.

"Won't he be looking for that card today, dearie?" Sandra chewed on a fingernail.

"You're right. I'd better turn it over to the police." Vlad turned sharply toward the door.

"Wait, there's more," Norm grabbed his arm. "The head thief is a master of disguise. He posed as an Italian buyer in Antwerp and dressed like a woman in Paris. He could be anybody, that's how good he is!"

"No fingerprints, no DNA?" Vlad said incredulously.

"Nothing. Not a clue left behind. The guy's a genius."

"But why would a master thief draw attention to the ship by stealing Katherine Beaumont's diamonds?" Sandra asked, still biting her nails. "Please explain before I need a manicure."

"Greed. Pure selfish greed. It was an easy job. Didn't think the yokels on the ship would catch them." Norm clenched his fist so hard Gaston let out a little yelp. "Remember, they didn't know I overheard their conversation. And I took the fall for the theft."

Vlad stared at him and said, "But now you're back on board. They'll know something's up"

"No, they won't cuz I'm not staying on board. Helga's waiting for me in a small speedboat docked by the side of the ship. I'm going on to Amsterdam with her." He rose and moved over to the door. "We'll connect with you there."

"I don't understand, dearie. Why can't you stay?"

"Part of the plan. You're going to act like I've been arrested for the theft. Mope around. Throw the crooks off guard. Keep an eye on Ollie and that fancypants. Wait for them to overplay their hand."

Vlad looked out the veranda door. "The fog is starting to lift. You better head back to the police boat. Just wait here while I run back to my room and get that credit card."

"Hurry up then!" Norm smiled. "Can't keep the lady waiting. She's not the patient type."

Vlad made the trip to his room and back in record time. He watched Norm disappear off the side of the ship, dropping down to the waiting deck of the small speedboat with a wave of his hand.

"I can't believe the police found Norm to be a credible witness, much less needing his assistance in locating a gang of jewel thieves. Now he's volunteering our help in catching them. And I thought this would be a romantic, relaxing cruise down the Rhine," he said as he shook his head, then loudly sighed.

At his side Sandra cackled and rubbed her hands together. "Oh boy. Now things are getting interesting, dearie. I can't wait for the action to begin. Bring on the jewel thieves!"

Chapter 33

BEATRICE ANSWERED THE DOOR WITH an awkward smile. "I suppose I made quite a fool of myself at the bar last night. And your poor shirt! Just throw it away. I'll buy you another."

"Consider it done. I wrapped it in the plastic laundry bag and dumped it in the trash can on the top deck."

"Thank you again for rescuing me from myself." She flopped on the chair and hung her head. "I'm such an idiot!"

"I'm to blame for driving you to take drastic measures. I was an idiot, too. I wish we could talk in depth about what happened yesterday. Sandra wisely pointed out the human heart is resilient. We may think it's broken but it's only bruised, and bruises heal eventually." He eased onto the edge of the bed across from her and took her hand, gently kissing it. She sat there, gratefully absorbing all his kindness, the way a cat lies in a patch of sun, visibly relaxed and restored. "Can we both grant each other a little grace and start today anew? I have some news from Norm that you're not going to believe."

"Norm! How could I forget? Even when I was flirting with Nigel, I was still more sleuth than sexpot. He didn't say another word about diamonds or the missing necklace. All he talked about on the dance floor was the Art Deco finds at the antique stores in Cologne. Frankly, a bit boring,"

"I saw Norm this morning and..."

She jumped to her feet. "You saw him? He's here on the ship? I want to see him, too. How's he doing? Did the police finally release him? What's with the Interpol comment?"

"Slow down! I'll explain. Sit back down. It's a long story and pretty extraordinary, even for Norm."

Instead of returning to the chair, Beatrice settled beside him on the bed, brushing her shoulder against his, then shifting away so she could meet his gaze. Hungover and tired, she still exuded an aura of wholesomeness and self-possession. Vlad found it hard to reconcile the wild woman from last night with the sweet lady sitting next to him. His lady, he hoped.

"First, no one knows he slipped on board except us and the captain. He concealed himself in the fog; a small police boat pulled up beside the ship to let him off. We're going to keep it a secret. Throw the thieves off balance."

Her voice rose with excitement. "So there are thieves on board? He was telling the truth about what he overheard."

"More than that. Not just a petty thief or two. The police think one of them is the mastermind of a group of criminals behind a series of unsolved jewel heists throughout Europe. The gang is very cunning, using clever disguises and never leaving behind any traces of their identities."

"A gang of professional thieves!" Her eyes widened. "Aren't they dangerous?"

"Not as dangerous as you would think. All of their heists have been pulled off without anybody getting hurt. They even shot a warning at the French Diamond Center using blanks. Besides, we're not going to confront them, just keep the suspects under surveillance."

"After my ridiculous behavior last night, they'll never suspect a thing! Miss Marple never threatened to dance on a table. I'm totally mortified at the spectacle I made of myself." She scowled at the memory.

"All the better. Keep them off guard. We'll act like we haven't heard from Norm, like he's still being held by the police. We can't let on that Interpol is on the case."

"That should be easy enough to pull off. Just keep on moping about like the last two days. I'm sure I can work up a tear or two when I think of your poor shirt."

"Shall we go to breakfast, Meryl Streep?" he stood up and held out his hand

She grasped it and pulled herself up. "I'd be delighted, Marlon Brando."

When they entered the restaurant most of the tables were still occupied by many of their shipmates lingering over their Bloody

Mary cocktails and mimosas. As they wandered among the tables they noticed Ollie deep into a conversation with the two ladies from the bar. He scowled as Vlad passed by and otherwise ignored them. Nigel, similarly engaged in a conversation with an elderly couple wearing matching cardigans, shrugged apologetically at the single empty seat next to him. Beatrice looked downcast and shook her head as Vlad gave a little wave of acknowledgement and steered her toward the back of the room. There, partially hidden in a corner, sat Dougie and Clarence, all alone at a table meant for six.

"Mind if we join you?" Vlad asked as he pulled a chair out for Beatrice and waited while she settled in.

Dougie waved a hand toward the empty chairs opposite them and said, "Go right ahead. Just a warning—Dad isn't feeling the best. He might be coming down with something. Might be contagious. You know how disease spreads quickly in a closed space."

"Thanks for the heads-up but we'll take our chances," Vlad said.

Beatrice blushed as she said, "I want to apologize for my behavior last night. I hope I didn't say anything to offend you. I'm not used to drinking."

"You were just a pretty lady on a night out. Everyone needs to let loose once in a while," Dougie said. "A lot of us are a bit hungover this morning. You should probably have a little hair of the dog that bit you." He lifted his Bloody Mary and took a sip.

"Who did that damn dog bite now? He was gunning for me last night," Clarence grumbled as he searched the crowded restaurant. "Is he here?"

"I'm not talking about the poodle," Dougie said loudly. "I was telling the lady she'd feel better if she had a little booze this morning."

"Well, why didn't you just say that. You got my heart pounding, and you know I had a bad night." He pounded the handle of his cane on the table with the last speech.

"Easy, Dad. Have another Bloody Mary and settle down. You don't want to draw any attention to us this morning." Dougie took his own advice and drained the glass. He waved it in the air, trying to flag down the wait staff. Catching Sam's eye as he carried a tray of dirty dishes toward the kitchen, he thundered his demand, "Waiter, bring my dad and me another one of these. And bring some for these two."

"None for me, thanks, Sam," Vlad said as he raised his hand like a traffic cop.

"None for me either, thank you," Beatrice echoed.

"Bring her a mimosa, and go light on the orange juice," Dougie insisted, watching the harried waiter disappear behind the swinging doors. "A little bubbly will do wonders for you."

"I really can't drink another drop," Beatrice said.

A slim waitress carrying two pots of coffee came over.

"Just black coffee for me—regular."

"Coffee for me, too." Vlad said. "And two large glasses of water, please."

"Sandra said you left in the middle of the night. I hope the phone call wasn't anything serious?" Beatrice said.

"Phone call? I didn't get any phone call. I had a bad case of indigestion. Didn't want to disturb the lovely lady," the old man said.

"Dad's right. Our androids don't work on board this ship. Told you we should have got some iPhones with SIM cards."

Vlad almost blurted out: *But I saw you on the upper deck yelling into a phone,* but he bit down on his lower lip instead.

Just then Sandra and Gaston entered the dining room but instead of joining them, she dropped into the empty chair across from Nigel. From her subdued outfit—purple pants suit and white blouse with violets embroidered on the collar—Vlad surmised she was undercover. She dabbed at her eyes with a handkerchief and, with a mournful expression, related the sad news about Norm to the folks at her table. Vlad nudged Beatrice with his foot under the table and flashed his eyes toward Sandra's performance.

"Bad news from our friend Norm," she said with a doleful expression.

"What's that?" Dougie said, leaning forward in his chair. "You finally heard from the poor dude?"

Beatrice answered in a tremulous voice, "Oh, yes. The police allowed him to contact us on the ship's phone. It seems they were able to corroborate the witness's story that put him outside the Beaumonts' room at the time of the robbery. He's waiting to talk to a public defender. It doesn't look good." Her voice cracked on the final sentence.

"Tough luck. I know he doesn't have the smarts to pull a heist like that off. Ever find out who IDed him?" Dougie asked as he slid his finger round and round the rim of the empty glass.

"Not a clue. They must be keeping the witness confidential. When we get to Amsterdam we're renting a car and driving back to Koblenz to see what we can do to help."

Beatrice sat up straight and said defiantly, "We know Norm is innocent despite what Katherine Beaumont thinks."

"It's not that Norm's not smart enough, he's too honest and goodhearted. Just watching out for her. She was flashing around those diamonds like she was asking to be robbed," Vlad added with a frown.

"I'm sure the German police will straighten it all out. It's their job to catch the crooks." Dougie said. He glanced toward the kitchen. "Here come our drinks."

The waiter placed the drinks brimming with celery and pickles in front of the two men and the mimosa near Beatrice.

"Took you long enough, Sonny. A man of my age could pass away while we were waiting," Clarence said, giving the waiter a crotchety stare.

"Here's to your friend Norm. Chin up, folks. Better days in Amsterdam." Dougie lifted his glass toward them before he gulped down half the cocktail.

Chapter 34

AFTER ATTACHING THE BRIGHT BLUE TAG to his large suitcase, Vlad set it outside his room with all the other collections of multi-sized bags as Lutz had instructed over the intercom. With the fog finally dispersed, the ship was sailing smoothly to Amsterdam. He gathered his passport and small stack of euros from the wall safe and tucked them into the inner pocket of his travel vest. After brushing his teeth, he put all his toiletries into the small black carry-on with his good gold watch and the delicate diamond he had purchased back in Crawford with such high hopes. He fought the urge to take it out and flip open the velvet case to gaze at it once more. No sense dwelling on lost opportunities. They were no closer to solving the mystery of the jewel thieves than to his proposal to Beatrice.

When he answered the soft knock on his door, there she stood, looking like a spring daffodil in her yellow sweater and flower print capris, purse, and green carry-on in hand.

"Let's pick up Sandra and head to the reception desk to check out. I didn't pay for gratuities yet. She probably hasn't even thought about settling up her account," she said.

"Plus, it's our last chance to put on our sad 'missing Norm' faces," he said.

No acting for Vlad; he truly felt mournful. Until Cologne the spark of affection between he and Beatrice had verged on growing into a full-fledged flame of passion. The chance encounter with Elke had doused the fire, and bitter embers of past failures threatened to derail his plans. However, their brief talk this morning rekindled his hopes, especially when she smiled at him like she was doing now.

"I'm glad the detective stint is almost over. I'll never complain about boring library work again," she said.

"I'm actually looking forward to department meetings with Chuck droning on and on about course offerings and accreditation. A refreshing break from this vacation."

They both laughed and fell into an easy silence. They walked to the stairs, weaving their way around giant suitcases and matching luggage sets. Two burly crewmembers hefted bags in each arm at the opposite end of the hallway, unnoticed by the remaining passengers preoccupied with checking out.

When they knocked, Sandra had changed into her orange paisley duster and orange sandals. Once again her make-up was expertly applied—no slashes of lipstick or dangling false eyelashes. Her blush blended in to accent her cheekbones, not a trace of mascara smudged below her eyes. In spite of the many wrinkles, she looked put together, not a hair out of place.

"You look great today," Vlad whistled as she picked up her glittery bag and Gaston's leash.

"If we get our picture in the newspaper for capturing the elusive jewel thieves, I want to look my best. I even brushed Gaston and put on his blingy collar. He needs to look his best, too. Right, boy?"

The dog in the rhinestone-studded collar gave a little bark.

"Besides, I want Clarence to eat his heart out over this." She slid her hands down her body. "A little reminder of what he'll be missing."

"I wish I had your optimism," Beatrice said, shaking her head. "I think it was Mission Improbable. We failed miserably at detective work."

"Don't be so hard on yourself, dearie. Your disguise last night as Mata Hari was a huge success. You could have stepped right out of a James Bond movie. Our Bea looked fabulous. Even knocked Luvy Puppy for a loop."

The poodle responded with a happy yip as Beatrice bent down to pat him.

"Thanks for the vote of confidence, but there won't be a repeat performance. I don't think Vlad's wardrobe can take another rescue like the last one."

"What do you mean, dearie?" she asked, knitting her brow.

Vlad abruptly said, "Never mind. It's a private joke."

Beatrice flashed him a grateful smile and moved toward the door. "We'd better get going."

"That's right. Jewel thieves await. Could you please set my trunk out in the hallway?"

As Vlad moved the huge suitcase, Sandra lingered in the doorway and swept her eyes around the suite. "I'm going to miss this place. Imagine an old lady like me having a grand adventure in Europe at my age. Wait 'til I tell my friends at the Senior Center. Master thieves on board our ship."

She closed the door with a wistful expression. "I never would have had this last cruise if it weren't for you sharing the reward money. Gaston and I thank you. Norm, too."

"It's not over yet. We have two days in Amsterdam," Beatrice said. "Imagine the canals and the quaint shops."

"It won't be the same. No shipboard romance. No undercover sleuthing. It'll be boring." She let out a little puff of air. "Gaston will be forced to eat dog food again."

They walked down the open staircase to the ship's lobby. Two long lines formed, stretching to the carpeted area of the nearby gift shop. As they inched forward, Dougie and Clarence joined the throng next to them. Gaston emitted a low growl the minute he saw them join the line, but a sharp tug on his leash silenced him.

"Gaston," Sandra hissed. "Mind your manners."

"I guess this is good-bye," Dougie said. "Dad and I booked cheaper accommodations in Amsterdam. We've had enough of all these expensive excursions."

"I'm going to miss you, lovely lady," Clarence said to Sandra. "But Sonny promised me a pot brownie."

"It was fun while it lasted. Reminded me of the good times on the burlesque circuit," Sandra sighed.

"You're still a looker, Sheila," Clarence said.

"Sandra," she corrected him. "Too bad you had to leave in the middle of our last night together."

"Sonny texted, said it was urgent." He jerked his head toward Dougie.

"Wrong, Dad. I never texted. Our phones don't work," Dougie snapped. "Don't you remember anything? When you came in the room you said you had indigestion, a bad gas attack, remember?"

"Oh. That's right. I farted like a cluster bomb going off. Didn't want to offend the lovely lady. Sorry if I woke you up, Beautiful," he said to Sandra.

"That explains why you left so abruptly. You're forgiven. I'm just disappointed I didn't get a proper good-bye." Sandra sighed. "With all the worrying about Norm, what's one more disappointment?"

Vlad looked at Beatrice, giving a little shake of his head as she rolled her eyes as if to say she was glad to be rid of these two clowns.

By this time they were at the desk. Vlad put his black bag on the floor as he went over the bill with the receptionist. Clarence and Dougie piled their bags next to his. Vlad leaned on the counter as he handed the lady his bill, an envelope, and his credit card.

"The invoice is correct. Two bar bills. No additional excursions. And the suggested fifteen percent gratuities. There's something special for Sam. He deserves a little extra for his exceptional service," he said as she took his card and submitted it to the machine for his bank's approval. Out of the corner of his eye he saw Clarence picking up his bag. He quickly pivoted and said, "Oh no, you don't. Not again. Clarence, you took my bag!"

"No, I didn't, you blighter. It's my bag." He clasped the black bag to his chest and glared defiantly.

"Give it to me. I'll prove it's my bag. If you let me open it, I'll show you my name taped on the inside." Vlad pleaded and grabbed the dangling strap.

"Let go, you moron. It's mine." Clarence clung to the handle of the bag in question and jerked back on it.

"I have a ring for Beatrice inside. I don't want to lose it," Vlad insisted. "The bag's mine."

In the background Gaston began to growl, and Beatrice gasped, "What? You got me a ring? I can't believe it."

Clarence continued to struggle, refusing to relinquish the bag as he shouted, "No, get away. Douglas, this bounder is trying to nick my bag."

Dougie stepped into the fray and said, "You're mistaken. It's Dad's bag. He's had it forever. Let go."

He pushed the old man aside and started a tug of war as he

grabbed the same strap Vlad held. Dougie yanked the bag toward him, and Vlad came along with it. He dug his heels into the floor and yanked back, throwing Dougie a bit off balance,

"I tell you it's mine," Vlad exclaimed. "Remember the suitcase your dad took. He's done this before to me."

By this time all the people in the reception area were staring at the scuffle, expressing a murmur of concern. The receptionist positioned her hand over the call bell as she watched them struggle.

Dougie shouted, "Not this time. It's ours!"

Gaston's ominous growls grew louder, and he lurched away from Sandra. The leash flew out of her hand as the dog hurled himself at Dougie, snarling and snapping, leash trailing behind him.

"Gaston, come back!" Sandra yelled as the dog sank his teeth into the man's ankle and held on with a vise-like grip.

"Damn you, Bullocks. Stop biting me." Dougie kicked at the dog, trying to break free from Gaston's jaws.

"Gaston, down, boy," Vlad said, alarmed at the growling dervish. "You'll get in trouble."

"That dog's a menace. He should be put down," Clarence said.

Vlad let go of the bag as he reached down to pull Gaston away from Dougie, still wildly thrashing about on one leg. The black bag snapped back, throwing Dougie off balance. He crashed to the floor, losing his grip on the strap as Vlad managed to disengage the poodle, holding tightly onto him as he growled and strained to attack the fallen man.

The bag landed upside down, and when the old man bent to retrieve it, the clasp gave way. The bag flew open, and the contents spilled out. Under the tumble of men's briefs and socks appeared a dazzling glint, then a gleam of crystalline shine. Clarence tried to kick his underwear over the offending strand.

"The missing diamonds!" a voice in the crowd exclaimed.

"I guess it **was** your bag," Vlad said, still grasping the collar of the frenzied dog. Gaston continued his frantic barking.

"No, no. It's your bag," the old man said. "You're a thief. You stole the poor woman's diamonds. Somebody call the police."

One of the brawny luggage haulers stepped forward. "No need. We're already here," he said. "We're undercover from Interpol. You're under arrest."

Dougie scrambled to his feet. He slipped a phone out of his

pants pocket and headed toward the open gangplank with his arm arced back like Aaron Rodgers about to throw a Hail Mary pass.

Vlad shouted, "Stop him. He's destroying valuable evidence."

He released Gaston, and the dog burst forward like a heat-seeking missile, leaping up to clamp his jaws on the uplifted arm. Snagging the edge of the billowy shirtsleeve, Gaston tugged the arm downward. The phone dropped harmlessly to the deck as Dougie screeched. Vlad scrambled to pick it up before the thief could kick it overboard.

"Ow. Sunovabitch is attacking me again." Dougie kicked at Gaston but the dog swerved, evading the profusely bleeding leg.

The desperate man shoved aside a woman standing openmouthed at the scene unfolding before her.

"Help! He's getting away!" she shrieked.

As he bulldozed toward the opening to the gangplank, Gaston chased after him, nipping at his heels. Suddenly, a uniformed policeman emerged from the shore and blocked his way. Other uniformed officers joined him, forming an impenetrable wall. Two of the officers grabbed Dougie's arms but he continued to thrash about while Gaston circled the group, still barking and flashing his teeth.

"You're under arrest. No clean getaway this time." The detective from Interpol slapped a set of handcuffs on the thief.

Clarence protested, "Those aren't the missing diamonds. They're just fakes. I got them to surprise my lady friend Shelia here. I'm just a confused old man. I'm no thief."

"You're the fake!" Sandra exclaimed. "Gaston had you pegged from the start." At the sound of his name, the little dog stopped barking and returned to her side.

"I should have paid attention to you more, Wonderdog," she said, picking up his leash.

Vlad handed the detective Dougie's phone. "I saw him talking on this to a possible accomplice. He lied about not having a working phone."

"I couldn't have stolen any diamonds. I was with my lady friend that night," Clarence said. "Ask her." He gestured toward Sandra.

"He wasn't with me all night. He left because of indigestion,"

Sandra said, turning to face him. "Clarence, I'm so disappointed in you. But you should have known better than to try to fool Gaston the Wonderdog. I told you he helped Vlad capture a terrorist."

"We'll sort this all out down at the station," said the policeman. "I'm afraid I'll have to ask you to come with us so we can get your statements. The theft on board the ship may be the tip of the iceberg. Now that we have these two in custody, perhaps we'll be able to finally crack a few more unsolved jewelry heists."

Just then Norm broke through the line of police, followed by a trim, well-built man wearing his tailored suit like a medal of honor. His demeanor brooked no challenge to his authority.

"That's my friends, the ones I was telling you about who brought down the terrorist in Crawford. They've been working undercover."

"Norm!" Beatrice exclaimed and dashed over to hug him. "I'm so happy to see you."

"We'll still need their statements," the steel-eyed man said. "We need all the corroborating evidence we can get with these slick operators."

"I told you not to put the diamonds in your carry-on," Dougie snarled.

"Bugger off, Sonny. You cocked up when you dropped the bag."

"Let's go, you two. Save it for the station," a uniformed policeman said as he led them away.

Beatrice stared wide-eyed at the men and said, "They sound British. They had us completely hoodwinked with their American accents."

"Masters of disguise, remember?" the Interpol detective said. "They're that good. We appreciate your assistance in putting them away."

"Happy to help any way we can," Vlad said.

"Will there be any newspaper reporters involved? I wore my best outfit." Sandra struck a glamour pose, one hand on hip, opposite arm overhead with her wrist bent. "I'm a former showgirl. I can use the publicity for my big comeback."

From: Chomskyv@crawford.edu
To: erinflamethrower@gmail.com
Watch for the news reports. We just thwarted a huge jewelry heist. Some international thieves were on board our ship. Gaston to the rescue! Tell you all about it when we get home.

From: erinflamethrower@gmail.com
To: Chomskyv@crawford.edu
OMG Trouble seems to follow you. Can't wait to hear your story

Chapter 35

VLAD GAZED OUT THE WALL-TO-CEILING window of their luxurious hotel in Amsterdam at the grand sight of the harbor. *The Haven* was parked somewhere along the piers. The beautiful Rhine rolled by, sunlight sparkling like diamond dust on its surface. He felt the inner pockets of his traveler's vest. Passport. Billfold. Ring. Today was the day. Come hell or high water or mad dogs or crazy friends, today he was going to open his heart to Beatrice.

Since the statements at the police station had taken so long, they'd missed the walking tour of Amsterdam. In appreciation for their assistance in clearing the ship's name from the robbery, the tour group had extended their hotel stay, rebooked a later flight back to the States, and Lutz had rescheduled a walking tour just for them. In addition, the hotel concierge booked a private boat tour along the canals. Norm, Sandra, and Beatrice were probably waiting in the lobby for him, but he looked in the mirror and practiced his speech several times.

"Beatrice, you are the sunshine in my days and the moonlight in my nights. My heart lives in darkness without you—no, too flowery."

He started again, "Beatrice, I think you know how I feel about you and…Beatrice, I've been waiting a long time to ask you this."

It all sounded so plain and pathetic, like a bad pop song. He trusted the right words would come when he held her hand. For God's sake, he was an educated man. He dealt in words day in and day out. Why were these so hard to say?

He caught his image in the elevator mirror on the way down. A shadowy half man with a thinning hairline, a khaki many-pocketed vest and sensible walking shoes. What he offered didn't seem like much—only everything.

The elevator door opened, he stepped out, and there she was, standing by a huge, glass water container filled with slices of mangos and tangerines, a few sprigs of basil floating on top. She was wearing a mango colored sweater with a softly hued scarf draped around her elegant neck and, he was happy to note, her sensible walking shoes, wide-toed and flat-heeled.

"Vlad, we're all ready to go," she said. The way she spoke sounded like wind chimes in a spring breeze, and his throat constricted with happiness.

"Look who's joining us," she waved her hand at a large woman whose back was toward them, standing near the leather couch. Broad-shouldered even in a pink cashmere sweater, its softness only accented the muscular biceps. Her brown trousers covered solid tree trunk legs. However, her ash blonde hair swirled silkily to her shoulders, and as she turned to greet him, Vlad saw it was PM Aschenbrenner shed of her harsh police uniform and severe ponytail. She extended her large hand in greeting.

"I hope you don't mind. Norman asked me along, and since I had the day off, I took a train to Amsterdam, and here I am."

As Vlad experienced her firm grip, Norm sidled over. Again he sported new clothes, a heather blue merino wool sweater over grey twill slacks. "Helga knows some good restaurants frequented by the locals. She's going to take us to one at lunch."

"My treat, in appreciation for your help in finally catching the White Panther gang's leaders. Interpol is drawing up search warrants as we speak, positive they'll find evidence for some of the unsolved heists."

"Leaders? Dougie and Clarence?" Beatrice squeaked. "I don't believe it."

"Believe it, dearie. They certainly had us bamboozled," said Sandra, rising up from the couch. "Except for Gaston. He knew Clarence was a phony from the start."

"Only his name isn't Clarence. It's Lawrence, Lawrence Pearce. Owns a seaside villa in Croatia and keeps a flat in London," Helga said. "His son's name is Alfred. Father and son jewel thieves."

"That's why that guy in Heidelberg called Dougie 'Alf.' He said it was mistaken identity. But it was all an act," Vlad said, slapping himself on the forehead. "If only I'd known…"

"Alf the Chameleon. Interpol knew him by that nickname. They thought he was a Serbian. Since the Baltic Wars ended, there are many soldiers of fortune for hire, professional thieves, very elusive. They strike and disappear. No one knows their true identities, only aliases. If one gets caught, they can't rat out the others because they don't know who they really are—only their talent and nickname," Helga explained.

"Talents like handling explosives or firearms or driving get-away cars," Norm added. "The gangs form and dissolve. Nothing permanent."

"But they talked like Americans!" Vlad shook his head in amazement.

"However, they are English. Pearce, the elder, had a stage career on the West End before he turned to crime. Even appeared in a few 'B' movies back in the fifties. Scotland Yard meets Charlie Chan mysteries," Helga said.

"Is that where he learned how the police in London work?" Beatrice asked.

"Possibly. He was learning more than his lines," Helga said. "Grew up in Liverpool and reverts back to that dialect under stress."

"Stress like when he got attacked by a trained undercover dog," Sandra said. "You should have seen him in action. He's ferocious. Right, Lovey Dog?"

Gaston emitted a single yip.

Lutz appeared with a middle-aged woman in tow who was wearing a weathered leather jacket, skinny jeans, and brown hiking boots. "This is Annalise, your guide for today. First, she will take you on the boat tour and then a brief walk to orientate you to this part of the city."

After the brief introductions, she warmly shook their hands and patted Gaston warily on the head.

"So this is the famous doggy that brought down the jewel thieves," Annalise said. "I'm honored to be your guide. If I have anything stolen, I'll know where to go for help."

She guided them outside the hotel and took them first to the nearby square. Hundreds of bicycles, in all colors and sizes, were locked in rows and rows of bike racks.

"This is Grand Central Square, nearly eight thousand bike stalls. You see why Amsterdam was voted the Most Bicycle-Friendly City in the World. Nearly one million bikes are in the city, more than cars."

Vlad watched a mother on a bike pass by with two children in an open box-like structure attached to the front. "Instead of a carpool to school, she has a bike pool. I wonder if Kaitlyn and Nicholas would enjoy that ride?"

"You will see many families traveling this way. People transport all kinds of goods in that carrier. So many bikes are parked here because your hotel is very near the train station." She pointed to a brick building with carved wooden trim, a white dome hovering overhead. "You can buy a three-day city pass for fifteen euros, which will be good for the remaining days of your vacation."

They followed her to the water where a canal boat was waiting. She ushered them into some seats in the open-air boat. The driver greeted them in English and started the engine. Beatrice reached for his hand and nestled her small palm in his. Vlad felt again for the ring in his vest as they traveled down the canal system. *Only three more days. She seems to have completely forgiven me. Why can't I bring out the ring and...? And what? Take a leap into the wide open?*

The boat passed by all sorts of houseboats. Some looked like freighters still sporting a mast, portholes, and engine room. Others were concrete barges with colorful houses built on top, ranging from small to luxury with several patio doors and floor-to-ceiling windows. Some even had a garden on deck, with beautiful potted spring flowers, statuary, and patio furniture including a grill.

"Houseboats became a popular way to avoid paying property taxes," Annalise said. "However, the government eventually caught up with them and now charge a docking fee. See the big *Open* sign on that boat. That's our Houseboat Museum."

The boat passed under quaint brick footbridges with wrought iron railings. The tall, narrow row houses were reflected in the water, some with small lovely classical statues set in the outer wall. Four elderly gentlemen, one with a cast on his foot, sat on a bench at the water's edge and gave a friendly wave as they drifted past.

"Amsterdam is so beautiful," Beatrice said. "I'm so glad you invited me on this trip."

The boat did a U-turn and headed back to the dock. Annalise offered to take them on a walking tour so she could introduce them to which sights and museums were available nearby.

"Gaston and I are just heading back to the hotel. My ankle is a little tender. No walking tour for us. Right, Lovey?" The dog barked in agreement. "Maybe we'll find some pastry in the coffee shop."

"I have some favorite spots I want to show Norm," Helga said. "Let's meet back at the hotel for dinner. We can share our adventures over some *bitterballen* and a beer."

"*Bitterballen*?" Beatrice asked.

"It's like a meatball with a crunchy breadcrumb coating. Dipped in mustard. Very tasty."

"I have a very important question to ask you," Norm said.

Vlad looked questioningly at Beatrice. *Had the romantic bug bitten Norm, too?*

"Yes, Norman?"

"I was wondering if you arrest a mime, do you tell him he has the right to remain silent?"

Helga laughed heartily and slapped Norm on the back so hard he jerked forward. "You are such a funny man. You always—how do you Americans say it?—crack me up."

"I love a woman with a sense of humor. Especially a policewoman. For once I'm on the right side of the law."

Norm and Helga strolled away hand in hand in the lovely May afternoon. Sandra tottered toward the hotel, the little poodle trotting with his head held high.

"I guess it's just the two of us on your tour," Vlad said.

"Wonderful. I won't have to shout to be heard or wear a device like I usually do. This will be more intimate," Annalise said.

And so it was that Vlad and Beatrice found themselves walking down narrow cobblestone streets in the shadows of tall, narrow buildings painted soft colors with sharp pointed roofs.

"What is that bar sticking out on the tops of so many of these buildings? It looks like some sort of pulley," Vlad said.

"That's exactly what it is. The stairs are too steep and narrow to carry furniture to the top floors so they haul big pieces up using that."

As they walked, Annalise told them about the wonderful museums, "The Rijksmuseum, with its Rembrandt collection and all the Dutch Masters, the nearby Van Gogh and Stedelijk, with its modern art. And, of course, you can't miss the Anne Frank House. And a little off the beaten path is our Jewish Museum."

"We'll have more than enough to keep us busy the next two days," Vlad said.

She brought them to the Dam Square, the historical center of Amsterdam. On one side was the majestic neoclassical Royal Palace and the beautiful Nieuwe Kerk (New Church) with its Gothic arched windows and four gingerbread steeples.

"Across from the church is the very upscale department store De Bijenkorf, and nearby is the Grand Hotel Krasnapolsky. You could enjoy a cup of coffee there. And, of course, our famous World War II monument is in the center."

The white stone pillar rose high before them. Four chained male figures were carved in relief in the front. "The figures symbolize the suffering of our people during the war. Above them is a woman holding a child, symbolizing peace, as do the doves ascending to the sky, for liberation."

Vlad stood silently gazing up at the monument, remembering all the sacrifices the Dutch people made so they could stand freely in this square and feel the warm sunshine on their faces.

"Here is a street map," Annalise said. "I've marked the way back to the hotel. I will leave you to your wanderings. There is much good shopping down that street and the best ice cream cone in the city for just one euro."

She scurried away, and Vlad and Beatrice were alone at last. They wandered down the crowded streets, browsing in gift stores and souvenir shops looking for the perfect gift for Maria.

"What about this?" Vlad held up a coffee mug with scenes of windmills and tulips.

Beatrice shook her head and picked up a silky scarf with a swirl of colors like Van Gogh's *Starry Night*. "Would Maria like this?"

"I think she would. She wears a lot of scarves with her suits when she shows houses."

"Good. Then we're done looking for souvenirs. Let's enjoy the sights of the city."

After the clerk handed him the bag with the scarf, she grabbed his hand, and they once again wandered the streets of the shopping district.

"Maybe we should look for that ice cream store," he suggested.

They noticed a small alcove tucked between two commonplace shops containing a bright, beautiful mosaic that depicted Jesus with a gilded halo. A gleaming cross soared above an arched entry.

"Is this a church?" Beatrice said.

"We'll find out," Vlad said as he pushed open the massive door with the iron handle.

As they stepped into the cool darkness, an elderly woman in a long black vest over a high-necked white blouse nodded at them and pointed to a sign: *Gentlemen, please respect this sacred place by removing your hat.* A simple altar was nestled between a statue of Madonna with baby and a saintly-looking bearded man under a gold cross. Sunlight shone through the stained glass windows rising behind it.

"It's so peaceful. Let's sit for a while," Beatrice said.

They sat quietly in the pew, admiring the stained glass figures smiling down at them. Totally alone in this sanctuary.

"I never imagined a tiny church tucked in the midst of the busy shopping district," he whispered.

"I like this better than all the huge cathedrals. I feel a deep connection to God in here, away from all the comings and goings of the street." She raised her eyes to the arched ceiling and folded her hands.

"And I feel a deep connection to you." He pulled out the small velvet box. "I've been waiting for just the right moment to give you this."

He flipped open the box. The diamond glinted in the light cast by the side sconces. Beatrice sat speechless as he removed the ring and picked up her hand.

"This is a token of my love. I know it doesn't have a high score on the four C's. It's simple and pure like my love for you. It can be an engagement ring, a promise ring, whatever you want it to be." He slipped it on her finger. "I love you. Could you see yourself married to me?"

Tears glistened in her eyes as she brought the ring hand to her heart. "Yes, yes, yes! I love you, too."

Then she flung her arms around his neck and kissed him. Her lips, so soft and warm, met his quivering lips. He closed his eyes and reveled in the luxury of her embrace, her delicate arms tightly woven around his neck. Her mouth opened slightly, and a hint of her tongue brushed his teeth. His tongue darted to meet hers, and his hands slid around her waist. He could stay like this forever.

"Ahem." The sound from the woman in the back broke their reverie. She stood behind their pew, arms akimbo, frowning slightly.

Gliding away from him, Beatrice shifted around to face her and held up her hand with the ring.

"We just got engaged," she told the woman.

"May I be the first to offer my congratulations?" she said. "But perhaps you'd prefer to take your celebration elsewhere?"

Blushing, Vlad stammered, "Yes, we would. We're so sorry."

He rose to his feet and pulled Beatrice up with him. "We'll always remember your beautiful little church. The perfect place to share our love. Thank you."

Still holding Beatrice's hand, he led her out of the dimly lit church into the dazzling sunshine. She paused blinking for a moment, then she smiled mischievously as she said, "Where's that map with the way marked back to our hotel? I know an even better place to celebrate."

Chapter 36

GIGGLING LIKE A MIDDLE SCHOOL GIRL at the roller rink, Beatrice dragged him into the elevator and pressed the button to her floor. The second the doors closed she was in his arms again, tilting her smiling face up to his. As he kissed her, he folded her in his embrace, seeing their happiness reflected in the mirror.

When they entered her room, she nudged him toward the bed, kissing him more fervently, catching his bottom lip ever so slightly with her teeth, then covering his mouth with hers. Unbuttoning his shirt, her hands moved across his chest, inching around his nipple, circling it with her fingertips.

Something hardened, too, despite his resolve to take things slow and gentle. Sudden excitement took on a life of its own. He moved his hands to the back of her yellow tunic top and undid the zipper. He slid it off her shoulders and moved his mouth from her lips to her bare throat. Vlad wanted to look into her eyes again, to make sure he hadn't imagined that glimmer, to lose himself in that place where nothing else mattered but them, and now. But Beatrice had already lowered her lids, masking the window into her heart.

She let out a small moan as he undid the clasp of her bra, slowly dropping it to the floor as his mouth moved down the sweet terrain of her chest bone to her breast. He cupped her breast in his hand as he bent down to softly lick her nipple. He felt it harden so he covered it with his mouth and kissed the strawberry tip of it, grazing the surface with his teeth. She moved her hand to his pants and undid the snap and zipper, pants and underwear joining the heap of clothing on the floor. As she slid her warm hand down and began to languidly caress him, sliding her hand underneath and cupping his roundness in one hand, he gave an involuntary groan

"I've been waiting so long for this moment," she said, and kissed him with more urgency.

"You are so beautiful," he told her as he deftly removed her capris and panties. The glimpse of her breast that day after her shower in no way did them justice—her rosy nipples, the firm weight of her breast in his hand. "So beautiful, like Venus rising from the shell."

He began to kiss her other breast, then dropped to his knees and kissed her stomach, determinedly inching his way down her body. No matter if he was a two-time loser at love. The third time's the charm. Throwing away all caution, he murmured, "So beautiful in body and mind. I love you so much."

"I can't believe this is happening." She moved back, breaking their contact. She held his fevered gaze for a moment, then framed his face with both her hands and whispered, "Because I love you, too."

He covered her hand with his, then brought it to his mouth and gently kissed her fingertips. He stood up and pulled her close to him, enfolding her in his arms, finding her mouth, exploring its softness with his tongue, putting all his unspoken passion into that one kiss. She eagerly returned the kiss for what seemed like a blissful eternity. Together they eased onto the bed, his hands slowly exploring her buttocks, her thighs, then reaching between her thighs to a silky wetness, a pulsating nub that he caressed softly.

"Whatever you are doing feels so good," she breathed.

Vlad wanted to make her happy, to give her pleasure in every way possible, because her pleasure was his as well. She reached for him but he brushed aside her hand, saying, "Wait! First, this is for you."

He slid her over to the edge of the bed and went down on his knees before her, delicately spreading her legs and sucking gently on the pleasure spot. She moaned and thrust her hips forward as he continued kissing and sucking until she shuddered and said, "I'm coming. Oh, God, I'm still coming."

The gush of her fluids, the sweet taste of her innermost part, filled him, and he could no longer hold back his throbbing member. He slid her to the center of the bed and eased himself into her, gently probing deeper with each thrust, enjoying her hip movements that mirrored his. Swaying each time longer inside, and deeper, until he couldn't tell where she began and he ended.

They moved as one. Slick with perspiration, he could feel his excitement growing, her skin damp and slippery; the beauty of connecting so completely with her overwhelmed him, he couldn't hold back. A final thrust was met by her arching hips. He made an animal sound, no language describing it, as she moaned in concert.

He fell trembling on top of her, body pressing against body, like clay in a mold, like they fitted together perfectly. He felt the whole of her under him, and she made him feel whole again, his entrance into the truly living, not just going through the motions of everyday existence.

Pushing her damp hair back from her forehead, he gently kissed her closed eyelids, then moved to her mouth, a butterscotch kiss. He slid over on his side so they faced each other, side to side. She opened her eyes, and he saw the look in her shining grey eyes. This time he was sure he was safe in her love.

"Thank you," he said, languidly caressing her neck, her throat. "You're lovely. Perfect. Splendid. I love you so much."

"I love you, too," she said, resting her ring hand on his chest. "Thank you for a magical day—full of surprises. A day I'll never forget."

They pulled the duvet over themselves and snuggled happily, his arm under her torso, her leg flung over his thighs, her hand still resting on his chest.

"I love this ring. It's so pretty. When you were fighting with Dougie over the bag and you blurted out about the ring, I didn't think I heard it right. You didn't say anything more about it."

"Because I was too afraid you'd say no to me. Then I'd be the one with a broken heart."

"Not broken, not bruised. Now mine's whole again and so full of happiness. I can't wait to tell our friends."

"Our friends. Oh, darn. We have to get dressed soon and meet them in the lobby," he groaned. "We're going somewhere for a beer and the meatball thing."

Sandra was ensconced on a love seat in the lobby with a white-haired gentleman wearing a black leg brace—so deep in conversation she didn't look up as they drew near. Gaston was contentedly curled up near her feet. She reenacted the fight over the travel bag with her gestures as the shaggy haired stranger hung on her every word. When they stopped at her side, she exclaimed, "There he is, the hero who fought the jewel thieves, Dr. Vlad Chomsky.'

The man clumsily rose to his feet and extended his hand. "I'm so happy to meet you. Sandra's been telling me about your adventures. Name's Alexander."

"Al's with a Rhode Scholar group touring the Netherlands on something called a Bike and Barge."

"Only I had a slight accident so the rest of the group went on without me. I'm recuperating here at the hotel where I had the extreme good fortune to meet this lovely lady. She's been regaling me with tales of her famous dog and his human associates."

"I hope she told you one of the jewel thieves was in his eighties. I'm certainly no hero," Vlad said as they shook hands.

"Ah, but you are," PM Ashenbrenner said as she and Norm walked up. "There was a reward for the capture of those two. Interpol found more evidence in their London home linking them to some unsolved heists. You are entitled to a substantial amount."

"Vlad, that's wonderful. I'm so happy for you," Beatrice trilled as she gave him a hug.

"Furthermore, that credit card you found belonged to an American who was pickpocketed in Cologne. Fingerprints on it also led to other unsolved cases. It looks like you also identified an international pickpocket."

"Yeah, Doc, that Ollie guy is a crook, too. Just not the one I heard on the balcony. So you're now an international crime fighter."

"And the American wants to give you a reward, too. Most of his money was recovered. He's so grateful he wants to give you two hundred dollars," Greta added.

"That's good news. But I have even better news. Beatrice and I are engaged." Vlad thrust his arm around her and pulled her close.

"Look. He got me this beautiful diamond ring." Beatrice held her hand out for them all to admire it.

As they all oohed and aahed, Gaston emitted a happy yip and jumped up on her.

"Congratulations! Dearie, like I told you, Bea and you were meant for each other once you talked it all out. Making up is the best part of a misunderstanding." Sandra winked at Vlad. "Looks to me like you've done a little celebrating already."

Beatrice blushed, and Vlad gave an embarrassed chuckle.

"Awesome, Dude. The cruise turned out to be romantic after all," Norm said as he playfully punched Vlad in the shoulder. "Congrats, pretty lady." He grabbed her ring hand and vigorously shook it. "I just have one piece of advice for you, Doc. Before you tell Beatrice something important, always take both her hands in yours. That way she can't hit you with them."

"I just love your jokes," Greta said. "You should be—what do you Americans call it?—a one-night stand-up?"

"You mean, a stand-up comedian. I never thought about performing. I got more jokes, lots more. Here's one: Love is blind, but marriage is a real eye-opener."

"Maybe you can tell us more over a beer and those bitter whatchamacallits?" Vlad said.

"*Bitterballen.* You're in for a treat," Greta said.

"After dinner, I think we should call the kids. Splurge on a long-distance call. With the reward money you'll be able to afford it," Beatrice said. "You can tell them all about the robbery."

"It'd be Friday afternoon there. Good way to start the weekend," Vlad added. "I'm eager to hear their voices. I missed them more than I realized."

"Do you mind if I join the party?" Alexander said. "As long as we're not going too far, I can manage to hop along."

"We're heading to the hotel restaurant. Sure ya can come along," Norm said, steering Greta toward the hostess in an elegant black dress at the entrance.

"We're all a little frazzled, dearie. It's been a long day. I hope the bartender can make dry martinis. And maybe extra *bitterballens* for Gaston. He's due for a new taste treat," Sandra said.

The group surged toward the restaurant, chattering excitedly, but Vlad grasped Beatrice's arm to stop her from following.

"Not quite the romantic candlelight dinner for two I envisioned to celebrate," he whispered.

"We'll have time for that tomorrow. I have a plan to ditch them all and spend the entire day on our own. Maybe we'll never leave my room. Hang out the *Do not disturb* sign and ignore all phone calls and loud knocking."

"We can always call hotel security," Vlad said. "Act like they are total strangers."

Suddenly, Norm stuck his head out the restaurant entrance.

"Hurry up, you two lovebirds, I'm getting ready to tell the joke about the princess who didn't want to marry the ugly king. It's a corker!"

Beatrice kissed him and said, "One thing I'm sure of, life with you will never be boring."

Acknowledgments

I thank my ever-tolerant husband, Michael, for listening to my first drafts and taking sacrificial naps so I could write in quiet.

I thank my writers' group for their continued support, especially Fran Milburn, Paul Marose, Bruce Benz, Dan David, and John Ashenbrenner who helped with information on German police.

I especially thank Karen Hodges Miller, my editor, who encouraged me to write this sequel when I thought one book was all I had to offer the world.

About the Author

Janice Detrie lives in Watertown, Wisconsin, with her husband, Michael, and her cat who thinks he's a dog. A former literacy coordinator, her reading tastes are eclectic—everything from biography to mystery to the classics to nonfiction. She has two children and two grandchildren. This is her second book featuring Vlad, Gaston, and their friends.

www.ingramcontent.com/pod-product-compliance
Lightning Source LLC
Chambersburg PA
CBHW072233170626
46813CB00003B/1200

* 9 7 8 0 9 9 9 8 7 3 4 2 1 7 *